THE SKELETON TAKES A BOW

continued . . .

A SKELETON IN THE FAMILY

"Adjunct English professor Georgia Thackery makes a charming debut in *A Skeleton in the Family*. Georgia is fiercely loyal to her best friend, Sid, an actual skeleton who is somehow still 'alive.' When Sid sees someone he remembers from his past life—who later turns up dead—Georgia finds herself trying to put together the pieces of Sid's past as she works to hunt down a killer. Amateur sleuth Georgia and her sidekick, Sid, are just plain fun!"

> —Sofie Kelly, *New York Times* bestselling author of
> *Faux Paw*

"No bones about it, Leigh Perry hooked me right from the beginning. An unusual premise, quirky characters, and smart, dry humor season this well-told mystery that kept me guessing until the very end. It's too bad Perry's sleuth is fictional—I'd invite Georgia over for dinner in a heartbeat."

> —Bailey Cates, *New York Times* bestselling author of
> *Magic and Macaroons*

"A delightful cozy with a skeleton who will tickle your funny bone."

> —Paige Shelton, *New York Times* bestselling author of
> *If Onions Could Spring Leeks*

"The first in a new series introduces a family that literally has a skeleton in its closet. What seems like an outlandish idea becomes a very touching and entertaining whodunit. The mystery is intelligent and nicely done with fun insights into academia and anthropology."   —*RT Book Reviews*

"Delightful characters . . . Perry uses dry humor and wit to bring Sid to life . . . A very original premise . . . Quirky and funny."
—*Deb's Book Bag*

"Enjoyable and engaging . . . Perry manages to achieve something I thought would be impossible: making a living skeleton who exists in the 'real' world somehow seem completely believable . . . The author's dry humor and ability to poke fun at the pretentious is always evident and this eccentric mystery proves to be surprisingly grounded and realistic. I loved this fun mystery and can't wait for a sequel that includes this bony and very likable sidekick."
—*Kings River Life Magazine*

"The first book in Leigh Perry's new series is one of the most unusual mysteries I've read in a long time. And that's a good thing. If you like cozy mysteries, I urge you to pick up *A Skeleton in the Family* . . . Georgia Thackery and Sid make a terrific team. It's an entertaining mystery involving a very special friendship . . . The book is a winner."
—*Lesa's Book Critiques*

"This is a really fun premise for a mystery series. Sid is a complete treasure . . . Very clever writing and thoroughly enjoyable. Funny and exciting and a great book to read on a chilly autumn evening. A terrific start for this new series."
—*Escape with Dollycas*

THE
SKELETON
HAUNTS A
HOUSE

Leigh Perry

BERKLEY PRIME CRIME, NEW YORK

An imprint of Penguin Random House LLC
375 Hudson Street, New York, New York 10014

THE SKELETON HAUNTS A HOUSE

A Berkley Prime Crime Book / published by arrangement with the author

ISBN: 978-0-425-25585-8

PUBLISHING HISTORY
Berkley Prime Crime mass-market edition / October 2015

PRINTED IN THE UNITED STATES OF AMERICA

10 9 8 7 6 5 4 3 2 1

Cover illustration by Ben Perini.
Cover design by George Long.
Interior text design by Kelly Lipovich.

To Joshua Bilmes,
who believed in Sid. And in me.

Acknowledgments

A skeleton is all about the connections, and I have quite a few connections to thank for their help:

My husband, Stephen P. Kelner, Jr., for a ludicrous amount of support.

Charlaine Harris and Dana Cameron, who dropped everything to beta read. Again.

My daughters, Maggie and Valerie, for letting Sid join the family.

My agent, Joshua Bilmes, who always has my back.

Robin Burcell and Sherry Harris, who shared their expertise and research about police procedures. Anything wrong in that area is my fault, not theirs.

Justin Turczak, for insider knowledge about working in haunted houses.

The Facebook hive mind. Someday I may find a topic about which my Facebook friends have no knowledge, but it hasn't happened yet!

I

Most people wear Halloween costumes in order to look scarier, but my best friend Sid picked his to look less scary.

He'd already climbed into the full-body fur suit, and I reached up to put the head on. "How's that? Is it straight?"

"I think so," he said, "but it's hard to breathe in here."

"You don't need to breathe." I wasn't being mean. Sid really doesn't need to breathe. In fact, he can't breathe because technically, he isn't even alive. He died over twenty years ago, and like most people who'd died that far back, all that's left of him is a skeleton. Unlike most people—unlike any other people at all, as far as I knew—Sid has come back to . . . Well, if not to life, then back to consciousness, movement, and a penchant for watching old cartoons. He also has a passion for Halloween, since it's one of the few times he can go out in public.

One might think that Sid's usual boney appearance was already right on target for Halloween and in previous years he'd dressed as Death, the Grim Reaper, and Jolly Roger.

However, recent incidents had linked skeletons and my family a little too publicly, and we'd decided that something a little more discreet was called for. Besides, Sid had run out of skeletal-themed costume ideas and was ready to try something new.

"How do I look?" He spun around slowly so I could see him in all his furry glory.

I reached up and straightened the green vinyl collar around his neck. "Not bad. I would never have recognized you." That was, of course, the point of a full-body-covering getup. "Let's hear the voice."

"Scooby dooby dooooo!" he crowed.

"Excellent!" It wasn't the best Scooby-Doo imitation I'd ever heard, but it wasn't the worst, either. "Why don't you practice moving around while I get my costume on? And remember you're over a foot taller than usual, and a lot bigger around. Be careful and don't step on the dog! The real dog, I mean."

Byron, my daughter Madison's Akita, had been solemnly watching the costuming process. I didn't think he acknowledged the cartoon Great Dane as a fellow canine, and even if he had, Sid's imposture would not have caused any latent affection to develop. Byron and Sid have a love-hate relationship. Byron would love to chew on Sid again, and Sid hated the memory of him doing so.

I left Sid stumbling around the living room, wincing as his tail nearly knocked a vase off an end table, and went upstairs to my room to get ready. Since I was going as Scooby's buddy Velma, my outfit was considerably easier to get on, and fortunately for my budget, had been made up of things in my house rather than rented from an expensive costume shop. I was wearing an old turtleneck sweater I'd dyed orange with a brick red corduroy skirt that I hadn't worn in years. Once I added orange knee-highs and an old pair of sunglasses from which I'd poked out the lenses, all I had left to do was curl my close-enough-to-Velma-brown hair under.

When I got back downstairs, I did my own twirl. "What do you think?"

He put his paw onto his chin. "Your skirt is too long."

"I hemmed it two inches shorter than any other skirt I own—that's as far as I'm willing to go."

"Isn't Velma's skirt pleated?"

"I didn't have a pleated skirt, and besides, have you ever tried hemming a pleated skirt?"

"I don't know about the shoes."

"I am not buying a pair of shoes for one night."

"And your hair is too long."

"Sid!" I said. "I'm only dressing up to keep you company, not entering a most-authentic-costume contest!"

"Yeah, okay. Just say your lines!"

"Jinkies! I think we have a mystery here!"

"And?"

I pulled the glasses off and put them behind me. "My glasses! I can't see without my glasses!"

"Scooby dooby doo!" He held up a paw for a high five, but managed to miss.

"Dude, I'm the one who lost my glasses!" I said, putting them back on my nose.

"Sorry. It's not easy to see in this head. Shall we go?"

"Just as soon as we go over the ground rules."

"Again?" He gave an exasperated sigh. "Don't take off any piece of my costume until we get back home. Don't go running around alone. Stay in character. Keep my phone handy."

The phone rule had caused some problems since the costume had no pockets and Sid wasn't wearing anything else, but I'd found a conference badge holder with a sturdy lanyard and a pocket big enough to hold the phone. Sid had it around his neck under the suit, and if necessary, could wriggle around to use it. It wouldn't have been possible for a normal human, but most of what Sid did was impossible for a normal human.

"Good." I checked that Byron's food and water dishes were filled, grabbed my pocketbook, and said, "Let's go!"

"I don't think Velma carried a purse."

"Sid!"

It took a little maneuvering to get Sid into the front seat of my green minivan with his head on. With anybody else, I'd have suggested he remove it for the duration, but since we didn't want to give any children nightmares from seeing a skull on top of Scooby's body, I just crammed him in and let him complain.

It wasn't a long drive, anyway, though it took more time than it did most days because of the traffic. We were heading for the Halloween Howl, Pennycross's annual celebration of all things spooky and scary. There were events scheduled at venues all around town, but McQuaid University—where I worked—was the epicenter. The Howl had started as a student Halloween party before morphing into the current month-long extravaganza. It wasn't as famous as the Haunted Happenings in Salem, but it drew pretty big crowds from the western part of Massachusetts. We were still three weeks away from October 31 but the fair that was the main draw would be running all three weekends leading up to the big day, fortunately on a Saturday this year.

Normally I enter campus at the main entrance on Elm Street, but the tree-lined street was closed to vehicle traffic for several blocks to make room for the carnival midway, whose lights I could see as I approached. Instead, I drove around to the back entrance, hoping the faculty parking pass that was one of the few perks of being an adjunct English professor would enable me to find a decent spot. Luck was with me—I snagged one of the last half dozen spots in the lot nearest the festivities.

The campus quad was normally a tranquil oasis of grass and stately oak trees, but tonight it was filled with tents for selling food and drink; campus club fundraising activities like a dunking booth and a cakewalk; a bandstand and dance area; and community arts and crafts displays.

I tugged my overly short skirt down a bit and helped Sid out of the car. After we made sure his head was on straight, I said, "Lead the way, Scooby. It's your night to howl!"

"Thanks, Velma," he said in a passable imitation of Scooby's accent, and grabbed my hand to pull me along.

I didn't blame him for being excited. Since Sid had come to live with my family back when I was six, ninety-nine point something percent of his time had been spent inside our house. Any opportunity to get out was a treat—being able to cavort in public was like Christmas.

He wasn't the only one cavorting—the campus was hopping. And dancing and slithering and creeping and all the verbs that went along with the Halloween Howl. The campus security officers were the only ones I saw who weren't in costume. Sid played his character to the hilt, pretending to be frightened of a crowd of zombies, boogying with a lady vampire, and joining the tail end of a conga line composed of masked superheroes.

By then it was fully dark and I was getting chilly, which Sid noticed despite the fun he was having.

"You okay, Geor—Velma?"

"I'm fine," I said, though I was starting to wish I'd rented a fur costume of my own. "I'll grab some hot cider. That'll warm me up."

"Wait! I know! Let's go to McHades Hall!"

"No, cider will be fine."

"Come on!" Sid said, and grabbed my arm again to pull

me through the crowd toward the front corner of the quad where a particularly bustling building loomed.

McQuaid Hall was the oldest building on campus, but the out-of-date, poorly maintained structure needed so many repairs that it was rarely used for anything but photo ops until a member of the McQuaid Scholars Committee realized that the place bore a striking resemblance to the Addams family mansion in the old TV show. So what better way to raise money for scholarships than to convert it to a haunted house attraction every year, and rename it McHades Hall for the occasion?

McHades was one of the star attractions of the Howl. I understood the haunt was one of the best in our part of the country, but I'd managed to avoid setting foot in the place. I was hoping to maintain that record, but three things were working against me. One, my sister, Deborah, was in charge of McHades this year. Two, my daughter, Madison, was working there. And three, Sid had a death grip on my hand.

As we got closer, we saw that the line of people waiting to get in snaked along the sidewalk. "Oh darn," I said in relief, "we'll never make it through that line. Let's hit the midway."

"Don't worry, Deborah will get us in," Sid said, pulling me past the gathered ghoulies, ghosties, and long-legged beasties to the tent where Deborah watched over a pair of ticket sellers, talking into a walkie-talkie.

Sid cheerily said, "Hi, Deborah! It's me, Scooby!"

Deborah looked resigned. My sister was a locksmith, which she said meant that she dealt in hard facts that made sense. Since Sid did not make sense, she had a more difficult time accepting Sid than I did. "I figured you guys would be showing up," she said unenthusiastically.

Sid lowered his voice to what he thought was a conspiratorial whisper. "I don't suppose you can sneak us past the line, can you?"

"You're in a fur suit," she said dryly. "Not exactly easy to sneak."

"Aw, come on, Deborah—"

"But as it happens, Madison reserved will-call passes for you two so you can go in with the next party." She handed an orange cardboard ticket to Sid, then tried to give me one.

"That's okay," I said. "I'll wait out here."

"You don't want to go in?" Sid said.

"Nope."

"Not even to see Madison give her spiel?"

"She did it for me at the house."

"You're not still freaked out about—"

"No, I'm not," I lied. "I just don't like going in front of all these other people. You go ahead."

"Are you sure?"

"The next party is leaving now," Deborah said, though I'm not sure if she was taking pity on me or getting rid of Sid. Either way, he scurried off to join a group. A young Snow White immediately announced that Scooby would protect her from any monsters, and reached up to hold his hand.

"Isn't that cute?" I said.

"It's not going to be cute when she comes out of the haunt crying." Deborah pointed at a sign on the ticket booth.

WARNING!
McHades Hall is too scary for the following:
People with weak hearts.
Those who faint easily.
Pregnant women.
Intoxicated visitors.
Children who frighten easily.
Enter at your own risk—no refunds!

"Yow. Maybe you guys should tone it down a little."

"If we tone it down, people complain because they feel cheated. We're not talking McKamey Manor or Blackout, but we are trying to scare people. That is the point, after all."

"I guess."

"Just because you don't like haunted houses—"

"I know, I know. I'm a wimp."

She shrugged. "You can see we've got plenty of customers without you." If anything, the line had gotten longer since we'd been talking. "Come Halloween, people are going to be waiting for two hours to get in. I just hope my cast lasts. All that screaming and scaring is hard work."

"I imagine so. So how long is Sid going to be in there?"

"It takes about half an hour to go through."

"Then I think I'll go get a hot dog."

"Bring back hot dogs and fries for me and my ticket sellers, and I'll pay for yours."

"Deal!"

I ran into my friend Charles along the way, and stopped to chat for a bit. Then with the line at the concession stand for hot dogs and the difficulty of carrying my load through the ever-increasing crowd, I was gone considerably longer than half an hour. When I finally got back, I handed Deborah the sack of food, reached in to grab a hot dog and a mustard packet for myself, and asked, "Isn't Scooby out yet?"

"Out and back in again. He was making a hairy nuisance—"

"Good one!"

"What?" She made a face. "God, you're as bad as he is. He was making a nuisance of himself while waiting for you, so I gave him another ticket."

"Jinkies. I guess he enjoyed it."

"Something weird about a . . ." She looked around and apparently decided too many people were in earshot. "About a guy like Scooby liking a haunted house, don't you think?"

"He loves Halloween. You know, he volunteered to work here for you."

"Madison told me. Thanks, but no thanks. We only hire fake spooks."

"Suit yourself." It was probably just as well. The other cast members might have noticed there was something odd about my pal.

I'd just finished my second hot dog when the first screams came. Well, to be fair, people had been screaming the whole time, attesting to the success of the scare actors' efforts, but these came via Deborah's walkie-talkie.

"What's going on in there?" she demanded of whoever was on the other end.

The response was loud enough that I could hear it plainly. "There's a dead body in here!"

2

"Say again?" Deborah's tone was determinedly matter-of-fact, but I could see how tightly she was gripping the walkie-talkie.

"There's a dead woman in the party room. A real one!"

"Who is it?" Deborah barked, and I knew she was thinking the same thing I was. My daughter, Madison, Deborah's niece, was in there. Sid was, too, but the voice had said "she."

"I don't know. There's blood and . . . It's real blood!"

"Don't go anywhere, and don't touch anything! I'm coming!" She keyed a different switch. "Security. Lock the haunt down—nobody in or out. Do it now!" Another switch. "Bring up all house lights and shut off sound effects. Room monitors, hold all groups in place and stay where you are! Tell your actors to drop character."

Then she pointed at her ticket agents. "You, call 911. Tell them to send cops and an ambulance. You, call campus security. I'm going in."

She headed for the front door, and I was right on her heels. "Where's Madison?" I asked.

"I'm not sure." Back on the walkie-talkie, she said, "Room monitors sound off." Deborah must have prepared them for an emergency because they started giving their names and statuses, including which scare actors were with them. Their voices were probably higher-pitched than usual, but they were holding it together.

Deborah led us in the front of the building, where a group of confused customers surrounded a young girl in a bride of Frankenstein costume. "Stay here!" Deborah ordered as we zoomed past, ignoring their questions.

There was a wide stairway in front of us, and though the glow-in-the-dark arrows painted on the floor pointed up, Deborah went past them to part a set of black curtains. The enclosure behind held control boards manned by college-aged kids in jeans and orange *McHades Hall Crew* T-shirts.

"What's going on?" one wanted to know.

"I'm going to find out. Stay here, stay safe."

We went through another set of curtains at the back, and I found myself in a narrow corridor made up of plywood walls. Deborah went forward and slid open a door. Just as we went in, I heard a room monitor on the walkie-talkie say, "Avery. I've got Madison and her group with me." I took a breath, wondering how long it had been since I'd done so.

The large room we'd entered was set up like a party, if you liked creepy parties. There was a banner hung on the wall that said *Delta Epsilon Alpha Delta Rush* in red, dripping paint. Along one side was a long table filled with nasty-looking refreshments like eyeballs in Jell-O, finger sand-wiches with human fingers shoved into them, and a head with brains hanging out. A bar had poison bottles, bloody Bloody Mary glasses, worms in the martinis, and maggots in the beer.

All fake, of course, but as gross as it was in normal light, I could only imagine how it would have looked if the scene had been set for customers.

In one corner of the room, half a dozen people in zombie costumes were huddled together. When they saw Deborah, they pointed to the opposite corner, where a woman was crumpled on the floor, lying on one side with one arm flung forward and wide-open eyes staring at nothing. And as the guy on the walkie-talkie had said, there was blood.

When I got nearer, I realized that she looked closer to girl than woman. I couldn't bring myself to look too long at her face, but her hands looked young. Her long blond hair didn't hide the fact that she'd been beaten hard enough that her skull was no longer shaped right and one arm was bent at the wrong place. She wasn't in costume, unless it was some character who wore blue jeans, white sneakers, and a dark blue hoodie.

Deborah knelt beside her and touched her arm. Then she checked for a pulse, something I hadn't realized she knew how to do. After a moment, she shook her head, took a deep breath, and stood. "Okay, the police are going to be here soon. Does anybody know who this is?"

There was a round of *no*s.

"Who found her?" Before anybody could answer, she said, "Never mind, we'll wait for the cops." She got back on her walkie-talkie to tell security to bring the police to the zombie party when they arrived. "Otherwise," she said, "nobody comes in, nobody goes out."

I whispered, "What about Sid?"

"There's nothing I can do about him, Georgia. We've got to preserve the crime scene."

She was right, I knew she was right, but the thought of what was going to happen when the police made my skeletal friend take off his costume scared me more than anything in the haunt could have.

3

We didn't have to wait long. It couldn't have been more than ten minutes when a guy in a bright orange *McHades Hall Security* T-shirt came in, followed by a pair of Pennycross patrolmen and a man in jeans and a button-down shirt.

When Deborah saw the fellow in jeans, she nodded a curt greeting. It was Louis Raymond, a member of the Pennycross Police Department. At one point, I'd been sure Louis was interested in dating her, but when Madison had been kidnapped some months earlier, he hadn't taken Deborah's instructions on how to respond, and she hadn't been pleased.

"We got a report of a woman being hurt," he said.

"She's over there. Dead."

He repeated Deborah's actions, then asked, "What happened?"

A college-aged guy spoke first. At least I thought he was college-aged. It was hard to tell under his makeup, which made him look as if his throat had been slit and putrefaction had set in. "We don't know! We were in the middle of attacking the group— I mean, not really attacking, but doing our scene, so we were chasing people all around. One woman went into that corner, tripped or something, and started yelling that it was a real body. We just laughed—you know, still in character—and she ran out screaming. But once she was gone I started thinking that there aren't any bodies in this scene, just us zombies. So I went to see what she was talking about and I found—" He swallowed. "I found her. I thought somebody had just moved a prop in here, but when I touched her, I could tell she was real. That's when we called Ms. Thackery."

"Do you know how long she'd been there?" Louis said.

The zombies conferred, but it turned out that they weren't sure. "That corner is really dark when the room is set, so we didn't notice her until that other woman tripped over her."

"I did a walk-through before opening tonight," Deborah put in, "and I'm sure she wasn't here then."

"How long have you been open?" Louis asked.

"Since five. So two and a half hours."

"She's not one of your people, is she?"

Deborah shook her head. "All of our people are accounted for."

"Then what about the group she came through the house with? Wouldn't they have noticed her disappearing?"

"Not necessarily," said a girl zombie with a fake eye hanging down one cheek. "A lot of parties get split up in the haunt, especially in this scene. They get so scared that guys forget their girlfriends and parents abandon their kids. It happens all the time."

I wasn't sure if I should be impressed or appalled by the effectiveness of their efforts.

"Have you checked security footage?" Louis asked.

"We don't have any cameras," Deborah said, and I could tell she was gritting her teeth.

He looked as if he was about to ask why when more responders started coming in: EMTs with a stretcher, additional uniformed officers, people in plainclothes with badges on their belts, and several campus security guards.

Louis waved one of the officers over. "Officer Burcell is going to take you out of the way and stay with you, okay?"

"What about the rest of the people in the haunt?" Deborah asked. "I've got cast and crew members, and I don't know how many customers are still in the building."

"We'll get to them as soon as we can," Louis said, "but it's going to take some time. Just hang tight."

Deborah got on her walkie-talkie and told her people that the police were on the scene, and that they should all stay exactly where they were until the police told them differently. There was some back and forth with the security crew outside the exit because apparently some people had escaped despite their best efforts to keep them contained, and some of the ones left were making noises about leaving. Louis sent a couple of officers out to deal with the situation. Then Officer Burcell herded Deborah, the zombies, and me to the end of the room as far as possible from the dead girl. Being at a distance was fine with me—farther away would have been better.

Deborah was glaring at Louis as he went to work, but I knew she wasn't really mad at him. She just gets argumentative when she's worried, and she was currently pretty worried. She was in charge of McHades, after all. Had she and I had a different kind of relationship, I'd have mirrored the scare actors we were standing with and offered her a hug or a hand to hold. But it was us, so I said, "You okay?"

She grunted in an affirmative way.

The niceties attended to, I said, "I guess Officer Raymond was off duty when the call came in since he's not wearing a uniform."

"He rotated to Investigations, so he gets to wear plain-clothes. Promoted to sergeant, too. Or so I hear."

I raised my eyebrows.

"What? We do still bowl on the same team. I have to talk to him sometimes."

In a better situation, I'd have probed more about just how much she had to talk to him, but it wasn't the time or place for sibling teasing. I think my unconscious was trying desperately to give me something to think about other than the dead body just a few feet away. At least the gathering responders meant I couldn't actually see her anymore. When I tried to think of something else, I started worrying about Sid instead. I wanted to borrow Deborah's walkie-talkie to call Madison and see if she knew where he was, but was afraid to draw any attention to him.

After some discussion between the various responders, Louis came over. "We're going to evacuate all of you people, plus the rest of the staff and customers so we can move the investigation along. McQuaid security has opened up a room in Stuart Hall, which I understand is close by, and we're going to walk you over there and ask everybody some questions."

"You want me to let my people know?" Deborah asked.

"If you wouldn't mind."

She nodded and used the walkie-talkie to spread the word. There was some grumbling, not so much from the cast as from customers who wanted to know what was going on, but Deborah just said, "Don't fuss at me. The cops want us elsewhere so we're going elsewhere."

"Thanks," Louis said when she was done.

"I don't blame them for wanting to leave," she retorted. "None of the customers upstairs or in the room before this one would have had a chance to kill that girl. It's the people who've already left you should be holding."

He held his temper admirably, and only said, "It shouldn't

take long to sort out the people who don't know anything, and we'll be trying to track down the people who left." Then he waved over another uniformed cop and a pair of McQuaid security guards and said, "These people will walk you over."

"Can we get our stuff out of the greenroom?" a zombie cheerleader asked.

"Not now," Louis said. "We're going to need to leave everything in situ until the forensics people get here."

"But I need to call my mom and let her know I'm okay," she said.

"You can use my phone," I said. "I didn't come in until after the body was found, so I don't need to leave my bag, right, Louis?"

"No, you're good, but as for calling . . . Look, I don't want to alarm the town with a bunch of rumors. So I'm going to ask you people not to make any phone calls, or e-mail anybody, or tweet for the time being. Once we identify the victim and get in touch with her next of kin, we'll give the okay."

The zombies and I nodded, and Deborah said, "Don't worry. They can wait."

Our escorts started leading the way out, two in front and two behind. I guess they didn't want anybody sneaking off. We went back the way Deborah and I had come, through the building to the main entrance, collecting staff and customers as we went. I spotted Madison, still in her vampire outfit, but didn't see Sid's Scooby-Doo head anywhere. I wasn't sure if that was a good sign or a bad one.

Once we were outside, the cops cleared a path through the curious crowd and took us to Stuart Hall, the sedate, ivy-covered building which held the plush dining room usually only used for university functions and suck-up-to-alumni dinners. The zombies and other made-up cast members looked particularly incongruous amongst the oak tables and solemn paintings of former deans and distinguished professors. A trio of maintenance people was busily setting up metal folding chairs all through the room, no doubt wanting to keep the fake blood and gore off of the upholstery.

People quickly divided up. Customers went to one side, grumbling and looking suspiciously at the scare actors. The actors were on the other side, comforting one another and chattering in a mix of excitement and upset. Deborah and I were left in the middle.

Madison found us quickly, and came over for hugs—in public—which showed how upset she was.

"Are you okay?" I asked.

"I'm fine," she said. "Did somebody really die?"

"I'm afraid so. And it looks like murder."

"Oh my gosh. Was it one of us?"

Deborah said, "Nope, a customer. I didn't recognize her."

"That's a relief," she said, then quickly added, "Not that it's good. I know I shouldn't care that it was somebody I didn't know but—"

"We get it," I said, and hugged her again. "I don't see Si— I don't see Scooby-Doo."

"I don't know where he is," Madison said. "He was with my group, but he slipped away when the lockdown was called."

"He couldn't have left the haunt," Deborah said. "Security said some people got through, but not a Scooby-Doo."

Madison said, "Then I guess he's still in there. What do we do if they find him?"

"Maybe they won't connect him with us," I said.

Madison gave me a look. "Mom, what are you wearing? Or should I say *Velma*?"

"Oh, coccyx, I forgot!" It wouldn't take a deductive genius to pair up my costume with Sid's.

"Besides which," Deborah reminded me, "my ticket takers saw you together. Didn't you notice them taking pictures? They thought you were cute."

"Next time, no matching costumes."

"If there is a next time," Deborah said ominously.

That pretty much killed conversation for a while, so we sat down to wait. Maybe fifteen minutes later, a man in a McQuaid sweatshirt and jeans came in, looking frazzled. He started for the clump of cops, but when Deborah called out, "Hey, Oscar," he swerved in our direction.

"You picked a swell night to take off," she said to him.

"I know. I should have known better on the first night of the Howl, but I wasn't expecting things to go crazy until closer to Halloween."

"Oscar, you've met my niece, Madison. This is my sister, Georgia."

"Oscar O'Leary," he said, shaking my hand. "You teach English, right?"

"Does it show?"

He grinned. "I don't know all the faculty, but having three professors with the same last name stands out."

"Oscar is McQuaid's chief of security," Deborah explained. "He's been helping me set up safety protocols at the haunt, not that they worked any too well tonight."

"Hey, we were planning for drunks and accidents, not murders." He patted her arm, and she actually let him. Madison and I exchanged quizzical glances. Oscar had sandy blond hair and dark brown eyes, and while I wouldn't call him handsome, he was definitely in the "nice-looking" category. I'd probably seen him around campus, but fortunately, hadn't had to deal with security in a while.

Deborah said, "So what's going on up at the haunt? Have they identified the girl yet?"

"Yeah, they found a purse dropped behind the curtains, and the picture on the driver's license matches the victim. Sergeant Raymond is calling her family. Man, that's not a job I'd want."

I took Madison's hand in mine and squeezed it. I didn't even want to think about getting a phone call like that.

"Anyway, Raymond is going to come take charge here when he's done, but in the meantime, I'm going to see about getting you people some drinks, maybe something to eat." He patted Deborah's arm again before walking on.

"He seems nice," I ventured.

"He knows his job," she said, which was high praise.

He certainly knew how to get things moving. Within minutes, the dining room personnel had rustled up coffee, soda, and cookies for everybody. I wondered which one of the dean's affairs would be short on refreshments as a result. Since I was never invited to such things, I took extra cookies.

Finally Louis showed up, and accompanying him were a trio of young women. All three looked as if they were a year or two older than Madison, with blond hair, and had such reddened eyes that I could tell they'd been crying. I assumed that they were friends of the murder victim, and I wished I could offer them a hug or some comfort. Madison looked at them as if she were thinking.

"Do you know them?" I asked.

"I'm not sure. They look kind of familiar."

Louis took a position near the front of the room, "May I have your attention please?" He waited for people to quiet down. "I want to thank you for your patience. I know this isn't the way you intended to spend your Friday night, but as you've probably heard, a young woman was killed at McQuaid Hall. We've identified her as Kendall Fitzroy. She lived here in Pennycross and attended Brandeis in Waltham."

There were gasps and murmurs from some of the scare actors, which I interpreted as recognition.

Louis went on. "We're going to speak with each of you to find out if you saw anything that can help us determine what happened. So if you can be patient just a little while longer, we'll get the process started."

As the cops organized themselves, one of the uniformed officers came over and said, "Miss Thackery?"

"Which one?" Deborah asked.

He looked confused, but said, "Sergeant Raymond said it's okay to let people make phone calls."

"Thank you," I said.

The zombie cheerleader must have heard, because she came over and said, "So I can use your phone now?"

"Sure." I pulled it out of my purse and handed it to her.

"Some of the others want to use it, too, if that's okay."

"Of course. Just don't get any fake blood on it."

"And make sure it comes back to her!" Deborah added.

The girl nodded, and took off with it. I didn't expect to see it for a while as she and other cast members took turns reassuring their families. I was just glad I had mine with me, other than my parents, who were out of the country on sabbatical, and, of course, Sid. I'd thought about calling his phone, but if he was hiding, I didn't want the ringing to give him away. Even the noise of receiving a text might be enough to alert anybody nearby.

In a matter of minutes, several tables were set up with teams of cops with notepads to take down statements and contact information. I'm no expert, but it seemed to me that the police did a reasonably efficient job of dealing with people in order of possible involvement.

First off, they spoke with Kendall's three friends, which was painful to watch because they were all crying so hard. I was relieved when the police finished with them, and Oscar and a Pennycross officer escorted them out. I hoped somebody would be driving them home.

Next, with Deborah's help, they sorted out the customers

who'd been caught in the first few rooms of the tour, meaning pretty much everybody on the second floor. Presumably they couldn't have killed Kendall because they'd been nowhere near her. After a few quick questions, the police sent them on their way.

The bottom floor consisted of three different rooms and an outside courtyard—Madison called them scare scenes—and the body had been found in the second scene of those four. Some customers had still been in the first and third scenes when Deborah called the lockdown, and a few more had been stopped in the courtyard just past the exit. The police questioned those people with considerably more thoroughness, and even pulled a few aside to search them.

As far as I could tell, none of them owned up to knowing the victim or, needless to say, killing her. The woman who'd found the body was in that group, and shrilly repeated that she'd never even heard of Kendall Fitzroy before finding her body, and I noticed that Louis made sure she had somebody to take her home, which I thought was nice. Or maybe she was a suspect and he was keeping an eye on her.

It was then that my phone finally returned, thanks to a girl who was all too convincingly made up as having had half of her face flayed. "Here's your phone, Dr. Thackery."

"Thanks," I said, and looked hard at the relatively undecorated half of her face. "Freshman comp last spring?"

She smiled, which made the effect even creepier. "That's right. I'm Linda Zaharee."

"And your final essay was about working in a haunted house." I don't remember all my ex-students, let alone their papers, but Linda had been attentive and enthusiastic with a fabulous head of red hair, and her haunted house essay had stood out in a sea of bland personal experience papers about overcoming handicaps, being bullied, and fighting racial prejudice.

"Yeah, I'm an old hand at haunting, though I've never seen anything like this before."

"Are you holding up all right?"

"Yeah, it's just that . . . Well, I knew Kendall. Not well, but we were at Pennycross High at the same time."

"So you two graduated what, a year and a half ago?" I said, trying to decide if Madison could have known the dead girl.

She nodded. "I hadn't seen her since graduation, which makes this so strange."

"Yeah," I said, and patted her shoulder, which seemed about the right level of contact between a one-semester professor and a former student, and she seemed to appreciate the gesture.

"Thanks for letting us borrow your phone, but I'm afraid we used up the battery."

"Don't worry about it."

It was just as well, I decided when she went back to her friends. If I'd still had power, it would have been awfully tempting to risk texting Sid, even though I knew it was a bad idea. But since I couldn't, I got another cookie.

I know it sounds nuts, because one would think being around an active murder investigation would be exciting in a morbid way or at least interesting, but it was mostly just boring. Madison went to check on her friends and Deborah was reduced to grunts and glares. With my phone dead, I had no games to play, social media to catch up on, or electronic books to read. That left the other people in the room as the only distraction from imagining what would happen if Sid were found.

Earlier Deborah had speculated that the killer had left the building before the body was found, and she was probably right, but I couldn't help looking at the other people waiting to give their statements, wondering whether any of them had blood on their hands, figuratively if not literally.

Unfortunately, nobody was stalking around looking like a serial killer or twirling a mustache like a more classical villain. It was just a bunch of people, many in costume, and some showing the signs of too much partying.

One guy did catch my eye. Not that he was acting particularly suspicious, but he seemed to be by himself, and not many people went into a haunted house alone. Other than Sid, of course, who was a special case in every way. Besides, this guy looked familiar, though I couldn't place where I'd seen him. He had reddish-brown hair and a small cleft in his chin, and his eyes were an unusually deep blue. He looked at me a couple of times, too, with that same air of almost recognition.

Eventually the police finished with the customers, and it was down to the haunt crew and me. Though I suspect I could have pointed out that I wasn't involved, I didn't mind staying with Deborah and Madison. Plus I wanted to keep an ear out for any news of Sid.

Louis stood in front of the room again. "Before we talk to the rest of you individually, I want to speak to you as a group about what happened." He consulted a note pad. "Kendall Fitzroy entered McHades Hall accompanied by three friends: Alexis Primo, Nadine Seger, and Vanessa Yount. Their tour guide was a young man, walking hunched over and wearing a hood."

"That was me," said a scare actor in the outfit described. "I'm doing Igor."

Louis wrote that down. "Do you remember seeing those young women?"

"Yeah, definitely. They were, you know . . ."

Louis waited for him to get it out.

"Well, I don't want to say anything rude with that girl dead, but all of them were pretty hot." One of the other actors punched him, and he said, "What? I like blondes."

Louis just nodded. "How many others were in that group of customers?"

"Maybe seven or eight."

"Counting the four girls, it was twelve," Deborah said. "We limit our groups to a dozen, and with so many people waiting in line, we didn't let any groups go in unless they were full up."

Louis made another note and asked Igor, "Did you notice anything unusual about the group?"

"Not really. There was a family with a couple of younger kids, maybe ten or eleven, so I was mostly keeping an eye on them to make sure the kids didn't get freaked out. We've got signals to tell the other actors to tone things down if a kid is about to lose it."

"Did you have to signal anybody?"

"Nah, those kids loved it. They'd scream, then laugh, and scream and laugh again. They were having a great time."

"And the victim and her friends?"

"They stayed to the rear of the group, and they were screaming at all the right places, but it wasn't panicked screaming."

"Did you know Ms. Fitzroy before tonight?"

He shook his head.

"Then how did you know her name?"

"I didn't."

"Somebody did. According to Alexis Primo, actors were calling out 'Kendall' in what she describes as a creepy, threatening manner."

Deborah said, "It's a classic haunt gag, Louis. If an actor knows a customer's name, we'll use it. It makes the experience more intense."

"So somebody at the haunt did know her?" he persisted.

"Not necessarily. One of her friends might have said her name where it could be heard, and someone picked up on it.

Then we spread the word to the rest of the cast." She looked over at the crew. "Who started the name gag with Kendall?"

"I think it was me," a timid voice said, and a werewolf in a lab coat stepped forward. "One of the blondes came into my scene, looked around, then went back to the door and said, 'Don't worry, Kendall, no zombies.' So when I did my transformation, I said, 'Kendall, drink this for extra credit.' Once they left, I told the room monitor that we had a name."

"Who was the monitor?" Louis asked.

"Me," said a boy dressed in black. "I used the walkie-talkie to let people know, in case they wanted to pick it up. Like Ms. Thackery says, it's something we do to make the experience more personal, you know."

"Good enough," Louis said, though I thought he looked disappointed that he hadn't happened upon a real clue. "After the group made it through the rooms on the second floor, they went downstairs. I understand the stairs are better lit than the rest of the house."

"No scares on the stairs," several actors said in unison, then broke into nervous laughter.

Deborah silenced them with a look. "It's a safety precaution. It's not strong light, because that would mess up everybody's night vision, but it's bright enough for people to get down the stairs, and there's nothing to scare them or make them fall."

"Good planning," Louis said. "As I understand it, the ground floor starts with a detention hall room, then there's a hall that goes into the zombie party room where Kendall's body was found. Did you notice anything unusual then?"

Igor said, "I was sticking with the kids when I gave my intro for the scare because the zombie party is one of our more intense scenes. Then the zombies came in and started chasing. At first the kids were all right, but one of the zombies got right up in their faces, and I could see they were getting upset. So I grabbed their hands and pulled them out of there. We waited in the hall for the rest of the group to come through."

"How long were you waiting?"

"Five minutes. Maybe a little less, maybe a little more."

"And you didn't notice you were missing somebody after that room?"

"It's a dark hall, and not very long, so it was crowded. I saw blondes toward the back of the group but I didn't realize that it was only three of them. Then I gave my spiel and took the group on to the next room. I kept hold of the kids, because I was worried the chainsaw would bother them. There's something about a chainsaw."

The scare actors nodded at that bit of haunt wisdom.

Louis said, "Vanessa Yount said she and Kendall were holding hands as they went into the party room because Kendall had a phobia about zombies, but a zombie ran at them and they got separated. Vanessa thought Kendall had gone on ahead, and that she'd catch up with her in the next room. Since she and the other two women didn't see her there or in the courtyard, they waited for her in the quad. When Kendall never emerged, they tried her cell phone, but got no answer. Finally they decided that she'd gone home without them, either because she was embarrassed about being frightened or angry because she thought she'd been ditched. Also, Nadine Seger said Kendall had mentioned wanting to call her boyfriend.

"At any rate, they went to the midway, not realizing that Kendall had never left McHades until we found her cell phone and retrieved their messages."

He looked at his pad again. "Can anybody explain why there might be a baseball bat in the building?"

"You found my bat!" said a zombie in a baseball costume.

"I mean, it's not mine, but I use it for the haunt. I swing it around and bang it on the floor—it makes a great noise."

"Can you describe it?"

"Aluminum, red tape on the handle. Just a regular bat."

"When was the last time you saw it?"

"It was in the greenroom. I left it there Thursday night after our final run-through. It didn't fit in my locker, so I leaned it up against the wall. Only it wasn't there tonight."

Louis wrote all this down.

"You're not saying . . . ?" The baseball player suddenly realized why the bat was important. "I mean, I didn't hit her. Ms. Thackery, tell him I lost the bat."

"Justin reported it missing first thing this evening," Deborah said. "No big deal—props get misplaced all the time."

"We thought the ghost took it," said a tall, thin boy in bloody academic regalia.

"Ghost?" Louis said.

Deborah sighed. "Every haunt has 'real ghost' rumors. You work in the dark with fake spooks all night, in an old creaky building, and your imagination starts to run away with you. I told you that, Austin."

"Then where did Min-woo's hat go? And Charity's gloves?"

"Why would a ghost need a hat and gloves? This many people, this many props and costumes, I'm surprised more stuff doesn't go missing."

"Somebody lost a pair of gloves?" Louis said with sudden interest.

"Yeah, our werewolf chemist Charity usually wears a pair of yellow rubber gloves, and those were misplaced, too."

Louis said nothing, but took a note. "What about the bat?"

"We hunted around, but when we couldn't find it, Justin went without it. And just so you know, he's one of our most experienced scare actors and would never hit a customer."

"Nobody said he did," Louis said. "I'm just trying to find out where the bat came from."

I said, "I suppose this is a dumb question, but wouldn't the killer have blood spatter on him or her?" Remembering what many of the scare actors were covered in, I added, "Real blood, I mean."

"Normally, yes, but it looks as if he or she was standing behind the curtain that ringed the room—"

"The scrim," Deborah said.

"Excuse me?"

"The curtains? They're called scrim. From the customer side, they look opaque, but people on the back side can see through them. So whoever was behind the scrim in the zombie party would have been able to see Kendall."

"How do you spell that?" Louis said, and wrote her answer. "As I was saying, the scrim had spatter, but the killer would have stayed mostly clean. But if he or she was wearing gloves, those gloves might show some evidence." He looked to some of the other cops, but they all shook their heads, which I took to mean that they had no other questions for the group. "Okay, now we want to speak to each of you individually. Deborah, I'd appreciate it if you could help us with names."

She went to join the cops, and the rest of us sat down to wait some more. It wasn't long for me. I was the next one called, and after Deborah explained I hadn't even come into the building until after the body was discovered, I was shooed away. I suppose that I could have insisted on staying, since Madison was a minor, but I knew Deborah would watch out for her favorite—and only—niece.

So I went outside to the quad and found a bench to sit on to brood. Had the police found Sid? If not, then where was he? And how long could a grown skeleton in a Scooby-Doo suit hide? After maybe ten minutes of my thoughts going round and round like a carousel, I got part of my answer. Two state troopers walked by. One was carrying Scooby's head and the other the body. There was no sign of Sid.

I thought about making a break for it, but it would only have postponed the inevitable. As Madison and Deborah had pointed out, I'd been seen with Scooby and my outfit made it patently obvious that we were connected. Plus I'd announced I'd be waiting for my daughter, so leaving would look more than a little suspicious.

I figured I had five or ten minutes before the police came for me. Since I was an intelligent, educated woman who was able to think on her feet, surely I could come up with an explanation in that length of time.

Maybe I could pretend that I'd dressed as Velma on a whim and just happened to run into a stranger dressed as Scooby-Doo and— It wasn't even worth finishing the scenario. The ticket takers at McHades Hall had seen me talking to Scooby, the tags inside the suit identified the store it had been rented from, and the store had all my information.

That's where my brain stopped. Neither education nor native intelligence helped at all, and as for thinking on my feet, I was sitting down. I was almost relieved when I saw Louis come outside the building, look around, and then walk toward me.

"Excuse me, Dr. Thackery?" Calling me Dr. Thackery instead of Georgia was a dead giveaway. "I understand that you were seen in the company of someone wearing a Scooby-Doo costume. Can you tell me who that person was?"

I have no idea what I would have said, though I was fairly sure it would have included a lot of *um*s, *uh*s, and at least one *well, you see* . . . But before I could begin to babble, a bass voice behind me said, "That would have been me."

I turned around and blinked. Twice.
Louis said, "And you are?"
"Dr. Thackery."
Louis looked confused.
"Dr. Philip Thackery," I explained. "My father."

4

For a man over six feet tall, my father isn't particularly imposing. Maybe it's the way he gently stoops to speak to others, or the elastic suspenders he usually wears to hold up his loose-fitting jeans, or the way his glasses magnify his light blue eyes. Certainly his amiable smile that night didn't hurt.

Louis said, "Can you tell me how you came to leave your costume inside McHades Hall, Dr. Thackery?"

"Inside McHades Hall? I'm afraid I don't know what you mean."

"Your Scooby-Doo costume was found behind some curtains along the wall of one of the rooms. Or rather, a Scooby-Doo costume was found."

"How extraordinary! It very likely is mine. That's why I came looking for the police, to report that it was stolen."

"Perhaps we should go inside to talk. Both of you, if you don't mind."

"Of course," Phil said. He gave me a wink as soon as Louis turned his back, and we followed him into Stuart Hall.

Deborah and Madison were standing next to each other inside, and neither of them looked surprised to see my father, even though he and my mother had been on sabbatical for over a year and weren't expected home for two more months. Obviously they knew more of what was going on than I did.

"Hello, Deborah, Madison," Phil said. "I wanted to report that my costume was stolen, but it seems it's already been found." He looked to where the fur suit was being examined. "Look, there it is. I was so worried we'd have to pay for it. I can't imagine that a suit of that quality comes cheap."

Louis escorted us to one of the interview stations and turned his pad to a fresh page to write down Phil's name. "Now you say you weren't in McHades Hall?"

"Actually, I was there earlier in the evening. Perhaps it would be best if I started at the beginning?"

"Please do."

Phil smiled the warm professorial smile that had made so many undergraduates adore him. "I suppose you know my wife and I have been on an extended trip out of town. Circumstances dictated that we return tonight, somewhat sooner than expected, to deal with an emergency with one of my wife's students. And of course I called Georgia to let her know about our imminent arrival."

I nodded, unsure if nodding along with a lie counted as lying.

"Georgia mentioned that Madison was going to be working at McHades Hall with Deborah, and we came up with the idea of my surprising them both by showing up incognito. Georgia rented my costume, and as you see, assembled one of her own to accompany me. So after I got into town, we came to the Howl and went to McHades Hall in order for me to infiltrate." He chuckled. "It's quite exhilarating to be someone else for a night, even a cowardly Great Dane."

Louis didn't seem inclined to discuss the joys of cosplay, so Phil went on.

"Georgia opted to stay outside to keep from inadvertently giving the game away to Madison, while I went inside and had a wonderful time. The young people—I believe they call them scare actors—do an amazing job. At the last minute I made myself known to Madison, and she was completely flabbergasted. I'm convinced she never guessed it was me."

I was convinced of that, too.

"Afterward Deborah kindly provided me with another ticket, but I had to attend to a call of nature. I realized I'd never be able to fit into a porta-potty in my costume, so I decided to leave it in Georgia's car."

"So you and your daughter went back to the car?"

"No, actually, Georgia was running some sort of errand."

"I was getting hot dogs," I said, happy that I could speak a true sentence.

"How did you get into the car?" Louis asked. "Wasn't it locked?"

"Of course. Georgia is very safety conscious. However, I know where she hides a spare key. So I divested myself and put the costume into the backseat, but here's the embarrassing part." He looked properly embarrassed. "I was in such a hurry to make it back to the conveniences that I must have forgotten to lock the car door behind me. By the time I returned, the costume was gone." He turned to me. "Don't worry, dear. Nothing else was taken."

"Did you call 911?" Louis asked.

"No, though I probably should have. I rather thought that the theft must be on the order of a prank—there were a lot of students drinking. I hoped that if I wandered through the crowd, I'd locate the costume and retrieve it myself."

"It would have been wiser to call for help," Louis pointed out.

"Indubitably, but I hated the idea of a prank getting a

student into serious trouble. At any rate, I never spotted it, and had decided to go find Georgia when I heard rumors of an incident at McHades Hall. Then I saw the police presence here, and thought I'd make my report of the missing costume in person, arriving just in time to hear you ask Georgia about it." He beamed at his good luck. "Now you say somebody took my suit into McHades Hall? Does that mean you caught the thief?"

"I'm afraid not. We found the costume abandoned, and have been trying to find who was wearing it."

"Why would anybody take off a costume in the middle of a haunted house?" Phil asked innocently.

"That's what we'd like to know."

There were a few more questions, during which Phil elaborated on his tissue of lies. Had I not known he was making it all up as he went, I'd have been taken in completely. My father was a law-abiding guy for the most part, but he was also a child of the sixties. So while he didn't mistrust the police as a general rule, neither did he feel they needed to know every little detail in every circumstance.

The only thing I thought Phil had overlooked was the ticket the imaginary thief had used to get into McHades Hall without having to wait in line, but when Louis asked, he said he'd left it on top of the costume because he didn't need it in the bathroom. Louis seemed convinced, though obviously annoyed that Phil hadn't immediately called the police. Eventually he decided that Phil and I could go, though Deborah and Madison had to stay with the rest of the McHades crew. I didn't like leaving my daughter, but I thought it would be good to get Phil out of there before he added any more quirks to his story.

I did insist on hugging Madison good-bye, and she whispered, "What about Sid?"

"Sweetie, he was smart enough to dump the costume—he's smart enough to stay still while cops are around. There's nothing we can do other than keep our fingers crossed that nobody realizes he's a real skeleton. We'll get him back as soon as we can." I wasn't happy about the situation, and figured that Sid wouldn't be, either, but I didn't have any other options.

5

The crowd at the Howl had dwindled to nearly nothing, with the midway shut down and the parking lot mostly empty. Still, I waited until we were safely in my car before saying, "Phil, what are you and Mom doing back in town? Not that I'm not delighted to see you, of course, but we weren't expecting you until after the first of the year."

"I know, we should have warned you, but it was a sudden change in plans. Your mother and I had intended to return to Edinburgh and to possibly spend more time in Cardiff as well, but one of Dab's doctoral students called with an emergency. They tried to work out the problem by e-mail and phone, but Dab realized that nothing short of a personal appearance would rectify the situation. She offered to return alone, but I was ready to come home. As lovely as the trip was, I've missed sleeping in my own bed. So we traveled home by the fastest route available. Dab was going to meet her student at the house so they could devise a strategy, but since I wasn't needed, I asked the car service to drop me off here so I could enjoy the Howl. I did attempt to call your cell phone when I arrived, but it went straight to voice mail."

"My battery died."

"I thought as much. I went to McHades Hall to look for you three, and heard about the murder. Then I texted your sister to find out what had happened and was in mid-text when the police carried out the Scooby costume. When I relayed that to Deborah, she explained that some creative prevarication would be required. I think I met that challenge."

"Oh, you nailed it."

"As for the costume being left at McHades, I expect that they'll eventually chalk it up to the thief not wanting to be caught with stolen goods."

He looked inordinately pleased with himself, and I couldn't blame him. "I missed you, Phil."

"I missed you, too."

We exchanged hugs as best we could while I was driving. Then he said, "Can I safely assume that it was our skeletal friend Sid who was wearing the Scooby-Doo costume?"

"Got it in one."

"An interesting choice. At some point, I need to hear more about your activities since your return to Pennycross."

I winced. The year I'd been back in town had been fairly eventful, but Deborah, Madison, and I had agreed that it would be better not to go into too much detail about some of the things Sid and I had become involved in, especially the more dangerous aspects. Of course, there were some things we'd had to tell my parents, and they had other sources of information as well. I expected they already knew more than I wanted them to.

Phil said, "I trust our early arrival won't disrupt you and Madison too much."

"Phil, it's your house!" My daughter and I had been living in the Victorian house where Deborah and I had grown up for over a year, and the fact that it had been rent free had meant that I'd been able to pay off my credit cards and sock away some extra savings, but I'd never forgotten that it was a temporary situation. Admittedly, I'd hoped to get through Christmas shopping without the burden of rent, but if I had to break out the credit cards again, I would.

Traffic was considerably less bothersome than it had been earlier in the evening, and we were soon back home. Byron came running when we went in the door, and woofed suspiciously at Phil.

"Oh, coccyx!" I said. "I hope Byron didn't give Mom a hard time when she came in."

Phil chuckled.

"What?"

"I see you've picked up your old habits, using bone names as invective."

"I'm afraid I have." When Sid had first come to live with us, his language had been a little salty, which we attributed to his coming to life in the middle of a carnival. Mom and Phil had asked him to tone it down around Deborah and me, and Sid had developed his own style of cussing, which I'd adopted, too. I stopped when I left home, but once I moved back to Pennycross and started spending more time with him, I'd reverted.

Byron paid no attention to our walk down memory lane. He started to leave the room, looked back at me, went a few steps, looked again, and repeated until I got the hint that I was supposed to follow him. He impatiently led the way to the kitchen, where my mother was sitting with a solidly built woman in black yoga pants and a grey sweatshirt. No wonder Byron was annoyed—there were strangers in what he considered his domain.

The two of them were talking earnestly when we came in, but as soon as Mom looked up and saw me, she broke into a smile and jumped up for a big hug. I returned it, with interest, then we leaned back to beam at each other. "You look great," we said in unison, then laughed.

Mom's gray hair was longer than I'd seen it in years, and she looked so bright eyed and trim that I knew the sabbatical had agreed with her. We hugged again, and I heard Phil blowing his nose behind me, though I knew he'd deny it if I accused him of getting choked up. He's a lot more sentimental than he'll ever admit.

"I want to hear all about how you and Madison have been doing," Mom said, "but can it wait a little while? Roxanne here is in mid-crisis, and we're plotting strategy. You remember Roxanne Beale, don't you?"

Now that I got a good look at her, I did. Roxanne had been a fixture at McQuaid for over a decade, first as an undergraduate and then as one of those perpetual grad students who was always on the verge of finishing her doctorate. Mom had actually inherited Roxanne from another professor who'd given up and retired before managing to get her to graduation.

"Hi, Roxanne, how's it going?"

"It's a disaster, a total disaster. I cannot believe this is happening to me." She looked so distraught I was thinking cancer or some other deadly disease.

Mom said, "I'm afraid Roxanne has nearly reached the time limit for completing her dissertation. She expected to be granted another extension, but she got a letter from the department that she has to be finished by the end of the semester."

"Oh, my," I said, horrified on her behalf. Okay, it wasn't cancer, but anybody who'd gone through the process of getting a doctorate had had the nightmare of never finishing and going through life with the letters ABD—All But Dissertation—as an ignominious end to a once-promising academic career.

"It's Dr. Eberhardt!" Roxanne said. "He hates the Romantic poets!"

"It's just a misunderstanding," Mom said. "I'll talk to him Monday and we'll get this all straightened out."

Roxanne nodded, but I don't think she was convinced.

"It's getting late, so why don't you go home and get a good night's sleep. Take the rest of the weekend off and relax for a change."

"Wait, what time is it?" Roxanne said, looking at the clock on the microwave. "I'm supposed to go down to the Howl and meet a friend. She's helping me crunch my research numbers. Has the haunted house closed yet?"

"As a matter of fact, it closed early," I said. "There was an incident. A woman was killed."

Roxanne went from disconsolate to panicked. "My friend Linda was working there tonight. It wasn't her, was it?"

"No, it wasn't any of the people working at the haunt. It was a customer named Kendall Fitzroy."

"Oh, good," she said, and sank back into her chair.

I'd felt the same when finding out that Madison was safe, though I was expecting her to add something like *Oh, but I'm so sorry that woman is dead.*

Instead it was, "If anything happened to Linda, I'd never finish my dissertation."

Mom winced, but said, "I'm glad your friend is safe. Here, let me get your jacket." In a moment, she had Roxanne out of the house.

"Wow," I said. "Was I that oblivious when I was working on my dissertation?"

"I think Roxanne has a special gift for being oblivious," she said.

"What's her dissertation on, anyway? Since when does a literature student need numbers crunched?"

"She's comparing word use and evolution of language across a number of Romantic Era poets. It's fascinating work and she has mounds of data, but has never been able to put it together in any useful way. I gather that this girl Linda is a gonzo statistician." She waved it away. "Enough of that. Come tell me what happened at the Howl."

While I told her, Phil started puttering around the kitchen, and soon a grilled ham and cheese sandwich and a soda appeared in front of me.

"Phil, you didn't have to do that. I should be taking care of you—you two must be jet-lagged out of your minds."

"Not a bit of it," he said. "I've traveled so much the past year that I never worry about what time zone I'm in anymore, and I'm delighted to have my kitchen back. Now eat up before it gets cold."

"I respect you too much to argue," I said, and dug in.

Some people would have bristled at suddenly having "their" kitchen reclaimed, but I admit to a complete lack of territoriality over cooking. I'm not a bad cook, and I do my best to keep Madison fed appropriate nutrients, but it's because it's part of my job, not because I particularly enjoy it. Phil, on the other hand, has always loved cooking and admitted one of his favorite parts about Madison's and my visits home was having people other than my mother and mooching grad students to feed.

Just as I finished eating, the door opened and Madison and Deborah came in. A bevy of hugging ensued.

"Any word about Sid?" I asked after we disengaged.

Deborah shook her head. "If they've found him, Louis didn't mention it to me. We may have lucked out."

"I wanted to go back and get him," Madison said, "but Aunt Deborah said we couldn't."

"The police wouldn't even let the crew get their street clothes," Deborah explained. "All they would let them do is get things like keys and wallets and phones, and they watched us the whole time. There was no way to sneak out a skeleton."

"It won't hurt him to spend the night in whatever hiding place he's found," I assured Madison.

She looked as happy about it as I felt, which was not very, but Deborah knows the best way to distract teenagers. She said, "Anything to eat around here? I'm starved."

"Coming right up," Phil said happily, and got busy grilling more sandwiches.

"What happened after Phil and I left?" I asked.

"Not much. It turns out some of my people knew the girl, but nobody saw anything that would help the cops."

"The awful thing is that I realized that I knew her, too," Madison said. "Or at least I met her. Her younger sister Bianca is part of choral ensemble and Kendall came to our Christmas show last year."

Madison was sitting between Mom and me, and we both reached over to offer hugs. Phil delivered a sandwich just then, too, which may have been more on point for a tired teenager.

"This is great, G-Dad," Madison said between bites. "So was that story you told the cops. How did you come up with it that fast?"

"Phil has years of study from all the excuses he's been given for why papers haven't been graded on time," Mom said affectionately.

"Of course it usually isn't a good idea to lie to the police," I said, realizing that we might not be setting the best example for my daughter. "Not that I'm saying that Phil did anything wrong, but this was a very unusual circumstance. You get that, right?"

"Yes, Mom," she said, and I knew she was resisting the urge to roll her eyes.

Deborah showed no such restraint, and followed an excellent demonstration of eye-rolling by saying, "Now that we've enjoyed our teachable moment, maybe we should make some plans. Once Sid gets back, you know he's going to want to involve himself in this murder."

"Don't worry. I'll tell him that the cops have got this one. They've got a body to work with, and Sid wasn't a witness, so there's no reason to interfere. I know the last thing you want is for him to be messing around McHades Hall. Right?"

"Wrong. I want Sid on the job. And you, too."

"Excuse me?"

"You heard me. I want you guys to investigate the murder."

"Who are you, and what have you done with my sister?"

Though Deborah had come through for me when I needed her help the other times I'd stuck my nose into police work, she'd made it plain that she'd have been considerably happier if I'd stayed out of it.

"Here's the thing," she said. "I was watching the cops mill around after you left, and it's pretty obvious that they think the guy in the Scooby suit was involved. I'm not blaming you or Sid—"

"Thanks so much."

"I said I'm not blaming you, all right! But you and I both know the police wouldn't be going in that direction if it weren't for them thinking a nonexistent thief snuck out of the haunt."

"Doesn't that make it my fault?" Phil said mildly. "Should I have come up with a different explanation?"

"No, Dad, you were great. If it weren't for you, the police would be leaning on Georgia, trying to find out who she rented that costume for. Now she's safe, but the police aren't going to be able to find the real killer."

"You don't know that," I said.

"I know every minute they spend searching for Scooby is a minute wasted. Look, Georgia, I'm not asking you to do anything you haven't done before."

"Ahem!" I said, looking at our parents.

Phil and Mom started one of their silent conversations, the kind made up of lifted eyebrows and significant glances that had infuriated Deborah and me while we were growing up. In fact, they still infuriated me.

"Georgia," Mom said gently, "we don't have all the details, but we do know that your recent research projects haven't been entirely academic."

"You do?" I said, eyeing both my sister and my daughter speculatively.

Before I could decide who'd spilled the beans, Deborah said, "Look, it's late and we're all tired. Just think it over, okay?"

Phil yawned pointedly. That started a round of yawns, and I knew I'd been outmaneuvered for the time being.

"Fine," I said. "We'll talk after we get Sid back."

But after Deborah left and the rest of us got ready for bed, I started thinking that there might be something my sister wasn't telling me. Plus, despite what I'd told Madison, I couldn't help worrying about Sid. I'd charged my phone as soon as I got home, but there'd been no word from him. Where was he, anyway? Was he okay?

It took me forever to get to sleep.

6

The phone woke me considerably earlier the next morning than I wanted to get up, given the night before. I was scrambling to answer it when I realized it hadn't rung a second time. Since Madison didn't have a landline in her room, I concluded that it had been a wrong number and the caller had given up. I punched my pillow into the proper shape and would have fallen asleep again had there not been a knock on the bedroom door.

"Georgia?" my mother said. "Deborah needs to talk to you."

Right. Mom and Phil were back. I grabbed my phone, and politely said, "What do you want?"

"I'm on my way over to the haunt."

"You aren't opening tonight, are you?"

"Are you awake yet? Of course we're not opening tonight—it's an active crime scene and they're still doing all that forensics stuff. Once that's done, Detective Raymond here wants me to walk him through the place, to show him how we operate. Then he should be able to let the cast come pick up their personal belongings. I thought you might want to bring Madison over to pick up her *things*."

"You mean I'll be able to get Sid, right?"

"Sure, if she left her school books here, she can pick them up, too."

"School books? What are you—? Wait, is Louis right there listening?"

"Obviously."

"Okay. What time should we be over there?"

"Sometime this afternoon, maybe one or two. I'll call when I know for sure."

"One or—" I looked at the clock. "Deborah, it's eight o'clock in the morning. Why did you call me so early?"

"No, no trouble at all."

She hung up before I could tell her what a miserable piece of sacrum she was, so I hung up my own phone and rolled back over, determined to get some more sleep.

Until I smelled bacon cooking.

I cannot fathom how anybody could have slept after that tantalizing scent wafted through the house. After five minutes of trying to resist, I gave up, took a quick shower, put on my Saturday loafing jeans and a Boston University sweatshirt, and made my way downstairs to find Phil once again at the stove.

"You really did miss cooking, didn't you?" I said.

"Tremendously. How do pancakes and bacon sound?"

"As good as they smell."

"I was going to make omelets, but there weren't enough eggs. There's not much maple syrup, either."

"I was planning to shop today," I said a little defensively.

"No problem. Your mother went to the grocery store to stock up. Oh, she had to take your car because we haven't picked ours up yet. Is that all right?"

"Sure," I said, trying not to sound annoyed. "It's low on gas, but there should be enough—"

"Don't worry, she'll fill up the tank on the way back. Now if you'll set the table, I'll have the pancakes ready in a couple of minutes."

I saw that Byron was in his favorite spot under the table, hoping that somebody would drop some food, and it seemed plain that he'd already adjusted to having Mom and Phil around.

"I should get Madison up to tend to the dog," I said.

"Oh, let her sleep. I took him for a quick walk when I got up."

"It's okay to wake her to take care of him, Phil. She knows Byron is her responsibility."

"I don't mind."

I made a mental note to remind Madison that she was not to take advantage of my father's willingness to help. Of course, I'd be more convincing if I weren't eating a batch of Phil's pancakes at the time.

Despite his apologies that he was off his game, I'd made it through a stack of them plus accompanying bacon when Mom got back with vast quantities of groceries, and it took all three of us to put it all away.

"Are you planning to feed an army?" I asked.

"I remember how much teenagers eat, and I expect Roxanne will be coming around."

"Funny how often grad students show up near mealtimes. Which reminds me, I should write you a check for Madison's and my share."

"Oh, don't worry about that," Mom said. "You can buy the next load."

Phil took advantage of the additional available ingredients to make omelets, despite my insistence that I'd already had plenty to eat. I only ate mine to keep from hurting his feelings.

Afterward, as we sat sated at the table, I said, "You know I'm really glad you two are back, but it did catch me by surprise. I haven't even started looking for a place for Madison and me yet."

Mom said, "Your father and I were talking about that last night, Georgia, and there's no rush. In fact, maybe we should consider making this a permanent solution. After all, the house was big enough for all of us when Madison was a baby."

"Are you sure about that?" I said. "Teenager Madison takes up a lot more space than infant Madison. Plus we've got the dog now."

Byron, who is no dummy, picked that moment to lean lovingly against Phil, who patted him and said, "Oh, Byron is no trouble at all."

"Well as long as we divide up the housework—and the expenses—I'm willing to give it a shot, but if you start to feel crowded or taken advantage of, speak up immediately!"

Mom patted my hand. "I'm sure things will work out just fine."

"Sounds great," I said, but I wasn't completely sanguine. I'd known a fair number of people in my generation who'd had to move back in with their parents for financial reasons—it was distressingly common among adjuncts—but I hadn't known any who'd enjoyed the process. Still, I was going to need a new set of tires on my car before winter set in, and if Madison and I could stand to share a house with my parents for even a month or two, it would help my bottom line quite a bit.

Since Mom had taken care of the grocery shopping, I got started on laundry. Madison eventually woke up, and after Phil fed her, I took her aside to tell her about the idea of sharing the house.

I was expecting a little pushback, since it had been just the two of us for most of her life, and adding Sid to the mix had required some adjustment. But she said, "Makes sense to me."

"You're sure?"

"It'll take a lot of the burden off of you if we don't have to move, so why not?"

"Sweetie, my job is to make life easier for you, not the other way around."

"I know, but seriously, the house is big enough for all of us, and you get along with G-Mom and G-Dad. Now if it were Aunt Deborah—"

"Don't even go there," I said. "Speaking of my beloved sister . . ."

"Please don't tell me you two are feuding."

"We don't feud. We just disagree some of the time."

"As in all the time."

"Some of the time," I insisted. After all, 99 percent of the time still counted as "some," and Deborah and I weren't that bad. I explained the plan for us to head to the haunt to get her things and retrieve Sid. "Are you okay with that?"

"Sure," she said. "I didn't have anything planned for today other than working at the haunt, and that's not happening."

"I mean are you okay with going back to McHades Hall after what happened there?"

"Well, I wouldn't want to go there alone in the middle of the night, but otherwise, it's no problem. I am just as glad I didn't see the body."

"I could have done without seeing her myself," I said, though it hadn't been my first dead body. I still wasn't sure how I felt about being able to say that. "Anyway, are you sure about going over there?"

"Mom, I go to PHS every day, and there was a murder, an attack, and an abduction there last year."

"True," I said, "but if you change your mind or want to talk to your therapist again, just let me know."

"Will do," she said. "What about you?"

"Wait, I'm the mother. I'm supposed to ask these things."

"I could call G-Mom and get her to ask."

Phil, who wandered through the living room at that point, cleared his throat.

"Or G-Dad," Madison said.

"I'm fine. Living with a walking, talking dead guy takes a lot of the scare out of it."

"I get that, but I meant going to McHades when you've got a thing about haunted houses. What's the story with that, anyway?"

Fortunately the phone rang, so I was able to dodge the conversational bullet.

"Thackery residence," I answered.

"It's Deborah. The police say people can come get their belongings now. Be sure to bring something big enough to carry all Madison's *stuff*."

"Message received." I hung up the phone and said, "Time to go get Sid."

7

Though it was just past one in the afternoon and the night's Halloween Howl festivities weren't due to start until four, there were more people out and about on the McQuaid quad than usual for a Saturday afternoon. A small horde of physical plant people and student volunteers were gathering debris and emptying trash cans, trying to get the grounds cleaned up before they all got messed up again.

The front door to McHades Hall was striped with yellow crime-scene tape, and there were signs that said *Closed until further notice* on the ticket tent and the front entrance. An extremely bored-looking Pennycross police officer was stationed at the door.

"Hi. My daughter works here and we were told she could come claim her belongings."

"Can I see some identification?" she asked.

I pulled out my driver's license and Madison handed over her student ID. The officer radioed somebody, gave our names, then handed back our cards. "You're clear."

"Is the press causing problems?"

She nodded, looking disgusted. "We gave them everything we could, and they still want to poke around. Head in and somebody will escort you to the greenroom."

That wasn't good to hear. I didn't know how we'd be able to sneak Sid out with a police officer in attendance.

The building was chilly, despite the sunny afternoon, and the place was dark thanks to the blackout curtains hung over every window to maintain the spooky atmosphere. An officer was waiting just inside the door and he said, "Come on up."

"I know the way," Madison said.

"My orders are to stay with you." He led us up the two flights of the main stairs, through a set of wooden double doors, and into a large room that looked as if it took up most of the floor. Despite all the dark woodwork, it was surprisingly bright, with skylights letting in the October afternoon sunlight.

"I think this was used for studio art classes when this building was first built," I said, remembering an article I'd read in the college paper. "It started out as the McQuaid School of Art, and then morphed into the university."

"I didn't know that," Madison said.

There was a handful of other people in the room: Louis, yet another cop, Oscar from McQuaid security, Deborah, and an assortment of young people I assumed were cast members, though I didn't recognize any of them without their guts hanging out.

"Hey, guys," Deborah said. "I hope you're not in a hurry. Louis says he has to inspect all the bags, despite the fact that they found the murder weapon last night." She made a face at a table where Louis and a uniformed officer were searching through a cast member's pocketbook.

"So much for our rescue mission," I said under my breath.

"Don't worry, I've got it covered," Deborah said. "So this is the greenroom. Men's room on one side, women's room on the other. A kitchen on the end. Lockers next to that for cast members to keep their stuff. I make them lock up their cell phones so they don't spend all night taking selfies and posting pictures of people looking scared on Facebook. There's always somebody on duty in here to help with makeup and wardrobe malfunctions, and somebody else mans the kitchen and the first aid kit. The crew takes breaks up here and waits for their shifts to start."

"Okay," I said, wondering why she was being so chatty.

"We've got chairs and couches for people to relax over there. Makeup tables by the wall, though a lot of kids do their own at home. That whiteboard by the door has the cast schedule and a place for them to sign in and out. They do get paid—not a lot, because the point is to raise money for the Scholars Committee—but paying them means they show up as scheduled. Most of the time. Everybody who was scheduled was actually here last night."

"Right." Looking at the list made me feel sorry for Louis. All of those people had to be considered suspects.

"Anything else you need to see?" Deborah asked.

"Like what?" Suddenly it dawned on me that she was assuming that Sid and I were going to investigate the murder. "Hey, what happened to 'we'll talk about it later'?"

She tried to look innocent. "Hmmm? I just thought you'd be interested in a behind-the-scenes view. It might be useful someday."

"Yeah, right."

Madison intervened by saying, "Maybe I should get my stuff."

"Good idea," Deborah said.

Madison's backpack was shoved into a locker along with an assortment of clothing and makeup. "Should I take everything, Aunt Deborah? Or is the haunt going to reopen?"

"That's between the police and the Scholars Committee,"

Deborah said. "The cops want it shut—the committee wants it open."

"Who's on the committee?" I asked.

"The McQuaid Quintet. Officially there are some others on the membership roster, but that's just for show."

I'd never met any members of the family who'd given the university its name, but their presence was often felt in town. "In that case, I'm betting it'll reopen sooner rather than later."

Madison hesitated, then put the spooky makeup back into the locker. Even high school students knew that when the McQuaids spoke, Pennycross listened.

Deborah checked the time on her phone. "We better get inspected. I think it's going to get really crowded in a couple of minutes."

Madison carried her backpack over to the table and unzipped it. Louis was thorough but professional, and didn't even question why my daughter carried three different bottles of scented hand sanitizer.

"How about that?" he said when he was done, nodding at the duffel bag I had on my shoulder.

"It's empty," Deborah said. "Some of the costumes and props need repair jobs, so I'm going to take them home. Is that okay?"

"Sure, that's fine," Louis said.

Deborah took the bag from me, went to a couple of lockers, pulled out the contents, and shoved it into the duffel, leaving the bag about three-quarters empty. Then she took it over for Louis to inspect.

He gave it a cursory examination and returned it. "You're good to go."

She promptly handed it back to me and said, "Here, make yourself useful. I've got to stick around, but one of the officers will walk you down. Bathroom break first, right?"

She shoved Madison and me in the direction of the ladies

restroom and closed the door behind us just as the officer from downstairs came in with seven or eight chattering cast members.

"What are you doing?" I asked her.

"Working around the cops," she said, looking at her phone again. "Okay, the next wave will be here in a couple of minutes. Come on."

She hauled us out, and said, "Hey, Louis, can somebody—?" Then she pretended to notice that all the cops were busy searching bags. "Whoa, bad timing on your part, Georgia. Hey, Louis, you want me to walk Georgia and Madison out while you inspect those bags?"

"If you don't mind," he said, looking harried.

"No problem. Come on, ladies."

I expected her to sneak off once we were out of Louis's sight, but she went straight down to the entrance hall, where more cast members had just arrived. The officer stationed there was on the radio with Louis, looking overwhelmed, and even more so as more people came in.

Deborah said, "Jeez, everybody came at once? You want me to watch the door while you take this batch to the green-room?"

"Yeah, that would be great," he said. "Okay, guys, let's head upstairs."

I saw Deborah mouth the word "stall" at a couple of the actors, who nodded and slowed to a snail's pace.

As soon as the cop was out of sight, Deborah said, "Madison, go halfway up and let us know when he's coming back. I'm hoping he'll stay up there to help search bags, but I can't be sure. I've got more people coming in as distractions, so I'll wait here. Georgia, you remember how we went last night?"

"Yeah."

"Go back through the control booth, and then turn right instead of going straight to get to the room on the end of the building. That's got to be where Sid is hiding. And make it snappy!"

"Got it!" The room where Deborah had sent me had a big sign on the wall—*Detention*—and was lined with cages. First up were cages inhabited by starved-looking mannequins clinging to the bars, then desiccated mannequins collapsed on the floor, partially denuded mannequins with red-eyed rubber rats in attendance, and finally, several cages of skeletons. Most of the cages had a single inhabitant, but the one on the end had two skeletons inside.

No wonder Deborah had sent me there—it was hard to beat the purloined letter approach.

"Sid!" I said.

Neither skeleton moved.

"Sid, it's me. Pull yourself together and we'll get you out of here." Still no movement. "Sid?" Surely nothing could have happened to him. As long as his bones were intact, he should be okay. Shouldn't he?

I started to reach for him, but something touched my back and I yelped and jerked around. Sid was standing beside me. Grinning. Of course, he was always grinning, but this time it was wider than usual.

"Georgia, why are you talking to a prop?"

"I wasn't—"

"You thought that was me, didn't you? You know somebody over twenty years—*twenty years*—and she doesn't even recognize you!"

"It's dark in here!" I said, though it really wasn't. "Besides, you have to admit that guy looks a lot like you."

"Please tell me you're kidding! Not only is that thing cheap plastic, not only is the spine one solid piece, not only is it a color not found in nature—"

"Sid, you're not exactly found in nature, either."

He ranted on as if I hadn't interrupted.

"Even if you ignore that, *that* is a female skeleton!" He pulled it out with a look of disgust, then shoved it into the cage from which he'd emerged. "Here's your room back, sweetie."

"Shall I leave the two of you together, or are you ready to go home?"

"Home, please. She's a lousy conversationalist."

I unzipped the canvas duffel and laid it flat on the floor. Deborah had been careful. Even with the clothes in there, there was room for Sid.

He stepped into the center of it, then fell apart in an orderly fashion. One finger bone landed outside the bag, but his other hand reached outside to grab it and put it inside. Then he zipped himself in.

It would have been fascinating to watch if we hadn't been in a hurry.

"Where's your phone?" I asked.

"It's in my skull."

Of course it was. I hefted the bag onto my shoulder. Sid's bones only weigh about twenty pounds, but added to the contents already there, it made a lot to carry. "Can you keep from rattling? I don't want anybody getting suspicious."

"Of course."

I'm not sure how he prevented it, but since I'm not really sure how Sid does any of the things he does, that was no big surprise.

I retraced my steps and just as I rejoined Deborah, Madison came down the stairs. "He's on his way back," she said. "Did you get Sid?"

"I'm in here," Sid said cheerfully.

"Shhh," I said, and poked the bag. I thought I heard a muttered "ow," but as long as the police officer didn't hear it, I didn't care. It wasn't like I could really hurt Sid anyway.

Once the officer was back at his post, Deborah said good-bye, adding, "Tell Mom and Dad that if they don't have plans for dinner, I'll come over and we'll order pizza."

"Sounds great," I said, hoping I didn't sound as phony to the cop as I did to myself. As Madison and I went out, I kept waiting for the long arm of the law to reach for me, but we made it safely to the car.

I just hoped none of the police had taken pictures of the room where Sid had been hiding, or at some point they might wonder why there was one fewer skeleton than before.

8

Madison and I barely got in the front door when Sid started yelping, "Put me down, I want out!"

"Stop rocking," I said as I gladly put down the heavy duffel in the front hallway.

The bag unzipped from inside, and in a process that always entertains me, the bones reassembled themselves and Sid stood up. With a joyful rattle, he bounded into the living room where my parents were on the couch going through mail that had arrived in their absence.

"Dr. T! Dr. Mrs. T!" Sid said, jumping between them so he could hug one with each arm. "You two are a sight for sore eye sockets!" I'd told him on the way home that my parents had returned.

"Thank you, Sid," Mom said. "You're looking well yourself."

"I think I've lost weight since I saw you last. Does it show?"

"It's very becoming."

"Tell us about the trip. I want to hear everything! Which place was your favorite? Did you like the food? Did you make it to Shakespeare's house? Did you see the Rosetta Stone? What about 221B Baker Street—you did go there, didn't you? And Scotland! Tell me about Scotland!"

"Sid, they can't tell you anything if you don't stop asking questions," I pointed out.

"Sorry, sorry. Was the White Tower awesome?"

Mom and Phil laughed and started telling stories ranging from spotting a rainbow in Stratford-upon-Avon that seemed to end at Shakespeare's grave to viewing the Crown Jewels but somehow finding the reproductions at Madame Tussauds Wax Museum more impressive to the near-religious experiences of visiting the British Library and Trinity College Library in Dublin.

I was as interested as Sid was, and even Madison stopped texting now and then to listen in, but I grew more and more distracted as time went on. As fascinating as the wonders of the Jane Austen tour were, my mind couldn't help but wander back to the murder at McHades Hall. So as subtly as I could, I pulled out my cell phone to start checking the Web.

The police hadn't given out much info to the press other than the fact of the victim's death and the usual "investigations are proceeding" line, but a murder in a haunted house was lurid enough to spawn a lot of interest. Add in the facts that Kendall Fitzroy had been young and pretty, and seemed to have no shadows on her background, and it was an irresistible story. There were grief-stricken quotes from her family, boyfriend, and friends, including the trio of high school buddies who'd been with her the night of her death.

Apparently they had a tradition of attending the Howl together, and even though three of them were attending college out of town, they'd all come home for the festivities. An enterprising reporter had found a photo from a previous

Halloween of the four of them dressed as Disney villain-esses. I couldn't decide if it was poignant or morbid.

Another reporter had researched deaths occurring in haunted houses, which turned out not to be unheard of, but all the others were suicides or accidents. I couldn't imagine why anybody would have gone to the trouble of committing murder in such a public location. Sure, it was dark and confusing, but there were so many people around. Could it have been a random murder of opportunity?

"Georgia!" Sid said, and I realized everybody else in the room was looking at me.

"Hmmm?"

"Do you know what time Deborah is planning to come over?" Mom asked.

Fortunately my sister texted me at that very moment. "She's on her way to Town House right now," I said. "What kind of pizza do people want?" After we negotiated our order, Madison and I went to set the dining room table and get drinks. We had everything ready by the time Deborah arrived, and we dug right in.

It was, I realized, a special occasion of sorts. Since Madison had only been formally introduced to Sid during Mom and Phil's sabbatical, this was the first time all six of us had sat down to eat together. Not that Sid actually ate, of course, but he was there at the table. I wasn't the only one who noticed, either. Sid was grinning to beat the band. It's not easy to have facial expressions when you're a skeleton and don't technically have a face, but somehow he manages.

After dinner was eaten and cleaned up, my parents went to their room to finish unpacking and Madison got picked up by a friend to hang at another friend's house. Deborah, Sid, and I ended up in the living room.

"So let's talk murder," Sid said. "Deborah, I know you'd

rather Georgia and I not stick our noses in things like this, but this time I think—"

"Stow it, Bone Boy. I want you to stick your nose in. Or nasal cavity, if that's all you've got to work with."

"You do?" he said, eye holes wide with astonishment.

She nodded. "It's Georgia who's balking."

He turned to me. "You are?"

"I just don't see why we need to get involved."

"Come on, we all know you're going to," Deborah said. "Sid is ready and raring to play Sherlock Bones, and you like being Dr. Watson."

"Why isn't he Dr. Watson?"

"Because Sherlock Thackery sounds lame," Sid said. "And you are a doctor."

"But—"

Deborah cleared her throat loudly. "Georgia, you can be Holmes, or Nancy Drew, or Jessica Fletcher. Just find out what happened to that girl. It's not like I ask you for much."

I couldn't argue with that. Over the years, my big sister had helped me with child care, loans, and keeping an eye on our parents while I was living elsewhere. Besides which, the way my mind had started wandering earlier, I knew I was already hooked. "If you really want me to—"

"Want *us* to!" Sid put in.

"If you want us to, we will. But knowing why could help."

"Fine! I want you to solve this because the murder was my fault."

"Excuse me?"

"What was the first thing Louis asked about? Security footage! I should have put cameras in there. If I had, that girl would be alive, or at least we'd know who killed her. But the McQuaids said there wasn't enough money in the budget, and I let it go. I should have insisted that they find the money. Or I should have put in more room monitors. Security is my business, and then I go and let one of my people—I let one of my customers get killed."

"Wait, back up. What do you mean one of your people? Kendall Fitzroy wasn't one of yours."

"I misspoke."

The patella she had! "Deborah, do you think one of your cast members killed that girl?"

"Well who else could it have been? Who but a cast member would have been able to attack her from behind the scrim, and know how to get out of there without being seen?"

"The police seem comfortable with the idea that an outsider could have committed the crime or they wouldn't be trying to find Scooby-Doo."

"Maybe," she said, "but they were questioning the cast members pretty hard last night."

"They're going to question anybody and everybody: Kendall Fitzroy's friends and family and especially her boyfriend. So of course they'll talk to your people. If nothing else, they may have seen something useful. That doesn't make them active suspects."

"I guess. It's just that all last night while I was watching the cops work, I kept thinking of things I could have done. Things I should have done." She took a deep breath. "This may not be something you get, because you've never been in charge of a business, but I've run my own place since I got out of school, and the first thing I learned is that when you're the boss, everything that goes wrong is your fault."

"'The buck stops here,'" I quoted.

"That's the way I see it, anyway. That girl came to McHades to have a good time. Maybe she was going to get scared and scream a little, but at the end of the evening, she'd be laughing because she knew it wasn't really dangerous. She trusted me to keep her safe, and I failed her. I can't bring her back, so I want to be damned sure the killer doesn't get away with it. I could sit on my hands and let the cops do whatever it is they do, but what if the stuff with Sid puts them off their game? Or I could try to snoop around myself, but I'm no good at that kind of thing. You and Sid are. You've solved murders the cops didn't even know about."

"They'd have been able to solve them if they'd known about them," I said.

"Possibly, and if they beat you to the punch this time, that's okay by me. But I'm not taking a chance on it. I want you and Sid on the job, if you're willing."

"Of course we're willing," said Sid. "Hang on while I get something to take notes on." I'm not sure that my grocery shopping notepad from the kitchen, complete with twee pictures of fruits and vegetables, was quite the right thing, but it was handy. "The police didn't say much where I could hear them last night, so I need you two to fill me in."

I rapped on his skull. "You are pretty hollow in there."

"Very droll. Facts, please?"

"Fine." I told him about how we'd found out about the murder, and what had happened since, with Deborah adding the details I missed.

Sid jotted down notes as we went. "Deborah, did you get anything else from your pal Louis? Did he tell you who he suspects?"

I said, "He suspects you, or whoever it was in the Scooby suit."

"Then he's an idiot, right, Deborah?" Sid said.

I expected her to join in on the Trash Louis party, but instead she said, "He's not that bad. You have to admit that your disappearance looks suspicious."

Sid and I exchanged glances, mine with raised eyebrows and his with no eyebrows at all. Was Deborah warming up to Louis?

Sid opened his jaw to say something, but I shook my head. Nothing would set Deborah off faster than teasing her about a romance that might or might not exist, and she'd already had a rough weekend.

Instead I said, "You spent a lot of time over at the haunt today, plus you were at Stuart Hall last night longer than I was. You must have heard something we can use."

"What about those three friends that were with our victim?" Sid asked. "What were their names?"

"I don't remember."

I didn't, either, and Sid looked vexed until I said, "The online news story I read mentioned their names."

"What about the boyfriend's name?"

"That's online, too," I said.

"Good. One always looks at the boyfriend first," he said solemnly.

"But the boyfriend wasn't in the haunt," Deborah said.

"He could have been," Sid said. "If he was in costume and managed to get into the same group as the victim, he could have killed her and been long gone by the time the body was found."

"There were also those people who scooted out when my security guys were trying to lock the building down. It's not like my guys could tase them," Deborah said.

"So for suspects," I said, "we've got Kendall's friends, family, and boyfriend. Plus the crew of the haunt and anybody who went through the haunt with Kendall."

Deborah said, "Actually, it could have been somebody from two groups before Kendall's to two after. When we're running at full capacity, it's four groups in the haunt at once. Technically their guides are supposed to keep up with them, but people get separated from their groups all the time. They get freaked by a particular room and go past very quickly, or they get freaked and freeze. Or they are freaks and stop and stare at a particular scare area. The guides keep things moving, but it's dark and it's confused. Just about anybody in the haunt at that time could have gotten to the zombie room, killed her, and then either gone on ahead or backtracked."

"So forty-eight more suspects," I said.

"Forty-seven," Sid said. "You don't have to count Kendall."

"Fine, only forty-seven. I'm so relieved."

"Forget the numbers," Sid said. "Let's try from the other direction. What do we know about the victim?"

I said, "I didn't get a chance to do a lot of research, but nothing I saw online gives a hint of why somebody might have wanted to kill her."

Deborah sighed. "This is starting to sound impossible."

"No, no, no," Sid said. "We're just getting started. You leave this to us. I'm going online right now to see what I can dig up." He was up the stairs in a bony flash.

Deborah looked at me.

"You asked for it," I pointed out.

"I guess I did." She hesitated, then said, "Just be careful, all right. I do want this thing solved, but . . . you know."

Another sister might have gone on to say how important I was to her, or that she hated the idea of even a hair on my head getting a split end, but Deborah wasn't that sister. Instead she said, "I'm going to Arturo's to get some ice cream. You want to come with?"

Spurred on by her ice-cream-sensing superpower, Madison texted me to ask for a ride home right after we left Arturo's, so we swung by to get her before taking the bounty home to share with my parents. They confessed to trying ice cream in many different places on their travels, but swore that nothing they found had compared to Arturo's dark chocolate. That led to more travel tales, to which I paid closer attention.

By the time they ran out of stories, it was time for Deborah to go home and for the rest of us to go to bed. Except Sid, of course. He'd kept us company for the ice cream party, but not having the demands of the flesh, as Phil put it, he didn't need to sleep. So instead he spent the night in his attic doing homework for the online class in art history he was taking and seeing what he could find out about Kendall Fitzroy.

When I got up Sunday morning, I found a neatly formatted dossier about the dead girl slipped under my bedroom door. Kendall Fitzroy had grown up in Pennycross and graduated from Pennycross High School, the same school Madison attended. Kendall was in her sophomore year at Brandeis University, studying business administration, and came home for the weekend every month or so. She'd been dating another student for several months, and there was no indication that they were having problems. Nor were there any broody ex-boyfriends around. Kendall wasn't known to have had any problems with her younger sister Bianca or her happily married parents. She had a ginger cat named Fluffy.

In short, she was as unlikely a candidate for murder as I'd ever heard of. Even Sid, whose theories were sometimes as ludicrous as his own existence, hadn't been able to come up with any reason anybody would have wanted to kill her. His best guesses were mistaken identity or a serial killer.

Despite my promise to Deborah, I couldn't think of anything else investigative to do that day, so while Sid continued to surf the Web for the latest and greatest news, I took my father out to retrieve his and Mom's Subaru from Deborah's garage. She'd been storing it for them, and being Deborah, had also kept it meticulously maintained, even starting it up every week or two to make sure it was ready to go at a moment's notice. I only wished I had somebody to lavish that much attention on my minivan, especially since I was worried it was on its last legs.

Then I finished up the laundry, graded papers, and made lesson plans for the coming work week. Right before bed, I went to Sid's attic to check on his progress, and though he said he'd typed his fingers to the bone—a joke he'd used so many times before that I couldn't even fake a laugh—he'd found nothing for us to go on.

I was ready to root for the cops.

9

Mondays are usually the bane of my existence because they insist on starting so early in the morning, but in a miracle unmatched in my adjunct career, I didn't have an eight o'clock class that semester. In fact, my first class was at ten, and though I then had to face three sections of English composition in a row, at least I could sleep in a little.

My parents also had plans to go to McQuaid that morning—Mom to meet with Dr. Eberhardt about her panicking grad student and Phil to visit with fellow faculty members—but I'd thought they were going to ride in with me. It was only when I got down to the kitchen that I realized they were already gone, and I remembered something I should have done as soon as I found out they were back in Pennycross.

Madison was at the table eating eggs and bacon cooked by my father, while Sid read the newspaper. "When did Mom and Phil leave?" I asked them.

"Maybe five minutes ago," Madison said, but Sid countered, "More like ten."

I grabbed my cell phone and punched in my friend Charles's number. "Pick up, pick up," I muttered.

"Dr. Charles Peyton at your service," the voice at the other end of the line said. Even at that hour of the morning, with caller ID so he knew it was me, Charles minded his manners.

"Charles, we've got an emergency. My parents have come home."

"Splendid! I'm sure you're gratified to have them back safe and sound."

"The problem is that they're on the way to McQuaid. Right now."

"Then presumably your father will want his office back?"

"Exactly." Charles was another adjunct, and like me, didn't own a home. Unlike me, however, he did not have a parental haven to live in. Instead he squatted in odd corners of the college or university at which he was working: unused classrooms, labs that needed rehab, and most often, the offices of faculty who weren't in residence for an extended period. Since my parents had given me permission to use their offices while they were on sabbatical, I'd shared the wealth with Charles by letting him live in my father's office while I worked out of my mother's adjoining space.

"They left five or ten minutes ago, which means they may already be at McQuaid. I don't know where on campus they're heading first, but—"

"I shall decamp immediately. Many thanks for the warning." He hung up, leaving me to wonder just how fast he could get his belongings packed and moved.

Madison, who'd watched me panic as she finished eating, said, "What was that about?"

"Sorry, but it's a secret, and not mine to tell." Not only was Charles embarrassed by his living situation, but if the powers that be at McQuaid ever found out, he would probably be fired unceremoniously. Of course, any adjunct could be fired unceremoniously at any time, but this version would include spreading the word to other colleges, making it nearly impossible for Charles to get another job. I'd only found out about his habits by accident and had been sworn to secrecy. I'd blown it by telling Sid, but since Charles had actually asked me not to tell another living soul, I was technically in the clear.

After making sure Madison got off to school, and checking to see that the doors were locked and both Sid and Byron were set for the day, I went to McQuaid so I could take care of some paperwork before class. I was also hoping to run into Charles to make sure that he'd gotten out in time, and was relieved to see him outside the adjunct office, chatting cheerfully with a man I didn't recognize. My friend, dapper as always in a tweedy suit with contrasting vest, looked more like a college professor than any other professor I'd ever met. He'd confided that his love for fine clothing was part of what kept him from being able to afford an actual home.

"Good morning, Charles," I said.

"What excellent timing, Georgia," he said. "I want to introduce you to one of my compatriots in the history department. Dr. Brownlow Mannix, American Studies. He'll be taking over for Dr. Donovan, who has to take leave a little sooner than expected."

"Is she okay?"

"The baby came early, but they're both fine," he assured me. "Dr. Mannix, this is Dr. Georgia Thackery, English."

"Dr. Mannix," I said out loud, though internally I was saying *Brownlow*? "A pleasure to meet you."

"Actually, we've met before," he said, taking my offered hand.

I took a closer look, which was nice because he was easy on the eyes. Also familiar. "Wait, weren't you one of the people the police detained after the murder Friday night?"

"Yes, I was. Were you there, too?"

"I was, though in costume—Velma from Scooby-Doo."

"Now I remember. But I was talking about an earlier acquaintance."

I went through a mental list of history adjuncts I'd met and/or worked with. "I'm sorry, I don't recall where we taught together."

"We didn't. You came to my family business about this time last year."

I'm sure I looked as blank as I felt.

He said, "Fenton's Family Festival? You were tracing a specimen."

Charles looked curious, but was far too well-bred to ask what his colleague was talking about. As for me, now I remembered. Fenton's Family Festival was the carnival where Sid had first come to life, and I'd visited the place when trying to trace his origins. The attractive Dr. Mannix was the carny who'd helped me while making it plain that he didn't believe a single word of my cover story.

I said, "Now I know why they call you College Boy."

He grinned. "Good memory." To Charles he said, "My father has a fondness for nicknames. It's a carny thing. I'm just lucky he came up with something relatively polite for me."

"How very interesting," Charles said. "Would you prefer that we refer to you as College Boy?"

"Brownie would be fine. So how's your skeleton, Georgia?"

"Still dead," I said and immediately changed the subject. "So you've run away from the carnival to join academia? Isn't that the opposite of the usual path?"

"Not so much running away as taking a break from. And not a very good one at that. The carnival is here in Pennycross for the Howl."

"Oh, your carnival is providing the rides. I hadn't realized because I never made it to the midway, given the circumstances."

"I heard about the murder," Charles said. "Terrible business. And you were both there?"

"My sister, Deborah, is in charge of McHades Hall this year," I explained, "and my daughter is working there. I just happened to be around when the body was found."

"I suppose you have even more reason to be afraid of haunted houses now," Brownie said.

"I was not afraid of your haunted house." When we'd first met, I'd been standing outside the carnival's zombie ride, trying to decide if it was where Sid had first come to life, and he'd concluded that I was nervous about going inside. I hadn't been—I'd never had any intention of going in. "What were you doing there? Checking out the competition?"

"No, our dark ride is no competition for an attraction like that. All we've got is mechanical jump-scares, no actors or chainsaws. With your place operational, our ride's business has been dead, if you'll pardon the expression. I've been trying to talk my parents into doing something more immersive, but they don't think it would be worth the extra staff we'd have to hire, let alone insurance liability. And having seen how things ended up Friday night, I've pretty much abandoned the idea."

"You can't blame the haunt's staff for that," I said indignantly.

"I don't, which is exactly why I wouldn't want to run something like that. We can vet our people all day long, but there's no accounting for towners."

"Towners?" Charles said.

"Sorry, I mean people who aren't with it, 'it' being the show."

"Such fascinating usage," Charles said. "It's quite evocative, isn't it?"

"You should hear his father," I said. "I didn't understand half of what he was saying."

"Dad does enjoy being colorful," Brownie said.

"I look forward to meeting him. Shall we go inside and get you settled into your new home away from home? I seem to recall that there's an empty desk close to yours, Georgia."

"There is. It's not on a wall, which inhibits privacy, but it's close to the front door for ventilation and there's a floor power socket handy so you don't have to deal with extension cords. The chair squeaks, but I've got some 3-in-One oil that would take care of that."

"Sounds like prime real estate," Brownie said, showing familiarity with the adjunct lifestyle. "I'm surprised it's vacant."

"There is the issue of the biologist who sits in front of Georgia," Charles said. "Dr. Weiss can be a little difficult to deal with. She's a longtime McQuaid adjunct, and likes to keep her finger on the pulse of the community."

I said, "By 'finger on the pulse,' he means nose in your business."

"Sara does have an inquisitive nature," Charles admitted.

"I grew up traveling with carnies who had nothing better to do than tell my parents what trouble I was getting into. I can handle Dr. Weiss."

"It's your funeral," I said as Charles opened the door for me to precede him into the casual cacophony that was the adjunct office.

I'd taught at schools that provided better accommodations for their adjuncts than a crowded, shared room, furnished with hand-me-down desks and chairs. Then again, I'd taught at schools that supplied no office space at all. Sadly, McQuaid was about mid-range.

Desks were not formally assigned. Instead, when an adjunct

LEIGH PERRY

joined the faculty, he surveyed the available spots and put his
name on the white board grid at the front of the room to stake
a claim.

I left Charles to explain the arrangements to Brownie while
I went to my desk, unpacked my bag, and looked to see if I
still had that can of oil. While I tackled the squeaky chair,
Charles took Brownie around to introduce him to the other
adjuncts. I watched their progress, trying to estimate how long
Brownie had been in academia. He only greeted one other
person as a friend, by which I estimated that he'd only taught
at two or three other schools. The longer one was an adjunct,
the more colleges and universities one had worked in, and the
more connections one had with other itinerant scholars. I usually knew four or five people at a school, showing I'd been at
it more years than I cared to count.

The ever-attentive Sara Weiss wasn't at her desk when
we came in, but she showed up ten minutes later and spotted
Brownie instantly.

"Who's the new guy?" she asked.

"Dr. Mannix, American Studies, and our new neighbor."

"Interesting." She fluffed her dark brown hair and smoothed
her eyebrows, which didn't change the fact that she was several
years older than he was. "Is he married?"

"No idea."

"You didn't check his finger?"

I shrugged, and went back to reading e-mail. It wasn't that
Brownie wasn't cute, and if Charles liked him he was almost
certainly a good guy, but the idea of bringing a date home
while my parents were in residence didn't stir my blood. It was
bad enough dating with Madison around, let alone Sid.

"Did you hear about the murder?" Sara said with a touch
too much glee for my taste.

"I did," I said, volunteering nothing more.

"A dead woman in a haunted house! I wonder how that's going to affect McQuaid Hall."

"The police have closed the haunt, if that's what you mean."

"But for how long? The building has to be in use for McQuaid to maintain ownership."

"You lost me."

She looked superior, which I admit she was good at, possibly because her upturned nose was so well designed for looking down. "Don't you know anything about the university's history? The McQuaid School of Art was established by noted local artist Persephone McQuaid, but enrollment dropped after she died."

"And the family gave the building to Pennycross to use for a university so long as they named both the college and the building after the family. I know that."

She waggled her finger at me. "Oh, but there was another string attached. McQuaid Hall was designed by Persephone herself, so part of the deal is that the building must remain part of the university."

"Meaning that it can't be torn down?"

"Meaning that it has to be in use. The administration has dodged the requirement for years by turning it into a haunted house for the month of October, but if the haunted house is closed, then it's no longer in use and the pertinent clause is enforceable."

"And the building reverts to the McQuaid family?"

"Not just the building. That whole part of the quad is part of the parcel that came with it. So the front entrance, most of the quad, half of Stuart Hall, and I think a chunk of Benson Hall as well. All gone!"

"Wow," I said, which was woefully inadequate for how much real estate the university stood to lose. I wanted to pick Sara's brain further, but a glance at my watch reminded me that it was time to get to the first of my trio of classes.

Though I do try to keep my mind on my teaching no matter what distraction is at hand, I confess that I spent a few minutes thinking about what Sara had told me. Not only was it juicy gossip, but unless I was wrong, it was also a decent motive for murder.

10

Once class was over, I texted my parents to see if they had time to join me for lunch. Phil was busy, but Mom said she'd meet me at Hamburger Haven, McQuaid's very own fast-food place. We got there at about the same time, went through the line to get our cheeseburgers and fries, and grabbed the last free table.

After applying ketchup and mustard as needed, I said, "How does it feel being back on campus?"

"Aggravating," she said. "I'm not overly impressed with Dr. Eberhardt."

I hadn't seen that much of the new English department chair myself. There'd been a short meeting during which Dr. Parker, the retiring chair, introduced Dr. Eberhardt to all the adjuncts. Then I'd dutifully attended the departmental welcome-aboard party and sipped my share of punch while listening to the dean extol his virtues and eaten a meal's worth of cheese and crackers while Eberhardt extolled his own virtues. While I knew there'd been buzz about hiring him from another school rather than promoting from within, it was hard for me to get my panties in a twist about internal people getting passed over when I was eternally external. So far, the only difference I'd noticed in his regime was extra paperwork for us adjuncts.

"I take it he wasn't very sympathetic to Roxanne's issues."

"Would you believe he quoted that old line to me? 'We call it graduate school because we want our students to graduate.'"

"What do you think? Politician?"

"Definitely."

We Thackery academics divided department chairmen into categories: the Fair-Minded, who only took the chair because it was his or her turn; the Rebel, who wanted to shake up the department, the university, and the world, in that order; the Functionary, who was a lousy academic but a decent paper shuffler; and the Visionary, who actually had a direction and a flair for management. Unfortunately Dr. Eberhardt was our least favorite: the Politician, who saw departmental power as the first step on his ascendancy to university dominion.

"At least he's fairly young," I said. Young Politicians didn't stay long on their hikes upward. "Maybe the next one will be better."

"Possibly, but it won't be in time to help Roxanne."

"So you couldn't get her an extension?"

"He said she could have through the beginning of next semester rather than the end of this one, but that was only because I'm still officially on sabbatical this semester and therefore can't oversee her final work. Roxanne is in a panic, needless to say."

"She *has* been taking a while to finish her dissertation. Technically she passed her deadline a while back." As in five years before, according to campus gossip.

"She's had a lot on her plate. She had to take a leave of

absence at one point because of family problems, and while she was gone, her thesis advisor changed jobs. Then her second advisor took over, but he retired, and she had to start over with me. Eberhardt just doesn't realize how valuable Roxanne's work is—you can't rush academic progress."

I nodded, but I thought Roxanne was one of those people who was afraid to graduate into the real world or even into academia. Grad school could be very cozy and safe, particularly once one had finished classes and qualifying exams, with only the research and dissertation to attend to. Of course, most people ran out of money sooner or later, but according to Mom, Roxanne's family was both wealthy and willing to fund her studies indefinitely. Since I had Madison during grad school, I'd had an urgent motive to get my own dissertation completed, so I wasn't overly sympathetic toward anybody who had time and money to burn.

I was, however, sympathetic for my mother's concern, so I let her fuss about Dr. Eberhardt, and made the right noises at the right places.

When Mom had gotten it out of her system, I asked her if she knew anything about the McQuaid family's string-laden bequest, but she knew less than Sara did about the situation. We moved on to other topics until we finished eating, and then both headed back to her office.

"I'll let my students know that I won't be seeing people in your office after today," I said. "Just be warned that a few of them will keep showing up for a while."

"No worries. I'll direct them to your office."

"Actually, I'll probably try to see folks in the Campus Deli. Or maybe pick out a corner in the student center."

"That won't be very private."

"It'll be more private than the adjunct office. You know what it's like down there."

"No, I've never seen it."

I described it to her, and the more I said, the more appalled she became. "That's . . . That's inhumane! How do they expect you to work that way?"

"I've had worse setups."

"This has to stop. I'm going to talk to some other professors, and in the meantime, you can keep using my office."

"Are you sure? I feel as if I'm imposing on you and Phil, first at the house and now here at work."

"It's not an imposition—we're glad to help. I'm just embarrassed that I wasn't aware of the situation before now. We're going to do something about this."

I smiled, but I didn't really expect anything to change. Mom wouldn't just be going against Pennycross administration, she'd be fighting what was being done at colleges and universities all over the country.

Phil was talking to a crony in his office when we arrived, so Mom went in to join them so I could close the adjoining door for my meetings. As far as I'd been able to tell at a brief glance, Charles had cleared out all traces of his stay, and I hoped that Phil would attribute anything that had been disturbed to my having used both offices.

There was a knock on the door, and the first of a steady stream of students started flowing in and out. Since I'd handed back three sets of graded essays that morning, I knew there would be requests for explanations of and/or arguments against their grades. It was the time of the semester when good students were buckling down and poor ones were starting to realize that they actually had to work to pass the class.

I ended up staying past my scheduled time, and even then had to firmly turn away a couple of students who'd come late. I might have stayed even longer, but Mom's grad student Roxanne showed up and anxiously asked, "Is Dr. Thackery here? I mean my Dr. Thackery. I need to talk to her."

"I'll check." I knocked on the door to Phil's office and when he answered, said, "Is Mom still around? Roxanne Beale is here to see her."

I don't think Roxanne heard Mom's sigh in response, but I did and understood it. "I'll be there in a moment," she said.

Usually I resent the fact that as an adjunct, I don't have the opportunity to mentor grad students, but in this case, I was glad I wasn't going to have to give Roxanne the sad news. Since I doubted she would take it well, I decided it was time to leave. As my mother came in the side door, I was on my way out the front. "See you later, Mom!"

I had other work to do and could have gone back to the adjunct office to tackle it, but home was a lot more appealing, especially since I wanted to compare notes with Sid. I still wasn't sure which one of us was Watson and which was Holmes, but I did know that his empty skull was great for bouncing ideas around.

Madison was home, so I stopped by the living room to say hello, pat the dog, and steal a handful of grapes before heading to Sid's attic.

When I tapped at the door, Sid yelled down, "It's open!"

I went on up the stairs to where Sid was sitting at his desk, tapping at his laptop. When I'd first moved back, the attic's furnishings were made up primarily of castoffs, but I'd managed to upgrade the desk, lamp, and chair to secondhand or even vintage, and while the sofa looked awful, it was pretty comfortable. At least Sid's laptop was decent, thanks to my educator's discount.

"What's the word on campus?" Sid asked. "There is nothing—and I mean nothing—new about the murder on the Web. I've been reduced to doing my homework for amusement. Please tell me you've got something."

"I've got an idea anyway. Have you found a decent motive for Kendall's murder?"

"I repeat, there is nothing new about the murder on the Web."

"What if Kendall's murder was a way to break the will that gave McQuaid Hall to the university?" I explained what Sara had told me about the odd bequest.

"Why would anybody attach strings like that?" Sid asked.

"Are you kidding? You've heard of Widener Library at Harvard? It's named that because Mrs. Widener gave them the money, but she had stipulations. One, there could be no additions or alterations to the building's facade, which is why they built a bridge to another building through a window, because that wouldn't disturb any bricks. When they needed to enlarge the library, the only way they could do it was to fill in the courtyard, which must have been a nightmare for the contractors. The other stipulation was that Mrs. Widener would be allowed to do landscaping on the grounds of the building, so that one wasn't so bad."

"Is something like that enforceable? Could the McQuaids really take back McQuaid Hall?"

"I'm no lawyer, but they could try."

"If they won, they could sell the building and land back to the university," Sid said. "You know the administration would be desperate to get it, even if it meant paying through the nose. The McQuaids could make a whole lot of money."

"Of course, the McQuaids are rich already."

"They wouldn't be the first rich people to be greedy or to spend beyond their means, no matter how big those means might be." Sid stroked his chin, which made a noise like two sticks rubbing against one another. "Interesting."

"Of course, if McHades Hall reopens, that'll blow the deal."

"If they've killed once . . ." Sid said ominously.

"That's what worries me. If the killer is picking targets at random, the next one could be Madison."

Sid instantly left the computer to come put a bony arm

around me, which was more comforting than it sounds. "Don't worry, Georgia. We're going to get this guy."

"I'm probably being silly anyway. It's hard to imagine one of the McQuaids sneaking around the haunt with a baseball bat."

"They could have paid somebody, and we know somebody snuck into the place. Unless you think it was one of the scare actors."

"Let's leave that idea alone for now. For Deborah's sake, I really hope it wasn't."

"Fair enough. For now, I've got something better to research. Like whether or not the will is enforceable and who exactly would get the money." He looked delighted by the prospect. "Any other grist for my investigative mill?"

I thought back over the events of the day. "I doubt this has anything to do with the murder, but we've got a new adjunct, and it's somebody you've met before."

"Somebody *I've* met?"

"Remember back when you were with Fenton's Family Festival? There was a little kid carny, and he grew up into the guy I talked to when I went to find out how you ended up in that carnival."

"Wait, are you saying that the midway at the Howl is Fenton's?"

I nodded. "It turns out that College Boy is Dr. Brownlow Mannix, and he's taking over for Kate Donovan because her baby came early."

"Now that's suspicious! I bet he'd know how to sneak into a haunted house."

"He wouldn't have had to sneak. He was at the haunt the night of the murder—I saw him with the other customers the cops took over to Stuart Hall."

"That settles it! Mannix killed somebody so we'd have

to close McHades Hall so the carnival could get more business at their haunted house."

"Don't you think that sounds a bit excessive?"

"Oh yeah? What if my Web hunt shows a correlation of haunted house murders and the appearance of this carnival in other towns?"

"If you find any such relationship, let me know. Otherwise, I'm chalking this up to prejudice against Fenton's."

"Do you blame me? They put me in a cage."

"Dude, they thought you were dead. Which you were. Did you ever think that if you hadn't been in that carnival, and hadn't seen me in trouble, you wouldn't have come to life? I know you wouldn't have come to live with us."

"That's true," he said, stroking his chin again, and I realized it was a gesture he'd copied from Sherlock Holmes movies. "Still, it's an interesting coincidence. Unless . . ."

"Unless what?"

"Unless they're looking for me."

"Why would they be looking for you?"

"Georgia, you told them I was here in Pennycross. Maybe they want to reclaim me and sell me. A robust skeleton like me is worth big bucks."

"I think you're safe." I patted his ulna. "I'm not letting anybody take you anywhere."

"Okay," he said, but I could tell he was nervous. Sid holds himself together purely by force of personality, so when he's anxious, the connections loosen. On a very bad day, he leaves bits of himself on the floor. Today he was still in one piece, but his connections had become noticeably looser since I'd mentioned Brownie Mannix.

To distract him, I said, "I read your dossier on Kendall. Very thorough."

"Nothing that wasn't in the papers and on TV. Today I looked at her social media, which her family has not yet deleted. It was set up as public so I could read just about everything. Which reminds me, you need to check your Facebook privacy settings. Madison, too. You never know who's looking."

"I'm pretty sure I don't have to worry about a strange skeleton other than you, but I'll take care of it."

"Anyway, she was active on both Twitter and Facebook. Her tweets and posts are all normal stuff: selfies, cat photos, life events. Lots of pictures, lots of comments about how much she loves college and her boyfriend and the Red Sox. She mentions a couple of social issues, but nothing controversial. She comes off as naïve, but well-meaning."

"Not much in the way of a motive for anybody to kill her, is there?"

"It's early days yet."

"Absolutely," I said as confidently as I could, but his bones were still a bit loose. I switched tracks to ask about his classwork, and after a few minutes of discussion about some of the readings, I was relieved to see that his bones were back to their normal level of attachment.

It's kind of surprising that Sid can be afraid—he is dead, after all, and he can't be hurt in the usual sense because he doesn't have any nerves—but thinking about the carnival made him think about being separated from me and our family, and that scares him silly.

II

I kept Sid company for a while as I did some actual work, stopping in time to go downstairs to see about starting dinner. Only Phil was way ahead of me, with homemade marinara sauce simmering on the stove and water boiling in readiness for pasta. "What do you need me to do?" I asked.

"You could set the table for five—Deborah just texted that she's coming over."

"Sure thing," I said, but I admit it rankled. Though I appreciated Phil cooking, I was used to choosing my own dinner, or at least being consulted about it. It seemed to me that it would serve Phil right if I announced that Madison and I were going out for dinner or ordering takeout. I'd have done it, too, if his sauce hadn't smelled so good.

"How long before Deborah gets here?" I asked once I'd finished.

"Ten minutes. I'm putting the pasta into the water now."

I called up the stairs. "Sid, Madison, dinner in ten!"

They'd just come down when I heard Deborah's voice in the kitchen. A second later, I heard another voice—it was a man's and it wasn't Phil's.

Sid gave me a wide-eyed look, then ran for the old armoire that was his designated hidey-hole when unexpected company arrived. He was moving fast, but was still in plain sight when the door to the kitchen started to open. So I slid one of the dining room chairs to block the door from opening, wincing at the sound of wood slamming against wood.

"What the—?" Deborah said.

I turned and saw the armoire door shut behind Sid. "Sorry. Just moving things around." I put back the chair, which was only a little worse for the wear.

Deborah came in, giving me a dirty look until I nodded at the armoire. "Come on in, Louis. My sister is finished rearranging the furniture."

"Hi, Louis," I said as he joined us. "I didn't realize you were coming over."

"He showed up just as I was heading this way and said he has some questions for us," Deborah said. "Dad forgot to mention dinner was almost ready. You may as well set another place at the table."

"Thanks, but I don't want to intrude," Louis said. "I can come back later."

"Nonsense," said my mother, carrying in a platter of garlic bread. "There's plenty, and your questions can wait until after you eat. There's one thing travel teaches you, and that's to grab every good meal you can because you don't know when you'll get another. Now come into the kitchen and get yourself a plate of spaghetti."

He looked bemused, but obeyed. A few minutes later, we were all settled around the table, laughing at how confused Mom had been when an English grad student asked to borrow a rubber. "All I could think of was that if I gave him one, I certainly wouldn't want it back. How was I supposed to know that 'rubber' means eraser over there?"

Louis said, "It sounds as if you two had a fascinating trip, Dr. Thackery. I've never been out of the country myself."

"Just call us Dab and Phil," Phil said. "With three Dr. Thackerys in the room, we'll never know who you're talking to otherwise. Would you care for more spaghetti?"

"I'm fine, Phil, thank you."

"Madison, how about you? Deborah? Georgia?"

"No thanks, Phil," I said. "It was great, but I'm stuffed."

"Georgia, can I ask you something?" Louis said.

"Do I need a lawyer present?" I asked, hoping I was kidding.

"Why do you call your father by his first name? Deborah doesn't, does she?"

I sighed, but of course Phil had heard.

"It's quite an amusing story," Phil said. "Georgia accompanied me to a departmental meeting when she was small, and noticed that the other professors called me 'Phil.' So when she needed help reaching something on the refreshment table, she called out, 'Phil!' The departmental secretary—an able woman, but perhaps too set in her ways—reproved her, saying, 'You shouldn't call him that. You should call him Father or Dad.' Georgia said, 'You called him Phil.' 'Yes, but I am his colleague.' Georgia looked her right in the eye and said, 'Someday I'll be his colleague, too; ergo, I shall call him Phil.'" He chuckled, and repeated, "Ergo! Clearly she was destined for academia. I didn't have the heart to correct her, and it stuck."

He chuckled again, Louis and Mom chuckled along, and Madison snickered. Deborah and I shared looks of disgust. In her case, it was probably because she'd heard the story more times than she could count—in my case, I could only imagine Louis wondering how that precocious colleague-to-be had turned into a barely scraping by adjunct. If I was being completely truthful, I'd admit I wondered the same thing myself.

Once dinner was over and the table was cleared off, Louis got down to business. "We've been going through witness statements, trying to track down the people who were in McHades Hall when the murder was committed and there are some people we haven't been able to identify. I'm hoping that one of the rest of you saw something. Well, not you, Dab, since you weren't there."

I saw Phil open his mouth to say he hadn't been there, either, but when I nudged him under the table, he shut it again.

"First off, of course, is Scooby-Doo. Unfortunately our lab guys haven't found any useful trace evidence in the costume so we're still trying to track him down."

"What's the big deal with Dad's costume?" Deborah asked.

"It's pretty suggestive that it was abandoned."

"Please," she scoffed. "The guy who took it just didn't want to get caught with a stolen costume. I doubt he had anything to do with the murder."

Louis gave her a sharp look. "Are you sure you don't know more about that costume than you've told me? And who was wearing it?"

Before Deborah could say anything, I said, "Deborah is looking out for me. I'm supposed to take the costume back this week, but if it's got something to do with the murder, you guys will need to keep it and I'm going to get stuck with a late fee."

"Don't worry," he said, "I'll call the costume place and take care of it. They won't charge you extra."

"Great," I said, hoping Deborah would let it alone. We really didn't want Louis getting suspicious. There were far too many holes in Phil's story, and if somebody started looking, it wouldn't take much effort to find them.

Louis went on. "We've got descriptions of half a dozen

other people who were seen at the haunt, but who left before they could be questioned." He pulled out a folder and put a picture on the table in front of us. "One of the customers took a selfie while waiting in line and this guy photobombed her."

"Do people realize how much of their life is documented in selfies?" Mom asked.

"It comes in handy for us. Do any of you recognize him?" The photo was of a girl in an angel costume next to one in a devil costume, and a guy wearing a hoodie was leering between them. "Deborah?"

"It rings no bells," Deborah said, and Phil and I agreed, but Madison took a closer look. "I remember that guy. He tried to get me to meet up with him later. When I wouldn't break character, he said I could bite his neck anytime."

"What?" I said, appalled.

"Don't worry, Mom. He was harmless."

"Did Harmless give you a name?" Louis asked.

"Rob or Rod, I think. He said he works at the movie theater at the mall, and he could comp me tickets."

Louis scribbled that down. "How about this guy?" He put down a picture of a man in a ninja costume, his face completely covered. The outfit struck me as ridiculous for a supposedly stealthy assassin. It had white trim on the sleeves, with a pair of hissing cobras encircling some sort of Japanese symbol on the chest.

Deborah shrugged. "I probably saw him, but do you know how many ninja we get?"

"Madison?"

"I remember a couple of ninja, but I think there was one with a design like that came in around that time. The trim really showed in the black lights in the chemistry lab scene. I didn't get a name, but he was a tough guy. Working hard not to be scared of anything, acting bored. Until the chainsaw. That's when he broke and ran. The chainsaw always gets them."

He jotted that down and looked at the rest of us. We shrugged. I hadn't noticed a ninja, and of course Phil hadn't.

Louis had four more people to ask us about: a witch, two guys in jeans and T-shirts, and a cowboy. He had photos of all but the cowboy, thanks to other selfies and camera phones, but we couldn't help him any more.

"Can I take another look at the pictures?" I said, and when Louis handed them to me, I held them up high as if trying for better light. In reality, I was giving Sid a chance to see them. After I thought he would have had enough time, I shook my head and gave them back. "Sorry, nothing."

"Have you come up with any reason why anybody would want to kill that girl?" Deborah asked.

"Investigations are proceeding."

"Come on, Louis, it happened in my haunt. Are we talking serial killer or drug hit or what?"

"Maybe somebody wanted to shut down the haunt for some reason," I said tentatively.

Louis raised an eyebrow. "Come again?"

"That building only belongs to the school as long as it's in use. If the haunt is closed, the building might revert to the McQuaid family."

"That's an interesting thought," he said. "I'll keep it in mind." But he didn't take any notes.

Louis had driven Deborah over, so after he thanked my parents for dinner, he took her back home. As soon as they were gone, I announced, "It's safe to come out."

"Ta-da!" Sid said, bounding out. "Good job on holding up the pictures for me to see, Georgia, but why did you give the cops our big lead?"

"It's not a lead, it's a theory. And I have to say that when I said it out loud, it sounded pretty improbable."

"All theories are improbable before they're proven. Anyway, I'm sure I saw the ninja."

"You did? What did he look like?"

From the angle of his skull, I could tell he'd have been rolling his eyes if he'd had any to roll. "Like a ninja. His face was covered."

"His whole face?"

Sid couldn't close his nonexistent eyes to concentrate, so he had a habit of covering his eye sockets with his hands in such circumstances. "His eyes showed. And a little of his forehead. So I could tell he was Caucasian and his eyes were hazel. That's it."

"But you're sure it was the same guy as in the picture."

"It looked the same—snakes with a Chinese symbol between them."

"Ninja are Japanese."

"And I'm sure the costume company did dissertation-worthy research to make sure it was an historically accurate ninja suit symbol for this oh-so-authentic ninja suit."

"Wow, that was an impressive amount of sarcasm."

"I do what I can. Anyway, despite your giving away our best lead, we've got plenty of new material to work with. A ninja, a cowboy, a witch, a harmless creep, and two random guys! This is great!"

"How?" I asked. "What are we going to do with this information that the cops won't?"

"Come up with more theories!"

He and Madison both went to work on homework, while Mom and Phil started watching some of the vast number of TV shows stored on their DVR. I tried to tackle more work, but was too restless to get much accomplished.

I didn't want to burst Sid's bubble, but I was feeling ridiculous for trying to get involved in Kendall's murder. What could we could possibly do that the cops wouldn't do better? They had experience and forensics and could ask people questions without having to come up with excuses. I had Sid, who was a computer whiz and a great spy, but who had some serious limits. And there was me—if assigning and grading essays and dealing with college students could solve a murder, I'd have it down cold, but otherwise . . .

Of course, Kendall had been a college student. Moreover she'd just started her sophomore year, meaning that many of her instructors had been adjuncts like me. Maybe there was something I could do the next day that the cops wouldn't think of.

12

My Tuesdays and Thursdays that semester were awkwardly scheduled. I had one class from eight to nine thirty, but my second wasn't until two. This time, however, I thought I could use that gap to my advantage.

After my first class, I headed to Mom's office. Luckily, she and Phil had errands to run and hadn't come to campus, so I had privacy. I was going to miss that luxury when my parents were back on campus full time. Despite their assurances that I could share with them, there was a big difference between borrowing space and having unlimited use of it.

My goal was to see what I could find out from my fellow adjuncts at Brandeis, a well-regarded private university in Waltham, Massachusetts. I'd never taught there, but I was hoping to find connections to exploit.

Before I'd left home, I'd asked Sid to search Kendall's social media for references to her classes, and when I checked my e-mail, I found that he'd sent a list of classes and instructor names.

With that in hand, I started looking through Brandeis's online faculty list. Kendall had been a business administration major, which made it trickier because I didn't have a lot of connections in business. Fortunately for me, Brandeis requires a writing seminar for all first-year students plus various core subjects, and those classes are mostly taught by adjuncts.

When I put the two lists together, I came up with the names of two people I could call.

I hit it lucky with my first target: Art Singer, a history adjunct I'd co-taught with as part of an experiment. He'd sent his classes' papers to my students for practice editing, and his classes had helped my composition students with research techniques. That gave me the excuse I needed, which was asking him for copies of the lesson plans we'd worked out—I couldn't claim that Byron had eaten my homework, but nobody argued with a hard disk crash.

Once Art had promised to send the files, we got down to every adjunct's stock-in-trade: gossip. We didn't just do it for fun, though of course that was part of it. It was to compare notes about working conditions and to find out which schools might have openings for adjuncts, and of course the gold ring, to see if anybody had tenure-track positions to fill. Neither of us had any hot news, but it did simplify moving the conversation toward Kendall Fitzroy's death. In fact, Art was the one to bring up the subject.

"I hear McQuaid is a dangerous place these days," he said.

"Hmm? Oh, you mean that girl who was murdered? Technically she wasn't on campus—she was at a haunted house. And she wasn't a McQuaid student."

"No, she was one of ours. Mine, in fact—I taught her last year in intro to American history."

"Oh, Art, that's awful. I'm so sorry."

"No, it's okay. I didn't know her well. Big class, and she wasn't exactly a model student. She was all about the partying."

"Freshmen," I said knowingly.

"You know the kind. Missed a bunch of classes, then came in right before exams to beg for extra credit assignments to make up for low test scores. I wouldn't bend, and I feel bad about it now."

"It's not your fault. You couldn't have known."

"Yeah, but still. Anyway, she managed to cram enough for the final that she squeaked through anyway."

We talked a little while longer, but that was as much as I was going to get from him.

My luck wasn't as good with my next connection. She answered my call, but was on her way to class and wouldn't be available until after lunch. That left me time to fill, but fortunately, having an actual job has a way of taking care of that nasty problem. There were papers to grade, e-mails to respond to, assignments to plan, journals to read—the bread and butter of academia.

Just before noon, I headed for the Campus Deli, and got there in time to get my Greek salad and soda before the lunch rush started and scored a table by the window. I was indulging in reading a book purely for pleasure instead of for work when I saw Charles looking for a place to sit.

"Charles!" I said, waving. "Over here."

"Georgia, what a lovely surprise."

"Won't you join me?"

"I don't want to intrude, and it's a double imposition because Brownie is joining me."

"He's welcome, too."

"Wonderful," he said, and took a seat across from me.

"I've been wanting to apologize for kicking you out of Phil's office without a warning."

"Not at all," he said. "You were more than gracious to allow me to stay as long as I did."

"Have you found a new place?"

"I'll be bunking with Brownie. I was ferrying my belongings to my car when I encountered him yesterday, and when I explained that I'd had to relocate, he invited me to stay with him."

"Then he knows about your living arrangements? I thought I was special."

"There are very few I've trusted with that knowledge," he said. "It's not that you are less trustworthy, but that Brownie is equally trustworthy."

"I'll count that in his favor. Where are the two of you living?"

"He has a compact, but well-designed, trailer currently situated on Elm Street. I'll be well housed until after Halloween."

"Elm Street? You mean you're living on the carnival lot?"

He nodded. "I'm anticipating learning more of the lingo during my stay there. It should prove to be quite an experience."

"I bet it will be," I said, trying to picture my natty friend picking his way past the discarded popcorn boxes and drink cups that infested every carnival lot I'd been on.

Brownie came over, and once we got the table arranged, I said, "How are you settling in to McQuaid?"

"It's always awkward picking up a class in midstream, but at least my predecessor left well-organized lesson plans."

"That makes all the difference in the world," I said. "Once I took over a composition class, and the guy had shifted his assignments around without updating the lesson plan. So I'm going by the plan, and it wasn't until three weeks in that one of my students told me they'd already done everything I was assigning. They'd just been handing in the same essays they'd handed in before, only they'd had time to correct the mistakes the other instructor had marked. Here I thought I had the most competent class ever."

"At least you had a lesson plan to consult," Charles said. "Once I had nothing but a stack of illegible index cards and a copy of the textbook with sections highlighted. To make the experience complete, the topic was one I'd never studied before, let alone taught."

That led to more war stories, each one funny in retrospect, though at the time I suspect we'd all indulged in words of the four-letter variety.

"One thing I've got to ask, Brownie," I said. "How do you juggle being an academic with being a carny?"

"In terms of time or philosophy?"

"I was talking time, but you'll get full credit for either approach."

"Time-wise, it's not as hard as you might think. The show shuts down after Halloween, and our winter quarters are outside Shrewsbury, which is near several colleges. Even when we go back on the road in April, we have a fairly stable route, and our usual stands are all in this part of New England. All I have to do is check with the colleges within commuting distance. It limits my options, but then again, if I can't find an adjunct job one semester, I just work more hours at the show."

"You like doing both?"

"I love doing both," he corrected me. "How about you?"

"Academia is home. Both my parents are English professors, and although they encouraged me to explore my possibilities, I decided this was the life for me early on. It hasn't turned out exactly the way I'd planned, but it's still good."

"What about living in Pennycross? You don't get bored staying in one place?"

"I haven't been back all that long. I grew up here, but since I got my doctorate, Madison and I have moved around nearly as much as you have."

"Madison is your partner?"

"You could call her that. I generally call her my daughter."

He nodded, and I caught his glance at my left hand, which was free of a wedding band. I hadn't even been eligible for a friendship ring for nearly a year, and snuck a peek at Brownie's hand in return. It was equally unadorned.

I was trying to decide if I wanted to take advantage of our mutually bare-fingered status when Charles looked at his watch and reminded Brownie that they had a meeting. So I went back to Mom's office to call my other Brandeis target.

Caroline Craig was an adjunct originally from Virginia, and she and I shared a love of pop culture, particularly comics. The cover story for her was asking if she had any recommendations for graphic novels I could use for a class I was proposing. To assuage my conscience, I did intend to suggest such a class to Dr. Eberhardt, but I didn't have any idea that he'd go for it. As far as I'd been able to gather, he thought "popular" and "culture" were diametrically opposed. At least I could pass the list on to Sid to add to his reading pleasure.

Once that was done, I brought up Kendall's death.

"That poor girl," Caroline said. "It just broke my heart when I heard."

"Did you know her?"

"I had her for university writing seminar last year, and I have to say I didn't think much of her. She didn't give two hoots about my class and was just barely scraping by with papers that were so bland I nearly dozed off reading them."

"Don't tell me: My Mother/Grandmother/Aunt Is My Real-Life Hero, How Racial Prejudice Diminishes Us All, and Bullying is Bad."

"Don't tell me you taught her, too!"

"I may as well have."

"Anyway, the only reason she was in my section was because there was a boy she had her eye on."

"Did he reciprocate?"

"Not right away, but she kept at him, bless her heart, and they finally went out partway through the semester. And here's the sweet thing. I think he steadied her down—she started putting some real effort into her classwork for a change. She still wasn't a gifted writer, but she improved enough to bring herself up to a B-."

"Good for her."

"I didn't have her this semester, but she came by my office a couple of times just to say hello. She even apologized for being such a pain in the tail end. Of course, she really hadn't wronged me any—it was herself she was hurting by not doing the work—but I thought it was sweet. I just hate that she died so young, after she'd really started turning things around."

I kept at it a little, but Caroline didn't know any more about Kendall's personal life.

Once I was off the phone, I checked my watch and saw there was no time to report back to Sid, so I grabbed my stuff and headed to class, figuring Sid wouldn't mind waiting.

13

Sid minded. If the flurry of increasingly annoyed texts I received over the next couple of hours hadn't clued me in, then the stony silence with which he greeted me when I got home and climbed up to his attic would have. Instead of speaking to me, he pretended he hadn't heard me come in, which might have been more convincing if I hadn't heard him scrambling around to get to his computer so he could act busy.

"Hi, Sid."

He kept typing.

"Come on, Sid, I didn't have time to call you."

No reply.

"Or e-mail you."

Nothing.

"Okay, I could have texted you."

"No, that's okay," he said with a sniff. "It's not like I'm your partner—I'm just a human search engine."

Had he been less cranky, I might have pointed out that calling him human would be a stretch. "You know I see you as a partner, but you also know my time isn't always my own. Somebody in this family has to bring in a paycheck so we can afford some of the new graphic novels coming down the pike."

"I suppose." He paused. "What graphic novels?"

"The list of really good ones that my friend Caroline gave me. She's got some free copies she scored at a conference, too, and was going to send them along, but if you're not interested . . ."

"Okay, okay, you're forgiven."

"Thank you."

"But comics later. What did you find out about Kendall?"

"Not a lot." I told him what I'd learned. "So she had freshman syndrome, but got over it long before she was killed. I don't think she was killed for turning over a new leaf."

"What about the boyfriend?" Sid asked. "If she was changing herself for him, maybe it was a *Fifty Shades of Grey* thing, and he was making her over in his own image. Eventually she started to resent it and wanted to break away. So he killed her rather than lose her."

"That's ugly, but possible. How did he get into the haunt without her knowing it?"

"He was the ninja, of course."

"That would explain why the ninja hasn't resurfaced. But isn't the boyfriend the first person the police would check alibis for?"

"He could have rented a ninja."

We looked at each other, and couldn't help giggling. It was in terrible taste, of course, but a rent-a-ninja was too funny not to laugh.

Once we'd recovered enough to be able to fake maturity, I said, "You know the police must have investigated the guy already."

"Not as well as I can," Sid said.

"Granted. But unless you find something, I think we have to look elsewhere."

"Kendall's family? Maybe she didn't get along with her parents, or had serious sibling rivalry."

"That's still something the police would look at." I held up a hand to forestall him. "I know, it goes without saying that you'll do a better job of digging into that, but I'm trying to come up with something I can do."

Sid and I both drummed our fingers, but the resulting duet neither caused brain flashes nor masked the sounds of loud footsteps from downstairs.

"Madison must be mad about something," I said.

"That's not Madison." A moment later, Sid was proven right when there was a knock at his door. Before he could answer, Deborah stomped in.

"I figured I'd find you two up here."

"Welcome!" Sid said, as delighted to see her as I was surprised. I couldn't remember the last time Deborah had come to Sid's room.

"What's up?" I said.

"I got a call today from the McQuaid Scholars Committee, namely Beatrice McQuaid. She was not pleased that I hadn't been calling her each and every day. The fact that nothing has changed since Saturday night makes zero difference to her. Bear in mind that Beatrice hasn't done a solitary thing since recruiting me—she hasn't even bothered to come down to the haunt. None of the committee have. The cast and I do the work, and they brag about how much money they make for scholarships."

"How did you get the job anyway?" I asked.

"I heard they needed somebody. The guy who ran it last year moved out of town, and since I've worked tech at haunts before, I got in touch. That's the last time I volunteer for anything."

"You did put together a good haunt."

"As if you'd know. If we reopen, are you going to come in?"

"It's kind of ruined for me now," I said, dodging. "With what happened and all."

"Uh-huh," she said, not believing me. "Speaking of scary things, Beatrice and the rest of the Quintet want to meet with me tonight."

"I wonder if they're going to tell you not to reopen the haunt."

"Why would they do that? No haunt means nothing for them to brag about."

"But it could mean a lot of money." I reminded her of what I'd told Louis about the McQuaid bequest being dependent on McQuaid Hall staying in use.

"So you think the McQuaid Quintet killed a girl to get the building and land back? Not that I'm saying they wouldn't, but if they had, why would they be bothering me about reopening?"

"They could be faking it to hide their real motive," Sid said.

"I guess," Deborah said, "but I can't see any of them getting their hands dirty."

"They could have hired somebody," I said, reminding myself to make no rent-a-ninja comments or else Sid and I would start laughing again, and Deborah would lose all faith in our deductive abilities.

She said, "If they're going to try to mess around with my haunt, they're going to have a fight on their hands."

"Go get 'em, and call me after the meeting."

"I thought you might want to come along, since you're nosing around."

I wasn't sure exactly what good I'd do other than lend moral support, but it was definitely something I could do that the police couldn't, so I was about to agree. Sid beat me to it.

"Good idea, Deborah," he said. "That would be a great place to continue our investigation."

"Yeah, no. You're not coming," Deborah said.

"You asked both of us to help. Georgia, tell her you need me as backup."

They both turned to me. I sighed, but after some negotiation, we came up with a compromise that made nobody happy. Including me, because I realized that I'd never agreed to go to the meeting.

We headed downstairs and told everybody what we were up to, and though Deborah made noises about heading home for a sandwich, Phil insisted on her staying for the stir-fry he was whipping up.

Over dinner, Mom pointed out that it might be better to dress upscale to meet with the McQuaids, so after we finished, I went to find something more suitable while Deborah made a quick trip to her place to change. By the time she got back, I was wearing my navy blue interview suit with heels, and had even put on makeup. I have a nice red briefcase I usually carry on such occasions, but this time I had to settle for a worn tote designed to look like an old-time doctor's bag. Even tying a scarf around the handles didn't disguise the scarred leather, but it was the only handbag I had that was big enough to squeeze Sid's skull into.

That had been part of the compromise. Since Sid's memory or soul or whatever it is that keeps him moving travels with his skull, as long as we had that, he was technically accompanying us. It was stretching a point to call him backup since about all he would be able to do in our defense was roll at people and bite them like a carnivorous bowling ball, but he was an excellent listener and might pick up something Deborah and I missed.

Of course he still grumbled. "This thing is too tight," he said from inside. "Great, now your cell is inside my skull."

I reached inside and pulled out the phone, then put it into a zipper section on the side of the bag. "There. Now keep your jaw shut or my wallet will be in there, too."

"You need to get a bigger bag, something with a see-through panel."

"I'm sure I can find a perfect skull touring bag on sale at Macy's, but until I do, you'll have to deal with this one. Unless you want to stay home, that is."

"No way! Sherlock Bones is on the case. And yes, you have to be Watson. You're the doctor, right?"

"Fine, I'll be Watson. Just remember, Watson is the one with a gun."

"Oh, please, everybody knows Holmes is the better shot."

"Sure, lying on the couch, but it's always Watson who's carrying the trusty revolver."

Sid and I continued our literary discussion until Deborah drove up and leaned on the horn to get our attention.

Like me, Deborah had a single good suit for those times when she needed one, but hers was a little sharper because she typically dealt with dress-to-impress businesspeople, not conservative academics. It was a rich burgundy, and since her legs were one of her best features, the skirt was shorter than mine. I comforted myself with the fact that my pumps were prettier than hers.

"Bone Boy in the bag?" she asked once I'd climbed into the car.

"You bet!" Sid chirped. "Hey, you two want me to wave at you from the attic window?"

"No!" we both said. Though Sid's ability to manipulate his bones at a distance was impressive, it might draw unwanted attention.

"Oh, come on," he said. "If anybody else sees me, they'll think I'm a Halloween decoration."

"That's why you shouldn't do it," I said. "Save it for Halloween night and you'll get a bigger reaction."

"Oh, good point."

Deborah shook her head in resignation. Just because she was used to the two of us, it didn't mean that she understood us.

"Where's the meeting going to be?" I asked as Deborah drove.

"At the McQuaid mansion."

"Of course. The better to cow us with."

"You know Beatrice didn't even give me the address. She just assumed I'd know where it is."

"She was right, wasn't she? Everybody knows where it is." At least everybody who'd lived in Pennycross for any length of time knew. I don't suppose the McQuaid family was all that rich or prestigious compared to folks in Boston or Long Island, but they were definitely the leading family in our little northwestern Massachusetts town. Not only had the college been named for them, but they were active in local politics and what passed for a social calendar. "I've always been curious about what that place is like inside."

"Me, too," Sid said. He might not get out of the house often, but that didn't keep him from taking fierce interest in Pennycross gossip. "Georgia, are you sure you can't keep the bag open for me to peek?"

Even if I'd been tempted, seeing the look on Deborah's face was enough to make me say, "Sorry, Sid. We can't take the risk of anybody noticing you. I'm a gate-crasher as it is. A gate-crasher with a skull in a bag wouldn't make the right impression."

"Spoilsport," he muttered.

Deborah pulled into the long, circular driveway in front of the McQuaid mansion and parked near the front door. There were five other cars waiting: two Mercedes sedans, a gleaming blue Lexus, a black Escalade, and a vintage seventies-era red-and-white Cadillac that was bigger than some of the apartments I'd lived in.

"Great, the whole McQuaid Quintet showed up. I mostly dealt with Beatrice, but I've met all the cousins."

"I thought they were sisters."

"A common misconception," Sid said. "Beatrice is an only child, but has four first cousins: Paige, Vivienne, and the twins, Edwina and Erika. Beatrice is the oldest, and the daughter of the oldest from the previous generation, which is why she inherited the mansion and the lion's share of oomph in town."

"How do you know this?" Deborah asked.

"From reading years' worth of faculty newsletters and Pennycross papers, added to lots and lots of eavesdropping. I know the names of their parents, husbands, ex-husbands, and kids, should you need them."

Deborah looked mildly impressed. "Maybe you're going to be more than just comic relief after all." She opened the car door before he got a chance to snark back at her. It was a dirty trick, but well timed.

I'd hoped for a butler or at least an aproned maid to answer the door, but instead it was Beatrice herself who greeted us.

"Ms. Thackery, thank you for coming," she said, then looked questioningly at me.

"My sister, Dr. Georgia Thackery," Deborah said.

"A pleasure," she said. "Won't you both come inside?"

We followed her across the black-and-white tiled foyer, past the dark wood accent table that would have seated five for dinner and still have had room for the exotic fresh flower arrangement that was all it was used for, and into an honest-to-gosh study, complete with leather upholstered furniture, a massive mahogany desk, an Oriental carpet, and built-in, glass-fronted bookcases. I was almost certain the room was as big as the one the adjuncts shared at McQuaid, even without the added space from the bay windows.

Four other women were waiting, all of them so meticulously groomed that I couldn't imagine how long it had taken them to get ready for the meeting.

"My cousins," Beatrice said. "Paige. Vivienne. Edwina and Erika." Paige was dark-haired, tall, and slim, while Vivienne was shorter and curvier. The twins were cute blondes, and looked considerably younger than I knew them to be. And Beatrice was elegantly slender, with her ash-blond hair cut in an asymmetric style that must have required weekly touch-ups to maintain its proportions. "You all remember Deborah Thackery. This is her sister, Dr. Georgia Thackery."

There were nods and pleasantries as Beatrice waved Deborah and me to armchairs, then joined two of her cousins on a long sofa while the twins took the loveseat.

"I'm sorry," Vivienne said in a tone that didn't sound particularly sorry, "but I'm confused as to why you're here, Dr. Thackery. You haven't been working at McHades Hall, have you? Are you representing the university or . . . ?"

Before I could spout my cover story, which was about as lame as most of the ones I'd devised, I got help from an unexpected quarter. Edwina said, "What difference does it make, Vivi? Deborah will tell her sister everything that happens anyway." Erika nodded in agreement.

Since either Deborah or I could fill a good-sized hard drive with things we'd never told each other, apparently Edwina and Erika were closer than we were. Maybe it was a twin thing. But since the other McQuaids were only children, they had no other basis for comparison, which may be why they let it slide.

"Of course Dr. Thackery is welcome," Beatrice said. "Deborah, I asked you to come over so we could discuss your plans for McHades Hall."

"I don't have any plans," Deborah said. "Until the police clear the building, I can't reopen."

Vivienne said, "That's ridiculous. They've had the building under their control for days. Do they think the murderer is still hiding in there?"

"I'm sure they're just being thorough," Beatrice said, "but I agree that it's unreasonable of them to interfere for much longer. It's important that we reopen this weekend."

So much for my theory that they wanted to keep McHades closed. I would have thought Deborah would be glad about that, but of course, she is Deborah.

She said, "Even if the police sign off on reopening, I'm not sure we should."

"Of course you'll reopen!" Vivienne said. "Why wouldn't you?"

"A young woman died in there. Don't you think it would be in poor taste to turn a murder site into a Halloween attraction?"

"Actually," Paige drawled, "you already have. There was a knife fight in the building decades ago, and one of the boys involved died. Also a young woman fell down the stairs and while on her death bed claimed that she'd been pushed."

Beatrice looked annoyed. "Paige is the family historian, but she knows full well that those incidents are neither here nor there. What's important is that the house reopen in order to raise the funds for next year's McQuaid Scholars awards. While that girl's death is a tragedy, depriving those students of their opportunity to attend McQuaid would only make it worse."

"It's only October—couldn't the committee put together

some other fundraising events in time to pay for the scholarships?" Deborah asked.

"I suppose we could," Beatrice said as casually as if they'd only have to search the sofa cushions for spare change, "but McHades Hall has been a tradition for how long now, Paige?"

"Eleven years," she said. "We McQuaids are simply slaves to tradition."

"Maybe we can name a scholarship after the dead girl," Erika said, giving Edwina a chance to nod emphatically.

"I'm sure that would be a great comfort to the family," Deborah said drily.

Beatrice said, "Erika, dear, we'll table that idea while we work on getting the haunted house running."

"Look, it's not my decision," Deborah said. "It's up to the cops."

"Who's in charge of the investigation?" Vivienne asked.

"Sergeant Louis Raymond."

"Call that idiot, Bea, and make him let Deborah reopen the place."

"I haven't said I'd reopen the haunt," Deborah said, her jaw set. Though I doubted the Quintet could tell, I knew she was mad. Part of it was their assuming she'd do what they wanted to, but I was pretty sure most of it was from Vivienne insulting Louis.

"What are you talking about? You have to reopen!"

I recognized Vivienne's tone. I'd heard it all too often from the helicopter parents who swooped in whenever a student didn't make the grade Mommy or Daddy insisted they deserved and moreover, needed to get into med school or law school or whatever. The fact that the grade had to be earned, not just demanded, left them as indignant as Vivienne was. I was sure there was a threat coming next, something about making sure that Deborah never worked in this town again, but Beatrice was smarter than that.

She said, "You did make a commitment, Deborah, but I realize that circumstances have changed, and that this has been difficult for you. It's just that we can't imagine who would be able to handle the situation as well as you have, or be able to pick up the reins. We'll understand if you're too distraught, but if you could see your way to continuing to run the project, we'd certainly let people in this town know how seriously you take your commitments."

It was all praise and bribe, no threat at all, which impressed me. It also made me wonder why Beatrice was spreading all that soft soap. Maybe the McQuaids weren't planning to reclaim the university's real estate, but perhaps there was something more at stake than bragging rights.

I could see that Deborah was about to agree, but I said, "Do you mind if Deborah and I step outside to discuss it? My daughter is one of her scare actors, and I want to share my perspective before she makes up her mind."

"Of course," the twins said simultaneously, then giggled. They were moving from cute to scary.

Deborah raised one eyebrow, but when I pointedly looked at my bag, she got the idea and said, "We'll just go into the hall for five, if that's okay."

"Certainly," Beatrice said.

I left the bag—and Sid—behind to follow my sister into the hall, closing the door behind us.

"What do you think?" Deborah said, and I knew it was for the Quintet's benefit, not mine.

"Well, you did make a commitment, and we've both seen some very promising scholars forced to leave school or go to a lesser university because of not having sufficient financial support. It would be a shame if McQuaid lost those students."

"That's true. My heart just aches for that poor girl's family. It was such a terrible thing. Really terrible."

I very much hoped nobody was eavesdropping, because we were terrible improvisers, but I played along for another five minutes until Deborah concluded our performance with, "I think I should carry on, despite the really terrible thing that happened."

Then she tapped at the door to the study.

Beatrice answered promptly, but I couldn't be sure that she'd been listening in.

We all took our seats again, and Deborah said, "Now that I've thought it over, I want to continue on as head of the haunt, but I do have conditions. One, obviously the police have to agree."

Vivienne started to speak, but Beatrice jumped in with, "I'll talk to them and make sure they've completed their examination. If they need more resources, I'll see if I can make that happen."

"Good enough. Two, my actors and crew may not be willing to come back or their parents may not want them coming back. I won't try to talk anybody into it."

"Of course not," Beatrice said. "If necessary, we'll help you recruit new people. Or perhaps offer higher pay."

"Three, I want security cameras. I'll use my connections to get them cheap and install them myself, but the committee will have to pay for them."

I was expecting the cousins to balk at the expense, but Beatrice said, "That's reasonable. I'm sure they'd make both customers and crew members feel more secure."

Deborah blinked, no doubt as surprised as I was at how quickly Beatrice had folded.

But before she could accept the terms, I added, "And four, Kendall Fitzroy's parents have to be consulted. They shouldn't read about the haunt reopening in the paper, and they can't be allowed to think that anybody has forgotten their loss."

"You're absolutely right," Beatrice said. "Vivienne knows them well, and we'll speak to them before we move any further."

"Then we have a deal," Deborah said.

"Thank you for your dedication," Beatrice said, and there were similar sentiments expressed all around. "We'll be in touch when I've had a chance to speak with the Fitzroys and the police."

She escorted us out, and this time I made sure to take my bag.

"That was odd," I said once we were in the car.

"What? Rich people wanting things done their way? Nothing odd about that."

"I mean that they really do want the haunt opened instead of having an excuse to reclaim that property."

"I told you, they'd rather have something to make a big deal about than more money."

"You're both wrong," Sid said from inside my bag. "Let me out and I'll tell you the real story."

I opened it, and pulled Sid's skull out to put on my lap, hoping that we didn't encounter any vehicles tall enough for the driver to look down and see him.

"Spill, Sid!"

"The McQuaids do want the haunt reopened—"

"That's what I said," Deborah said.

"But you don't know why. The bequest is involved—"

"Which was my theory," I said.

"But it's not involved the way you thought," Sid said. "Now both of you stop interrupting!"

"Sorry," I said. Deborah grunted.

"The Quintet knows about the bequest, but they don't

want it revoked because the building wouldn't come to them." He paused dramatically, so I figured I was supposed to ask him a question.

"If not to the McQuaids, then to whom?"

"Oh, it would go to a McQuaid, just not any of those McQuaids. There's another McQuaid. Nobody knows where he is, but he's the real heir."

14

"Hold on, there are more McQuaids around?" Deborah made a face. "Isn't that batch enough?"

"Tell us what you heard, Sid," I said.

He cleared his throat, or rather made a useless throat-clearing noise. "As soon as you left— Leaving me in there to eavesdrop was a great move, by the way."

"Thank you, but you can compliment me later."

"As soon as you two left, Vivienne said something like, 'This is ridiculous. She has to run the haunted house because we'll never be able to find somebody else fast enough. You'll have to make her do it, Beatrice!' Then Paige asked how they could be sure you two weren't in league with *him*. The twins, who I can't tell apart, said they'd be humiliated if *he* came back and destroyed the family's legacy, and that they'd have to leave town. Then they all fussed about how *he* had even found out about the will, and there were some accusations back and forth about who it was who'd given away the secret. Vivienne blamed Paige, because Paige discovered the clause in the first place, and Paige blamed Vivienne for telling somebody. It turns out that the twins don't have a hive mind after all because one went along with Vivienne while the other agreed with Paige.

"Eventually Beatrice calmed them all down. She said that she was sure Deborah would reopen the house if they didn't push her too hard, and that Paige was just being paranoid because there was no reason to believe you two even know about the will. Of course you do, but I wasn't going to tell them that. As for *him*, she said, 'If our long-lost uncle shows up, we'll do what we have to.'"

"A long-lost uncle?" I said.

"I know, isn't it just too *Downton Abbey*!" Sid said. "I thought I knew the whole McQuaid family tree, but I sure missed that branch."

I said, "I don't know how Sara Weiss finds out the things she finds out, but she's got some great sources. Maybe I can get more dirt from her tomorrow."

"Not that gossip isn't fascinating," Deborah said, "but what does it have to do with the murder?"

"Are you kidding?" Sid said. "This proves that— It means that—" He hesitated. "You tell her, Georgia."

"It's possible that the missing uncle killed Kendall, or hired somebody to do it, to get McHades shut down so he could take advantage of the loophole in the will," I said.

"If somebody wanted the haunt shut down, I can think of a dozen better ways to do it," Deborah said.

"I can come up with a few, too," I admitted. "The fact is, this might have nothing to do with the murder. Most of what Sid and I find out has nothing to do with the murders we're investigating. We never know what's important until the killer is found."

"It's not exactly methodical, is it?"

"You can't expect us to act like professional detectives,

Deborah. If you want us to stop—" I put my hand over Sid's mouth before he could object. "If you want us to stop, we will, but otherwise, we're going to keep finding out stuff that may or may not be related, and coming up with ludicrous theories. Can you deal with that?" In one respect, I was in total agreement with Beatrice—I knew better than to try to push Deborah into anything.

She drove for a minute or two, then said, "Okay. I shouldn't have expected anything different. I mean, you're an English professor and Sid is . . . Sid's Sid."

Only then did I move my hand from Sid's mouth.

Deborah dropped us off at the house without coming in, and I found Mom, Phil, and Madison watching a DVD of *Guardians of the Galaxy* while sharing a bowl of popcorn. Byron was sprawled nearby, close enough for pats and stray pieces of popcorn, but jumped up as I pulled Sid's skull out of the bag.

"Back off, kibble breath!" Sid snapped.

Byron looked disappointed, but retreated as Sid's headless skeleton came lumbering down the stairs, reaching out blindly.

Once he'd plopped his skull into place, Sid said, "Hi, Thackerys! I'm heading upstairs to work."

My family didn't even react to any of that. I wasn't sure if it was a good sign or not.

Before I headed to McQuaid the next day, I got a text from Deborah:

Beatrice called. Kendall's parents don't object but cops won't release house. Evidence gathered, but worried about security. Weekend looking iffy. Any progress?

I wasn't happy about my reply, but I hadn't had any grand revelations and I was fairly sure Sid hadn't either.

Nothing. Sorry.

I went to tell Sid the latest and found him pounding madly at his laptop.

"The cops have actually defied the McQuaid Quintet, so no word on when the haunt will reopen."

"Uh-huh," he said, not looking in my direction.

"Louis must be tougher than he looks."

"Uh-huh."

"In fact, I like him so much I'm going to marry him and have little police detective babies. Is that okay with you?"

"Uh-huh."

"Dude." I waved my hand in front of the screen, blocking his view. "What's wrong with you?"

"I've spent ten hours straight trying to find some mention of this McQuaid heir, and there's nothing. Not one thing. Oh, sure, there are McQuaids. There are a gazillion McQuaids, and if I had a first name or age or anything but the last name—"

"And gender."

"Unless he's transitioned, or has died and it's his heir I should be looking for. Which might mean somebody with a different last name entirely."

Sid threw up his hands in exasperation, a gesture that's literal for him, so he had to reattach them before continuing to rant. "I found a family in Medford, Mass., but there's no connection, and I tracked a paleontologist in Colorado until I realized it's a woman about forty years too young. I even located a branch of the McQuaids in Germany, but they aren't related. I'm starting to think I'm not going to be able to find anything! How can that be?"

"Not all records are online. Some stuff still has to be found in record offices and libraries."

"That's crazy talk, Georgia, everything important is online."

Of course the real issue was that Sid couldn't go to town hall to look up birth records or hunt down ancient newspapers in the library. "Well, we don't know for sure the heir is even involved."

"I don't care. I refuse to stop looking."

"Okay. I've got to go to work."

"Sure, whatever." He turned back to his laptop.

15

With Sid working so hard on tracking down the mysterious missing McQuaid, I felt justified in not even thinking about murder for the rest of the day. Had I run into Sara, I would have tried to pick her brain for McQuaid family lore, but our schedules didn't mesh. Instead I was forced to pay attention to my job. It was oddly relaxing.

After my trifecta of classes was over, I went to my parents' offices. Mom was deep in conversation with Roxanne and a horror-makeup-free Linda Zaharee.

"Sorry," I said. "I didn't mean to interrupt."

"Georgia, this is Linda. She's a math major and is helping Roxanne with the calculations for her paper."

"Actually, Linda is one of my students, or at least she was," I said. "And Linda, your skin has cleared up nicely."

Mom looked shocked, but Linda giggled. "Dr. Thackery saw me made up for McHades Hall."

"That's a relief," Mom said. "We're working on Roxanne's dissertation."

"So I gathered." Every available surface was covered with papers, open books, journals, two laptops, and an iPad. "Is Phil around?"

"No, he's doing a guest lecture for another professor, then they're going to talk shop over lunch."

"Okay. I was going to ask if you wanted to go eat, but under the circumstances . . ."

"There's no time," Roxanne said. "I can't even think about food."

Upon seeing a pained look on Linda's face, I said, "Could I bring you guys something?"

"Would you?" Linda said. "I'm starved."

"No problem." I took orders and money, headed for the Campus Deli, and brought back sandwiches, chips, cookies, and drinks for all. As I lugged, I realized it was my second stint as a delivery person in recent days. Maybe I could start a service on campus and work for tips. It might make for a nice supplement to my per-class pay from McQuaid.

That day's delivery was particularly lucrative because Mom insisted on paying for my share, and I didn't want to argue with her in front of company. But even without that, I would have been glad I'd made the offer. While Roxanne barely touched her meal, Linda went through hers like only a hungry college student can, and accepted Mom's cookie, too.

Later that afternoon, I was even more glad that Linda had gotten something to eat. By then, I was at Phil's desk grading essays. A couple of students had come by for office hours, but I'd quickly dealt with their concerns, leaving me time to work in relative quiet. I was just wrapping up when there was a tap at the door.

I opened it to find Louis Raymond, a state trooper, Officer Burcell, and Oscar O'Leary, McQuaid's chief of security.

"Can I help you?"

Louis said, "We're looking for Linda Zaharee, and we were told she might be here."

"She's next door in my mother's office."

While they went to knock on Mom's door, I opened the adjoining door.

Mom was already at the door and Roxanne was saying, "Not more distractions!"

Louis stepped in and said, "Linda Zaharee?"

"Yes," Linda said.

"Do you have to do this now?" Roxanne asked. "We're in the middle of something important."

Louis ignored her. "Ms. Zaharee, when we spoke to you on Friday night, you said you hadn't known that Ms. Fitzroy was in McHades Hall. Is that correct?"

"Yes. I only found out she'd been there when you told us."

"And at that time, you said you knew her from high school but hadn't been in contact with her since then."

"Right."

"Then can you explain the e-mails you exchanged with Ms. Fitzroy on the day before she was murdered? In which you planned to meet up the day after her death?"

She looked distressed. "Kendall e-mailed me out of the blue. I know I should have told you, but since I didn't have a chance to meet her, I didn't think it mattered. I guess I didn't want to get involved."

"Can you tell me why you were meeting?"

"She wouldn't say. If you've got the e-mails, you know that."

"And you had no idea what it was about?"

"No. I swear, I barely knew her at PHS."

"Then can you explain these?" The trooper handed him a plastic bag labeled *EVIDENCE*. Inside was a pair of yellow rubber gloves with dark-brown streaks and smudges. The stains could have been fake blood, but I didn't think they were.

"Those aren't mine," Linda said.

"Are you sure of that?"

"Of course I'm sure."

"Then can you explain how they were found inside your dorm room?"

"What? I didn't . . ."

"Your roommate found them there and called us."

"But they're not mine. I've never seen them."

"Really? Because they match the description of the gloves that are missing from McHades Hall."

"I didn't take them!" Her voice was getting shriller and shriller.

"Excuse me," Mom said in her most professorial manner, "are you intending to arrest Ms. Zaharee?"

Louis said, "Yes, ma'am, I'm afraid we are."

"Then Linda, I advise you to say nothing further until you've spoken to a lawyer."

"Look, Dab," Louis started to say.

"That's Dr. Thackery, Sergeant Raymond."

He looked unhappy, but said, "Dr. Thackery, don't you think it would be in Ms. Zaharee's best interest for her to tell us the truth?"

"I believe there's some sort of warning you're supposed to read now," she said pleasantly.

"Yes, ma'am. Linda Zaharee, you're under arrest for the murder of Kendall Fitzroy." And just like on TV, he read her her rights. I thought Linda was going to faint, but she pulled herself together and allowed the officer to handcuff her.

"Is it necessary to humiliate her by walking her across campus like that?" Mom said.

"I'm afraid it's procedure," Louis said.

But Oscar said, "Have you got a jacket, Miss Zaharee?"

Linda nodded at a McQuaid fleece hoodie that was still on her chair.

Oscar draped the jacket over her cuffed hands, making it look as if she was just holding it. "Is that acceptable, Sergeant?"

"That'll be fine."

Oscar nodded at Mom and me, then he, the state trooper, and Officer Burcell led Linda away. Louis stayed behind and asked, "Is either of these laptops hers?"

"Why?" Roxanne said.

"If you prefer, I can take both."

"No!" she said, grabbing one of them and clutching it to her chest. "This one is mine. That one's hers."

"Fine." Louis packed it in the bag Mom identified as Linda's.

"How long will Linda be gone?" asked Roxanne, who clearly didn't understand what had happened.

"Don't worry, dear," Mom said, "we'll get this squared away as quickly as we can." She looked at Louis. "Unless you intend to arrest somebody else, I suggest you leave."

He started to speak, but I think he'd finally realized where Deborah got her uncompromising streak. As soon as she closed the door behind him, Mom said, "Roxanne, do you have Linda's parents' number?"

"No, just her cell."

"Then I'll get it from the registrar." Normally university registrars won't share information like that, but Mom was well known enough at McQuaid that she got what she wanted. "I'm going to let her parents know what's happened. Georgia, you better call your sister."

I retreated to Phil's office to do so, but when Deborah didn't answer, left a message for her to call me back ASAP. I could hear my mother explaining the situation and telling somebody to get a lawyer for Linda right away. She even had recommendations.

I took the opportunity to call Sid. For obvious reasons, he doesn't normally answer the landline, but he usually enjoys getting calls on his cell phone. Not this time.

"I still haven't found the McQuaid heir," he snapped as soon as he answered.

"That's not why I'm calling. The police just arrested Linda Zaharee for Kendall's murder."

"Who's Linda Zaharee?"

"One of the scare actors." I told him what Louis had said.

"Deborah's going to flip her cranium if she finds out one of her people was the killer after all!"

"We don't know that she's guilty."

From the open door I heard Roxanne say, "She's not guilty of anything! She's a statistician, not a murderer!"

I wasn't sure that one necessarily contradicted the other, but was glad to know that Roxanne was showing loyalty to something other than her dissertation.

Sid said, "I'll see if anything about the arrest has hit the Web. Call me if you hear anything else."

"Will do."

As soon as I hung up, the phone rang again.

"What?" Deborah barked.

I went through the story again, but when I finished, heard nothing from the other end of the line. "Are you there?"

"Yes."

Another pause.

Finally she said, "I'm going to the police station to find out what I can. I'll call later."

I went back to Mom's office in time to hear Roxanne say, "Dr. Eberhardt can't hold me responsible for my stats maven getting arrested, can he? He has to give me an extension now."

I don't know how Mom kept her voice cordial, but her years of soothing manic grad students must have paid off. "I'll make sure he knows, but I'm afraid it might not affect his decision."

"Do you suppose the police will let Linda use a laptop in jail? Because I could e-mail her my data and she could—"

"Why don't you just work around the numbers for now? Keep polishing your introduction, and then put together a table with your raw data. We'll get to the results section as soon as we get this straightened out." She helped Roxanne pack up her papers and other detritus, and ushered her out the door. Then she took a long, deep breath.

"I told Deborah," I said. "She's on her way to the police station."

"With luck, Linda's mother and a lawyer will meet her there."

"Should I be concerned that you were able to recommend a criminal lawyer without any research?"

"Do you know how many protests I was involved in back in the day? Of course I know lawyers."

"Mom, I think there are stories you've never told me."

"Another time, dear. For now, we've got to focus on getting Linda out of trouble."

"Are you that sure she's innocent? I thought you only just met her."

"You're right, I don't really know her well enough to say. It's just that seeing the police handcuff her in my office brought back some very bad memories."

"Mom, you really have to explain that someday."

She just smiled. "I don't know about you, but I'm ready to go home."

16

As soon as Mom and I came in the door, I saw Madison's school books dumped on top of the coffee table and noticed that Byron was missing, and cleverly deduced that my daughter had taken the dog out for a walk. Then I checked to make sure all the downstairs curtains were drawn before yelling, "It's me and Mom, Sid. It's clear!"

A moment later, he came clattering down the stairs. "Any more news?"

"Not yet. Deborah was heading to the police station the last I heard."

"I would not want to be in Louis Raymond's shoes when she gets there," Sid said.

"How about you? Anything about the secret McQuaid on the interwebs?"

"Nada. Nicht. Not one ossifying thing."

"Let it alone for a while. Either you'll come up with a new approach, or we'll find out something else to go on. In the meantime, you can keep me company in the kitchen."

After witnessing Linda's arrest, I was too restless to do anything that required concentration, so I did something I hadn't done since my parents got back: I cooked. Fortunately we had the ingredients I needed to make the chili Phil had dubbed Enamel Chili because it was so hot it could melt the enamel off of teeth. It had the distinction of being one of the few dishes I could make better than my father could, and was comfort food for Madison and me. With Sid's help, I got to work on a pot full of comfort.

Phil got home shortly after that, but when Mom and I started to tell him about Linda, he said, "I've heard. The story is already all over campus." We gave him more details anyway, and when Madison returned with a well-exercised Byron, we went through the story again.

"I can't believe it," she said. "Why would Linda kill Kendall?"

I said, "I have no idea, but the police must think she has a motive. How well do you know her?"

"I thought I knew her pretty well," she said, absently scratching Byron. "She's done McHades for three or four years, so she was somebody I'd go to when I had questions about how things worked. She has mad makeup skills, and she's an awesome scare actor, totally committed to the part without ever stepping over the line with the customers. I told her she should audition for a play sometime, but she said she couldn't act on stage—she just liked scare acting. When she's in her usual clothes, she's kind of quiet, but as soon as she puts on her makeup, it's like she's a different person."

"She would have been in costume when the murder was committed," Sid said. "And from what Louis said, she'd been in contact with the victim and then lied about it."

"Still," Madison said.

"I taught her one semester," I said, "and Mom has been working with her, but neither of us can see it, either."

I could tell that Madison was upset about her friend, because she brought her books into the kitchen to work on homework instead of retreating to her room. Mom and Phil stuck around, too, and we talked of nothing in particular while I got the chili onto the stove to start cooking. Sid was even nice to Byron—he gave him a pizzle stick.

I stalled with the chili, expecting to hear from Deborah, but finally baked some crescent rolls to go with dinner and got Sid to set the dining room table. We heard the back door open just as we were sitting down.

I don't think I'd ever seen Deborah look so dejected. Her shoulders slumped, and if she'd been Sid, I'd have expected her to be leaving a trail of bones behind her.

"You're just in time for a bowl of Georgia's chili," Mom said. Then she caught each of our eyes—or eye sockets in Sid's case—and gave a little shake of her head, a clear message that we should hold off on questions until Deborah had eaten.

I was just as glad. Though I've spent an alarming amount of time discussing murder, I prefer not to do so at the dinner table.

Phil and Sid carried the conversation, talking about the art history class Sid was taking online which segued into movies with historical settings which led to the TV show *Rome*, which Sid had recently binge watched. By the time they got to speculating about whether HBO would ever make a third season, we'd finished eating, wiped the table, and cleaned up the kitchen.

Deborah, who'd uttered nothing more substantive than "Pass the butter," since she arrived, said, "I guess you want to know what happened at the police station."

There was a round of nodding, and we all sat back down.

"By the time I got there, Linda had lawyered up and wasn't talking to anybody, so I found Louis to ask him what was going on. It's not public yet, so don't go spreading it around.

Louis only told me as much as he did because of my running the haunt and us being friends. But it looks as if they've got a pretty good case against her."

"We saw the bloody gloves," I said.

"Plus they found those e-mails between her and Kendall. There was a phone call, too, earlier that day. Linda lied about all of that."

"But why would she kill Kendall?" Madison asked.

Deborah shrugged. "An old grudge from high school is their best guess. You remember those friends of Kendall's who were at the haunt with her? They say that Linda was always jealous of Kendall because she was popular in school, softball star and all that. Louis isn't sure if it was premeditated or not. One scenario is that Linda saw Kendall or heard people calling her name and realized who it was. Then she targeted Kendall in the zombie party, thinking she wouldn't be recognized in that makeup. Only Kendall did recognize her and said she'd get her into trouble, and Linda struck in self-defense."

"What about the baseball bat?" I asked. "That says premeditation to me."

"Maybe Justin left it in the party room after all, and Linda found it."

"Sounds pretty convoluted."

"Yeah, Louis was trying to make me feel better. The likelier scenario is that Linda knew Kendall was going to be at the haunt because of that phone call, and hid the bat and gloves where she could get to them."

"But the police are sure she did it?" Sid asked.

"They don't have the whole story, but they've got enough to keep her in custody until they get the rest."

"I can't believe it," Madison said sadly.

I was having a hard time, too. Maybe it was just because it felt so anticlimactic that after the theorizing Sid and I had done, it was something so obvious. "Wait a minute. I read in the news that Kendall and her friends made an annual trip to McHades, and Madison told us that Linda had worked at the haunt for several years. Why did she snap this year? Had she been under any kind of stress?"

"I only chatted with her a little while," Mom said, "but she told me that she was breezing through her courses, which is why she was able to take the time to help Roxanne. Apparently she's quite brilliant with statistics."

"What about personal problems?" Sid asked, following my reasoning. "Madison, you spent time with her."

"She didn't mention anything like that to me. She liked her roommate, gets along with her parents, and doesn't have a boyfriend or girlfriend, so no problems there."

"How about you, Deborah?" he asked. "Did you see signs of anything going on with her?"

"Sure, Sid, I could tell she was about to go homicidal," she snapped. "That's why I kept her around."

"Deborah," Phil said reprovingly. "Nobody is blaming you."

"I'm blaming myself, Dad. I hired a murderer and let her loose on the public. Don't tell me that I'm not being logical. I know that, and I don't care." Before any of us could try to comfort or argue with her, she said, "We don't know what Linda and Kendall talked about in that phone call, or what it was they were going to meet about. When the cops find out, we'll know why Linda went off the deep end."

"You're probably right," I said, but it still didn't feel right. One glance at Sid, and I knew exactly what was going on in his nonexistent brain. "If it's all the same to you, I think we're going to stay on the case for now. Something about this smells off. Linda just doesn't seem like a killer."

"Don't you ever watch the news?" Deborah said. "Every time they catch a killer, his idiot neighbors and stupid family and clueless coworkers bleat about how he seemed like such a nice guy. So this time I'm the clueless coworker."

"But—"

"Georgia, the cops are satisfied so stop trying to prove that you're smarter than they are."

I started to count to ten, but didn't get past three. "Let's get this straight. I got involved in this cluster because you asked me to. After all, I'm a lady of leisure. I just have five sections of expository writing to teach every week with all those papers to grade. So of course I was dying for a chance to play detective."

"Okay, fine, I get—"

"But since you did ask me to get involved, I have been trying my best, and I do not believe that girl is guilty. Neither do you."

I glared at her, she glared at me, and our glaring might have lasted all night if Mom hadn't intervened.

"Before we raise our voices any further," she said, "let's consider this logically. Either Linda is guilty or she's not."

Had it been anybody but our mother, Deborah would have snarled at her for stating the obvious, but she managed to control herself and just say, "Okay."

"If she's guilty, it's not going to hurt for Georgia and Sid to continue their investigation, is it? The worst that could happen is that they'll find more evidence against her. In fact, that would be a good thing because we'd all rest easier."

Deborah nodded.

"If Linda isn't guilty, then the only way that she's going to get out of jail is if the police find the real killer, or at least some evidence that it's somebody else. Only the police aren't likely to find anything because they aren't looking."

Deborah nodded again.

"So in either case, it makes sense for your sister and Sid to stay on the job. Isn't that right?"

"Georgia said she was too busy with work," Deborah muttered.

"Georgia, do you want to continue this investigation? Because you don't have to, and you certainly don't have to prove anything."

I wanted to tell her that of course I knew that, but maybe part of me really was trying to prove that I was smart. I didn't care what the police thought, but I did want Mom and Phil to know it, even if my academic career hadn't been stellar. Except that if that were my only aim, I'd be writing academic articles, not solving a murder. So why had I gotten involved in the first place?

Deborah had asked me to investigate, but I could have turned her down. Sid was always eager to snoop, of course, but he'd never make me do something I didn't want to. I couldn't pretend I'd been protecting Madison because the easiest way to do that would have been to pull her out of the haunt. Nor could I claim I was selflessly trying to rescue Linda—the world was filled with people being treated unfairly, and I wasn't rushing to help them. With all that, why was I refusing to give up? I didn't know what the answer was, but I did know one thing. "I am busy, but I want to do this."

"Good enough," Mom said. "Now since your father and I have plenty of free time until next semester starts, Phil will continue to take care of the cooking, I'll deal with household chores, and either of us can grade essays if you run short on minutes. And it goes without saying that we'll help with the detective work if there's anything we can do." She looked from one of us to the other. "All right?"

Deborah and I nodded.

"Then it's settled. I'm getting started right now by washing a load of laundry."

She bustled out, and Phil ambled after her. Madison stayed where she was, as if afraid that any movement would set Deborah and me off.

My sister and I weren't glaring at each other anymore, but we weren't smiling, either. Finally she said, "I guess Mom's right. You go ahead and do whatever it is you do."

"I'll try my best."

"Okay. I'm going home." She got up, but stopped long enough to say, "Good chili."

"Thanks. Glad you liked it."

After she was gone, Sid said, "Whoa. I've never known Deborah to apologize so profusely before."

"What apology?" Madison said.

Sid patted her on the shoulder. "Kid, trust me, I've known Deborah for most of her life. That was as close as your aunt ever gets to saying she's sorry."

"And she knows I've accepted it," I said.

"Very graciously, too," Sid said. "A genuine Hallmark moment."

Madison looked back and forth between the two of us, probably trying to decide if we were pulling her leg, but we really weren't. Deborah and I may not have a greeting card kind of relationship, but we understand each other.

Madison went to tackle her homework, but when I offered to help Mom with laundry, she told me I had more important things to do. Sid and I ended up back in his attic.

"Any ideas?" Sid asked.

"Not a one. You?"

"Maybe. If Linda isn't the killer, then the killer is framing her."

"And doing a pretty good job of it, too."

"Why?"

"What do you mean?"

"The usual reason to frame somebody is to divert suspicion

away from oneself, right? But the police didn't have any suspects, unless you count Scooby-Doo. Who was the killer diverting attention from?"

"That's a good question, Sid. Maybe the real killer was nervous, and thought the police would find him if they kept looking."

"Possible, but it occurs to me that there are two things that happened as a result of Linda being arrested. One, Roxanne's screwed on her dissertation."

"Why would anybody go to so much trouble to keep Roxanne from getting her Ph.D.?"

"Anything scandalous in the dissertation? Something somebody wouldn't want published?"

"It's about word use in Romantic Era poetry, so it doesn't seem likely. Besides if there were anything that was going to cause a stir, Mom would have warned her about it. Dissertations are supposed to be original, but students are steered away from outright controversy."

"How about a competitor with a similar project who's afraid Roxanne will beat him or her to the punch?"

"Given how long she's been working on this thing, anybody who wanted to beat her to the punch could have done so a long time ago."

"Then maybe somebody really hates Roxanne. You have to admit, she's kind of annoying. I've never even met her face-to-face, and she annoys me."

"All grad students are annoying when they get this close to finishing their dissertation. When I was in the middle of mine, I went out to dinner with a friend of mine the day she got a book contract—an actual 'I've sold a book to a New York publisher and it's going to be published' moment—and all I talked about was my research topic. If that had been a viable murder motive, I'd be dead."

"Still," Sid insisted, "there might be something in Roxanne's background to make somebody despise her."

"Okay, we can check into that, but even if we find an enemy, that won't explain why somebody would frame Linda. Why not just kill Linda? Or Roxanne, for that matter."

"To cover his tracks. Nobody would expect a plot so complex."

"That's a point." I know I didn't expect it to be true. "What's the other result?"

"I bet the haunt will reopen."

"Weren't we thinking the murderer wanted to close the haunt?"

"Right, right." He drummed his finger bones against the desk. "What if the secret McQuaid heir killed Kendall to get the haunt closed so he can claim the property? The Quintet found out about it, but won't go to the police for fear of besmirching the fair name of McQuaid. So they're framing Linda to get the haunt reopened without the secret heir coming into it, so the heir will slink away in disgrace."

"How did they get the bloody gloves?"

More drumming. "One of them broke into the heir's hotel room and stole them."

"Then why frame poor Linda?"

"She beat one of the Quintet kids out for the math award at PHS? Or maybe they know Roxanne and think it'll be funny if she doesn't ever get her doctorate. Or maybe—"

"Sid, just stop. I'm not saying your theories don't make sense." They didn't, but I wasn't saying so. "The thing is that we don't need more theories—we need some facts or evidence or proof."

"Yeah, I guess we do." He started drumming again, and I thought I saw his bones loosen a touch.

"Don't worry," I said, patting his scapula. "I don't know what we can find that the cops didn't, but—"

"Georgia, if you say that one more time, I'm going to bite you. Haven't we solved murders before? If you don't take your abilities seriously, at least take mine seriously!"

"I'm sorry, Sid," I said, surprised by his vehemence. "I don't mean to disrespect you, but this murder feels different from the other ones. Then there were things we knew that the cops didn't. Now it seems as if they know everything we know, plus they've got the forensics and all that going for them."

"But with all that, they've still got the wrong person, don't they?"

"We don't know for sure . . ."

He snapped his teeth threateningly.

"Yes, they've got the wrong person."

"Which proves that we already know something they don't, right?"

"Right."

"Okay then. Now you go get some sleep, and I'll troll the Web and see what else I can find that the cops missed."

"If it's there, you'll find it, Sherlock," I said, and leaned over him to plant a kiss on his skull. Kissing bare bone is an odd sensation, but no more so than when I kissed my first car when nobody was looking, and my car didn't smile afterward the way Sid did.

I followed his advice, and though I didn't wake up inspired Thursday morning, at least I was well rested, which was a good thing because the first news of the day wasn't promising. Sid had prepared more dossiers overnight, this time on Roxanne and Linda. Roxanne did so little other than work that she hadn't had time to create enemies, unless you counted the person who claimed she'd co-opted her carrel at the library. Linda was the opposite, with lots of on-campus activities, but she seemed well liked. In other words, Sid had found nothing that would show why somebody would want to prevent Roxanne's doctorate or get Linda thrown in jail.

Fortunately for my peace of mind, the day got more interesting later on. After my first class, I received a text from Deborah.

> Beatrice called. Haunt reopening Friday. Meeting with crew and cast @McHades @6. Tell Madison.

Before I could respond, she sent another.

> Want to come?

I was checking my schedule to make sure the timing would work when yet another appeared:

> Bring Sid.

If she and my parents had that much confidence in our detective work, maybe I should, too. I texted back that we'd be there, then let Madison and Sid know that I'd pick them up at five thirty.

17

Phil was right about the news of Linda's arrest having spread. When I went to the adjunct office after class, I was immediately approached by people asking if the rumor was true. Once I gave the bare-bones account of what had happened, I claimed I had more work to do than I actually did and got busy on my laptop. Of course, that made no difference to Sara Weiss. She showed up a little after eleven, and even before she sat down, said, "Is it true?"

I was tempted to mess with her by pretending not to know what she was talking about, but since she might know something useful, I didn't want to annoy her. "About the arrest? Yeah, the police arrested a sophomore named Linda Zaharee for the haunted house murder."

"Handcuffs and everything? In your parents' office?" She sounded aggrieved that it had happened in a place to which she had no access.

I nodded.

"Did she resist arrest?"

"There were four cops. What could she have done?"

"I don't know. She could have still had the murder weapon."

"The baseball bat was left at McHades Hall," I said without thinking.

"How do you know? Do you have a connection at the police department? Did they release more details?"

Great. If I told her I'd been one of the first on the scene, she'd want to know all the gory details, and there'd been more gore than I wanted to remember. So I hedged. "That's what somebody told me. What have you heard?"

For the next twenty minutes, Sara bombarded me with rumors, facts, and total speculation mixed together indiscriminately. I know she must have breathed during that time—she wasn't Sid—but I'd have been hard-pressed to say when she had the opportunity. Unfortunately she had no useful facts except the fact that the ninja, the cowboy, and Scooby-Doo were still unidentified. She wound it up with, "I'm just glad they've got the killer behind bars. I know I'll sleep a lot easier tonight."

"I don't think Linda is guilty."

"Of course she's guilty."

"I don't know her well, but I taught her, and my sister, mother, and daughter know her. She doesn't strike us as a killer."

Sara gave me a pitying look. "Good grief, Georgia, don't tell me she pulled the wool over your eyes? You can tell from her picture in the paper that she's a stone-cold killer. She's got dead eyes, like a shark. Why do you think she worked in that haunted house? I mean, what kind of weirdo spends all night scaring people?"

"People like my daughter and my sister."

I thought that might give her pause, but I hadn't reckoned

on Sara's insatiable hunger for gossip. "Really? Did they see the body? Was there a lot of blood?"

I'm not often speechless, but that time I was. How tactless could one person be?

"Hey, Georgia!" a voice behind me said. "Are you ready for our lunch date?"

It was Brownie Mannix, and as far as I knew, we hadn't made a lunch date, but when he gave me a wink, I got the idea.

"Is it that time already?" I said, packing up my things as quickly as I could. "See you later, Sara." I think she was starting to ask if she could join us when we went through the office door, moving just short of a run until we were sure she wouldn't follow. Then we slowed down to a more normal pace.

"Thanks for the save, Brownie."

"No problem. It looked as if you were ready to slug her, and though that would have been entertaining, I didn't want you getting into trouble."

"It's my own fault. I answered a question about the arrest in my mother's office, and that got her started. Then I made the mistake of admitting that I know something about the murder that she doesn't."

"I wonder what she'd say if she knew I was in the haunt when it happened?"

"Have you ever seen a lamprey?"

He laughed.

"Anyway, the least I can do after my rescue is buy you lunch."

"Thanks, but one of the perks of having the show right outside campus is that I can eat at the cook shack for free."

"Another time?"

"Or you could join me instead. It's not fancy, but Stewpot is a good cook, and Thursday is chicken and dumplings day. Plus you can't beat the price."

"Isn't it against the rules for you to sneak me in?"

"My mother owns the carnival."

"In that case, I would be delighted."

As we walked across the quad to the main campus gate, then onto Elm Street where the carnival was set up, I admit to curiosity about the people Brownie worked with outside of academia. Carnivals have always struck me as being contradictory. On one hand, people take their kids there for fun and excitement. On the other, most people I know assume that the carnies running those merry-go-rounds and Ferris wheels were at best uneducated, and at worst unsavory. I had no idea of what to expect.

What I did not expect was to find Dr. Charles Peyton ensconced in the center of a small ring of tables and chairs next to a trailer from which wafted tantalizing smells. He was sitting with a woman with short, silver hair and eyes the same blue as Brownie's and a man with wispy gray hair escaping from his Red Sox cap. Both were wearing the purple polo shirts that identified carnival employees.

Charles saw the two of us approaching and beamed. "Georgia, College Boy, please come join us."

Brownie sighed, but bowed to the inevitable. "Georgia, you may remember my parents. Mom, Dad, this is Georgia Thackery, one of my colleagues from McQuaid."

"Glad to see you again, Mr. and Mrs. Fenton."

Mrs. Fenton smiled, but Brownie's father said, "It's Mannix, but just call me Treasure Hunt." He eyed me. "How do I know you?"

Brownie said, "Georgia came to the lot about a year ago, checking on the provenance of a specimen."

"Right. How's the skeleton?"

"Still dead."

"Did you ever lick it?"

It was Treasure Hunt who'd shared the tried-and-true way of determining whether or not a skeleton was a reproduction. A real skeleton is porous, so if you lick it, your tongue sticks. At least he said so—I'd never tested it myself. "A lady never licks and tells."

Treasure Hunt made a noise which I can only describe as a guffaw. "Sit down, Georgia. College Boy, are you going to let this gal starve to death? Go get her something to eat."

Brownie made the exact same sound I made when my parents embarrassed me in front of friends and said, "One plate of Stewpot's chicken and dumplings coming right up."

While he was gone, Charles said, "Treasure Hunt and the Boss have been educating me on the use of carnival lingo."

"Not me," Mrs. Fenton said. "I usually find English is good enough."

"I use English," Treasure Hunt protested. "I just think that only a comic book idiot wouldn't bother to learn the right way to talk to people."

"Comic book idiot," Charles repeated, rolling the words around in his mouth. "What does that mean?"

"That's a carny so lazy and stupid that he'd rather read a comic book than tend to paying customers."

"Or we could just call him lazy," Mrs. Fenton said.

"Where's the fun in that?" Treasure Hunt protested.

I could tell this was an old argument between them.

"Nice to see you again, Georgia," she said, "but I should get going. Somebody has to work today—not all of us are comic book idiots." She gave Treasure Hunt a quick kiss on the cheek that took the sting out of her remark.

Treasure Hunt watched her go with a grin. "That's my girl!"

Brownie arrived with a tray holding two canned Cokes and

two plates of food. He put one of each in front of me, along with paper napkins and plastic cutlery. "Bon appétit."

"It smells wonderful, but there's no way I can eat all of this." The dumplings were piled high and wide on the over-sized plastic plate.

"Just try a bite."

I did so, and immediately started thinking about seconds. "This is amazing."

"Family recipe," Treasure Hunt said. "Stewpot said his grandmother was the meanest woman he ever met, and his grandfather left her more times than he could count, but he'd always come back for those dumplings."

Charles patted his stomach. "I've never eaten so well in my life as I have during my days on the lot. Treasure Hunt, are you sure I can't pay for my board?"

The older man waved. "Your money's no good here, Britannica."

"Britannica?" I asked.

"My new nickname," Charles said proudly. "It's because I mentioned to Treasure Hunt that I specialize in the Pax Britannica period."

"No, it's because he talks like he swallowed an encyclopedia."

"I like it." I noticed Treasure Hunt eyeing me speculatively, and I was worried that either he was going to bring up Sid again or bestow a nickname on me, so I said, "What other words have you been learning, Charles? I mean, Britannica."

"A clem is a gullible local, particularly in a rural area. Other terms for those not with it—meaning people who are not part of the show—are towner, townie, chump, or rube. As in, 'Hey, rube!'"

"Don't say that too loud," Treasure Hunt warned.

"My apologies." Charles lowered his voice and said,

"'Hey, rube,' is the traditional call when a carny finds himself in dire need of aid. All showmen within hearing range are honor-bound to drop whatever they're doing to come to his assistance. Though I understand some shows now use the phrase, 'It's a clem!'"

"Or they just use their walkie-talkies," Brownie said.

"What do you know?" Treasure Hunt said dismissively. "You screw the carnival and then come eat for free."

"He isn't saying that Brownie was dishonest," Charles assured me. "'Screw the carnival' means that he left the show before the season was over."

"Which I haven't," Brownie said. "Was I screwing the carnival when I took over as talker for the merchandise wheel, or spent an hour finding a short in the popper?"

Treasure Hunt shrugged. "Maybe working at the egghead farm hasn't completely ruined you. Yet."

Brownie shook his head ruefully—obviously this was another old argument. While Charles asked for an explanation of the new terms, I was happy to finish emptying my plate.

"So I hear they arrested one of your students yesterday," Treasure Hunt said.

Brownie looked chagrined. He'd rescued me from Sara only to have his father get onto the same topic.

"They did," I said, "but I think they've got the wrong person."

"Wouldn't surprise me none. Cops always go for the easy answer, whether or not it makes sense. Our patch has been working overtime squaring things so they don't try to blame one of us. Cops love blaming carnies."

"A patch is like an ombudsman for the show," Brownie explained. "She takes care of customer complaints, and liaises with the police for permits and so forth."

"We should never have come to Pennycross anyway."

Treasure Hunt looked disgusted. "Hockey Puck Wilson usually takes this stand, but he burned the lot last year."

"I don't remember a fire," I said, "so I'm guessing that means he made the lot too hot somehow."

"Got it in one. Hockey Puck's show was infested with grifters, short-change artists, and pickpockets, which added up to unhappy towners. So the sponsors found us, and the Boss accepted without asking me. I never did like this town—no offense. Besides, we should have canceled after what happened at our last stand."

"What happened?" I didn't really think a murderer had been stalking the carnival, but it wouldn't hurt to ask.

What Treasure Hunt described was considerably less fatal. "I caught a first-of-May eating peanuts at the duck pond, and when he saw me coming, he tossed the shells right on the ground! After that, I knew we'd never make our nut here."

Charles and I looked to Brownie for a translation.

"For a carny to eat peanuts in his tent is supposed to be bad luck, especially if he throws the debris on the ground. And 'making our nut' means covering expenses, which we've been doing nicely, no matter what my father says."

"The stand isn't over yet," Treasure Hunt said. He stood and stretched. "Well, maybe you academic types don't mind spending all day sitting and talking, but I'm a working man. I'm going to take a visit to the donniker, then go get busy."

"That's the restroom," Charles explained, though I'd kind of figured.

"So now you've had a chance to see the glory that is my family," Brownie said after his father left. "Eccentricity defined."

"Are you kidding? My parents are English professors, my sister is a locksmith who runs a haunted house for fun, and my daughter is an otaku slash science fiction geek. Eccentricity is my life." And that was leaving out Sid.

"Nonsense," Charles said. "Both of your families are perfectly charming. But what is an otaku?"

That moved the conversation away from carny to the equally confusing vernacular of nerd culture, and I think that by the time we headed back to campus for afternoon classes, we could all agree that my family was just as weird as Brownie's.

18

My plan for the rest of the day was simple. I'd teach until three thirty, then spend an hour at my mother's office, fortunately unoccupied for the day, to grade papers or meet with any students who came by. After that I'd head home in a leisurely fashion to pick up Madison and Sid to bring them back to McQuaid for the meeting at McHades Hall. Given the amount of food I'd had for lunch, I wasn't worried about eating, but if I did get hungry I'd have plenty of time for a snack.

Unfortunately, my plan didn't allow for a student who came running up after I'd already locked Mom's office and was on my way out. It was vitally important that we talk right away so he could explain why I shouldn't lower his grade even though his weekly essay was going to be late. It took fifteen minutes to convince him that I disagreed. Then when I got to my car, I remembered I needed to stop at the gas station, where there was a line.

With all that, it was already five thirty-five when I burst in the back door, calling out, "Sid, Madison, are you ready?"

Then I stopped. Roxanne and my mother were at the dining room table, again surrounded by papers and books.

"Excuse me. I didn't realize we had company."

"We're doing what we can while we wait for the police to do the right thing about Linda." Mom's voice was strained, and I could see the entreaty in her eyes, but all I could do was give a little shrug since I'd neither found the real killer nor broken Linda out of jail.

Madison came downstairs, carrying her old backpack. "I'm ready. Here's your bag."

I automatically reached out for it, but was about to ask why when I noticed it had a skull-sized lump in it. "Okay then. We better get going."

"What about Sid?" Roxanne said, though up until that moment she'd seemed so intent on a printout that I'd have thought Sid could have walked into the room in all his bony glory and performed a solo from *Swan Lake* without her noticing.

"Excuse me?"

"You were calling for somebody named Sid."

"Oh, it's a nickname. For the dog. And I was kidding because I'm not taking the dog." I was ready to kick myself as soon as I said it, but Roxanne just nodded as if it made perfect sense for me to give a dog a nickname, and went back to her printout.

Mom said, "Will you be back for dinner?"

"We'll grab something on the way home." It wasn't an unreasonable question, but I wasn't used to having to run my schedule past anybody else other than Madison. I knew I should probably have a talk with Mom about boundaries, but I'd rather have had a root canal without anesthesia.

The police guard and crime-scene tape were gone from McQuaid Hall, but the door was locked and we had to wait for Deborah to let us in.

"We're meeting in the greenroom," she said.

Madison and I started up the stairs, but Deborah said, "You sure you're all right to come inside, Georgia?"

"I've been in here before."

"Yeah, but it's nighttime." Then she smirked.

I held up three fingers. "Dancing in public. The feel of rubber bands. Inflatable arm-flailing tube men. Let she who has no phobias cast the first fear."

Her eyes narrowed. "Fine. Go on up."

From inside the backpack, I heard Sid whisper, "I didn't know about the tube men thing."

"Shhh."

The greenroom was already well filled, and at about ten after six, Deborah came up and the crowd quieted.

She said, "First off, I want to thank you for coming. What happened last week was bad, and I wouldn't have blamed you if you'd quit the haunt."

Somebody said, "The show must go on!" and there were general sounds of approval.

"That's the way I see it, too," Deborah said. "As you've probably heard, the police have a suspect in custody that they're satisfied is the right one. So we're reopening tomorrow night."

There was a cheer.

"But!" Deborah interjected. "I'm not assuming anything about our safety from here on out. First off, I've already begun installing security cameras, which I will be monitoring personally." She looked around sternly. "Camera footage will be for security only. We will not be putting embarrassing videos of our customers up on YouTube. Is that clear?"

Heads nodded vigorously.

"I'm also going to station more room monitors, in more places. That's going to mean longer shifts."

She paused to allow for the inevitable groans.

"It also means more pay. The McQuaid Scholars Committee has agreed to double your hourly rate, and it'll come out of their budget, so we'll still make the same amount of money for funding scholarships."

The reaction switched back to cheers, though I suspect it was for the extra pay and not the size of the scholarship fund. As for me, I was applauding Deborah for getting the McQuaid Quintet to pony up the bucks. Knowing that they were worried about the missing heir must have given her the edge, even if she couldn't allude to it directly.

After that, she broke the meeting into groups to deal with details like scheduling, costume repairs, and shuffling the scare actors to make up for the cast members who'd been frightened off by the murder.

That's when I felt a nudge from the backpack, telling me that Sid wanted to consult. So I went to the bathroom, made sure nobody else was in any of the stalls, then unzipped the backpack to pull out his skull.

"Phew!" he gasped. "I wasn't sure I was going to make it! What rotted in there?"

I took a whiff, and remembered why the backpack had been retired. "Madison left a carton of milk in there over a long weekend, and it spilled. And spoiled. We thought it would air out eventually."

"And you used me to test the theory?"

"How often do I have to remind you that you don't breathe?"

"It's the principle of the thing. So where are we?"

"The ladies' room."

"I can't be in the ladies' room!"

"Well I'm not going into the men's room, and you don't use any bathroom, so what difference does it make?"

"It's the principle of the thing," he said again. "You're disrespecting my manhood."

I thought about pointing out that he was lacking that

portion of anatomy that bestowed "manhood," but decided it would be too cheap a shot. "I figured you were enlightened enough not be bothered by what is, in fact, a gender-neutral bathroom."

He radiated suspicion, but nodded. Well, without a neck it wasn't really a nod, but he did kind of bob his skull.

"Now what did you want?"

"I think we should tour the building."

"You went through the haunt the night of the murder."

"Those were just the public spaces. I want to see the rest, including the scene of the murder."

"I saw enough of that already."

"I know it's upsetting, Georgia, but—"

"No, you're right. We should look around now that we've got a chance. I don't know that we'll see anything the cops didn't—"

"Ahem!"

"Sorry, sorry." I would have apologized further, but the bathroom door started to open and I shoved Sid back into the backpack just as one of the scare actors came in.

"I thought I heard voices," she said, looking around.

"I was on the phone," I lied. Then I washed my hands and went back into the main room.

Deborah was talking to the costume crew, so I found Madison and said, "Since your aunt is going to be busy for a while, I thought you could show *us* around."

She looked at the backpack and nodded. "Got it. What do you want to see first?"

"How about the control room or whatever you call it."

"We call it the control room." She led the way down to the first floor and into the curtained enclosure Deborah and I had gone through in such a rush on the night of the murder. "That's the—"

"I can't see anything," Sid said from the backpack.

"Sorry." I unzipped it and held it in front of me, so he was hidden but could still look out. "How's that?"

"That'll do. Now start over."

"Sound board, light board, and since I haven't seen those screens before, they must go with the new security cameras."

"It's a shame they weren't there before, or that the room monitors didn't see anything," Sid said.

"Come on, dude, you were there. You know how dark it is, and confusing."

"No, no, I get it. I just wish we had more to go on."

Madison looked only partly mollified. "What next?"

I said, "Sid? This was your idea."

"Can you walk us through the haunt as if we were customers? I want Georgia to get a feel for the flow, and I've got some questions about the setup."

"Do you want me to see if I can turn on the special lighting and effects?"

"Thank you, no," I said firmly.

"Okay, then." We went back to the entrance hall. "Here's where the tour starts. Each group is met by a guide who shows them through the house."

"That's what you do, right?" I said.

She nodded. "The group is supposed to stay together for the whole tour, but it doesn't always work out that way. People get scared and run ahead, or sometimes they freeze in place. Plus we're trying to keep people moving, so we can't always keep track of every single person."

"Madison," I said, "nobody blames the tour guides for Kendall getting killed."

"Are you sure? The cops kept harping on it, especially with the guide who had that group."

"Which one was that?" Sid asked.

"Liam. He does an Igor riff."

"Write that down, Georgia. I didn't bring a pad. Or my hands."

"I think we can remember. Go on, Madison."

"Anyway, each guide has a spiel. Like 'Welcome to McHades University, where all your worst college nightmares come true.' Blah blah blah."

"The blah-blah-blah part is particularly frightening," I said.

"Mom, it's kind of hard to get into character under the circumstances."

"Fair enough."

She cleared her throat, then spoke in a much lower, more ominous tone. "I'll be your resident advisor, though my first advice is that you transfer out now, while you still can. Because once you enroll, you can't ever leave again." She laughed evilly. "No? Then don't blame me if you don't make the grade."

Madison led us up one flight of stairs, then turned to the left. The wide hall was lined with black curtains that were covered with spooky messages painted in Day-Glo colors: *Go Back*, *Help Us!*, and my personal favorite, *Too Ghoul for School*. "Time for your first class: chemistry," Madison intoned as she gestured for me to step into the first room.

In her regular voice she said, "This is the lab, obviously. Normally the stuff would all be bubbling, and we'd have dry ice making steam." There was a long lab table covered with various pieces of glassware with poison markings. A mannequin with a look of horror had his hand in a beaker labeled *Acid*, only the hand was a skeleton hand. "The scare actor in here has her back to people as they come in, and she pretends to swallow some stuff in a beaker. Then she grabs her throat, screams and groans, and turns around so people can see that she's changed into a werewolf. She jumps at them, and I rush people out and say, 'Quickly, before Mrs. Howl-ley gives you homework!'"

"Nothing scarier than homework," I said.

"Where does the room monitor stay?" Sid asked.

"In that closet. We took the door down and put in a scrim so she can see the whole room, but you can't see her at all."

We went back into the hall and on to the next room. "Next up, history. What education could be complete without learning about the black plague, Countess Bathory, and Jack the Ripper?"

This room was broken into three tableaux. The first was a pile of faux corpses with faux rats with faux red eyes.

Madison said, "We light up the rats' eyes, and the joke is that Purell hasn't been invented yet. We've got one radio control rat, and the room monitor stays in that corner, all in black, making it jump at people. Some people have a real issue with rats."

"Who wouldn't have an issue with rats?" I said.

The next tableau was a curvaceous female mannequin in a bath tub with a red-stained, naked body and a satisfied smile on her face. A trio of mannequins in peasant dresses was sprawled across the floor, each painted to look as if her throat had been cut. "We fill the tub with fake blood every night, and those are the virgins Countess Bathory supposedly drained to stay young. If the group is old enough, I'll say it's harder and harder to find enough virgins every year. We have a scare actor in that same outfit acting like her blood is draining into the tub saying stuff like, 'Help me! Save me!'"

"How can somebody talk when her throat is cut?" I asked.

"It depends on if it was the trachea, the esophagus, or an artery that was cut," Sid said cheerfully.

"Sorry I asked." I didn't want to know how he knew.

Next up was a dead woman mannequin in vaguely Victorian garb, with bits and pieces of her insides on the outside.

"That's gross," I said.

"Kind of the point," Madison reminded me. "I tell people that Professor Ripper really gets into his subject, and hates it when people cut class. We have a guy in a black frock coat who pretends to be a dummy until they get close enough, then he turns around and comes at the people with a knife."

"A fake knife, right?"

"Totally fake."

"Good."

We went to the next room. "This is the school cafeteria—it's your basic cannibal theme. There's a scare actor for the cook with a cleaver—a fake cleaver—and kids pretending to be students pretending to eat body parts."

"Also gross. And yes, I know that's the point."

"Room monitor?" Sid asked.

"One of the cannibals is the monitor—he drops character if he needs to."

We'd reached the end of the hall, and started back in the other direction to reach psychology class, which featured a mannequin strapped to a table and being subjected to electroshock therapy, a scare actor confronting his arachnophobia by being trapped in a cage full of rubber spiders, and a scare actor in a straitjacket writhing and screaming about exams. The monitor doubled as the professor taking notes about the various experiments.

English class was a lot like history, except the three tableaux showed fictional horrors instead of historical ones. So we had an exorcist trying to help a really grotesque mannequin, a woman in a shower being stabbed by a psycho, and the two creepy little girls from *The Shining*.

"This is more movie than literature," I said.

"I know, but we have to make sure the customers recognize the visuals. I suggested a stoning out of 'The Lottery,' but Aunt Deborah was worried we'd hit somebody in the eye. Anyway, the exorcist, the psycho, and the creepy girls are all actors. With that many in the room, we haven't had a separate monitor, but Aunt Deborah may add one now."

We moved down the hall. "The last room on this floor is the campus health center. You've got your insane nurse, your blood-covered doctor, your patient strapped to the table begging people to let her out, and amputation jokes. The spiel is that you better stay healthy, because if you're not in pain when you come to the health center, you will be when you leave."

"Cue creepy laughter?" I asked.

Madison nodded. "Creepy laughing is surprisingly hard on the throat."

Back in the hall, she said, "That's it for the rooms on this floor, but there are also pop-outs along the hall."

"What's a pop-out?"

"We station scare actors in these alcoves." Though the wall was lined with curtains, Madison knew which one to pull to reveal a gap just big enough for somebody to stand in. "They'll reach out, or jump out, or just scream, depending on how energetic they're feeling. We always have one near the door at the end of the hall to move groups along. Linda is a pop-out specialist."

"So she could have had time to kill Kendall?"

"Right. But she didn't, did she?"

"Definitely not," Sid assured her.

Madison opened a door at the end of the corridor to show another flight of stairs. "The stairs are always lit, by the way, and the guides make sure nobody runs or pushes. And absolutely no scares on the stairs."

Once down, we went through a short hallway to another room. "Detention hall."

"This is where I hid," Sid said.

"I figured," Madison said. "For a haunted house, we really don't have many skeletons."

"Why would you?" Sid asked. "Skeletons aren't scary."

Madison and I shared a look.

She went on. "I say something about making sure you do

your homework or we'll put you in detention and forget to let you out. Some of the props are motorized to rattle around, but there haven't been scare actors or monitors before now. It's not a big scare area, more a place to let people catch their breath before the big scares."

The end of the room opened to a hall with the requisite black curtains, and signs pointing the way to the dorms, with more spooky warnings.

"Any pop-outs along here?" Sid asked.

"Nope. We want to lull people into a false sense of security."

I knew the next room a little too well.

"This is our zombie party scene where . . . you know," Madison said. We all looked over at the corner where the body had been found. Sid had no questions other than asking about the monitor, and I was happy to keep moving.

The room opened onto another hall. Madison said, "And on to graduation."

The final room looked like an old-fashioned lecture hall with rows of seats on a gentle incline down to a platform with a podium and blackboard. At one point, seats must have filled most of the room, but there were only three rows left, and from our vantage point, we could see what looked like mannequins wearing mortar boards seated in the chairs, watching in rapt attention. But as we moved around, it was obvious that it was only heads on spikes, with the faces in various expressions of horror, pain, and madness, and appropriate amounts of pretend gore trailing from their severed necks. They looked kind of cheesy, but I could see how the scene would be horrifying with the right lighting.

Madison said, "There's a scare actor behind the podium, and I introduce him as the headmaster. Get it?"

"Very witty," I said.

"He welcomes the group to commencement, and says

they were such good students he doesn't want them to leave. Ever. Then he pulls a chainsaw out from behind the podium and chases people around. By this point, they're softened up by the rest of the haunt and even the tough ones tend to lose it if somebody is chasing them with a chainsaw."

"A prop chainsaw, I assume."

"No, it's real."

"You're kidding."

"It's a real chainsaw—there's just no chain. The headmaster could still burn somebody with it if he put it right up against somebody's neck, but he's not dumb enough to do that again."

"Again?"

"Just kidding. Aunt Deborah only lets mature cast members handle the chainsaw. Anyway, in case the headmaster isn't freaking them out enough, random professors pop out with fake axes and knives and things. That's why we took the chairs out, so there would be plenty of room for chasing. I let the customers run and scream for a while, then I open the door and yell for them to escape while they can."

The exit led to what must have originally been some sort of courtyard or maybe a sculpture garden. Now it was tricked out as a cemetery with tombstones and a shed painted to look like a mausoleum.

"And that's the end?" I asked.

"Nope," Madison said with a grin. "They think they're safe, but we've got random monsters out here to give them one last scare. That keeps them moving until they're out the gate. Then they're really safe."

"That last bit scares the piss out of people," Sid said with a snicker.

"Sometimes literally," Madison said.

"You mean people really wet themselves?" I asked.

"Sometimes. And worse."

"Oh. Ew." Now I knew I'd made the right decision in not going into the haunt.

"What else do you guys need to see?"

"Didn't I hear something about secret passages throughout the building?" Sid said.

"They aren't secret passages, exactly. We've got paths along the edges of the hallway and some of the bigger rooms so our people can get to and from without being seen. It's all just plywood walls and scrim."

We went back inside to see the maze of cramped, confusing pathways. Madison pointed out the black light bulbs and arrows painted in florescent paint that enabled the cast and crew to sneak around unseen for more effective scaring.

We ended up back at the front door. "That's it," Madison said.

"Pretty scary," I said.

We'd intended to go back to the greenroom, but people were already leaving, so we decided to wait for Deborah downstairs. I zipped the backpack to prevent unwanted skeletal exposure, and we leaned up against the wall to kill time. Well, that, and I was thinking about the haunt layout, and hoping I could figure out something brilliant about the murderer's approach. Apparently I couldn't.

We'd been there a few minutes when Madison asked, "Mom, can I ask you a question?"

"Sure."

"What is it with you and haunted houses?"

"I just don't see the point, that's all. If you're scared, you feel bad for being a coward. If you're not scared, you feel stupid for having wasted your money."

"And it has nothing to do with something that happened in high school?"

"Did Sid tell you? He pinky swore!"

"It wasn't me!" said Sid from inside the backpack.

"All he said was that you quit going to haunted houses after high school, so I figured something must have happened."

I sighed. "Okay, I may as well tell you. It's just kind of embarrassing."

"I won't judge."

"Me, neither," Sid said.

I bopped his skull through the fabric of the backpack to remind him that he was supposed to be incognito. "Junior year, a group of us drove over to Springfield because we'd heard they had a really good haunted house, but we weren't impressed at first. The guy there was doing an abysmal Boris Karloff voice, and the props all looked as if they came from the Halloween decoration aisle at Target. Their fake blood looked like catsup or cherry pudding or something, and it was all over, so the place was sticky and stinky. The layouts in the first two rooms weren't very good, and we could see the people getting ready to jump at us long before they moved. We just laughed at them."

"Scare actors hate that."

"We couldn't help it. Then came the third room, which was all dark, and that was scary because we could hear some-body else in there moving around. Plus he kept laughing a crazy laugh. Since he knew the room and we didn't, he kept circling to come behind us and laugh some more. We were trying to find the way out, but got jumbled together, and some-body knocked my pocketbook off of my shoulder. I told my friends to wait so I could find it, but they didn't hear me. So they found the way out while I was scrambling around to find my bag. When they realized I wasn't with them, one of them called out, 'Georgia! Where are you?' The next thing I know, the guy in the room with me started calling out 'Georgiaaaaa' in a creepy voice that was even worse than the laugh. Of course, if I'd been thinking, I'd have realized he'd heard my name and was just messing with me. But—"

"Dark room, creepy voice," Madison said.

"Exactly. And that was just the start. I don't know if the scare actors had walkie-talkies or what, but when I finally made it to the next room, which was a gory butcher shop set, the people in there knew my name, too."

"So they were all calling you?"

"Worse. One of the actors started singing."

"Singing?"

"You know the song 'Georgia On My Mind'?"

She nodded.

"That's what he was singing. Only it was in this eerie voice, and other people joined in. Maybe it wouldn't have bothered me normally, but by that point . . ." I shivered, even all those years later. "I don't think they knew the lyrics, so they were kind of muttering and mumbling, but that made it that much scarier. My friends had gone on ahead, so I was by myself, and I was almost too afraid to move. Finally I made myself run out to the next room and when I caught up with my friends, they said I was as white as a sheet. Later, I realized it was all just a trick and that I was never in any danger. But it wasn't fun, and I never wanted to go into another haunted house. What can I say? I'm a wimp."

"Anybody would have been freaked by that. At least you didn't wet yourself." When I didn't respond immediately she quickly added, "Not that there would be anything to be ashamed of if you had."

"No, I did not wet myself," I said, though I might have if I hadn't gone to the bathroom immediately before entering the haunted house. "But I really hate that song!"

Madison leaned against me in the time-honored way in which teens show their affection and Sid was kind of nudging from inside the backpack, so I did feel better. "Madison, can I ask you a question?"

"Sure."

"You scare actors get irritated when people don't get scared, don't you? Laughing instead of screaming, making fun of your best bits, and so on."

"Absolutely. We work hard to scare people."

"But when people are really scared, and have involuntary fear reactions in their pants, you mock them unmercifully. So how are people supposed to act?"

She looked sheepish. "We're not exactly fair, are we? What we love are the people who play along. They jump and scream, but then they laugh because they know it's not real. And they don't hit us!"

"People hit you?" I said.

"Sometimes. Nobody has hit me, but Liam got hit a bunch of times last year. He was in an optical illusion room, all painted in black and white squares with strobe lights, and he wore a black and white suit so people didn't notice him. Just as the audience decided it was a mind-twister instead of a scare, he'd start moving. He didn't jump at them, just came closer, but he got socked in the stomach three times in one weekend. The people claimed it was a fear reaction, but Liam says one guy did it because he was mad about being scared. Anyway, Aunt Deborah was careful with the haunt layout. Other than in the chase scenes, nobody gets that close to the audience, and we watch out for anybody getting violent. It's much safer."

I nodded, but wasn't entirely happy with my daughter working in a place where she could get hit. Then I started thinking. "What if Kendall hit one of the scare actors? Then he or she hit back in self-defense, and—"

"Now you're scaring me."

"Sorry," I said, making a mental note to save my more bizarre theorizing for when I was alone with Sid.

Deborah came down the stairs, herding the rest of her crew ahead of her. When it was just us Thackerys, she said, "I wondered where you guys had gotten to. Have you eaten? I'm starved."

"I was planning to get something on the way home. What sounds good, Madison? Burgers, subs, Chinese?"

"Chinese!"

"Chinese it is."

When we got May Chung's, Deborah did the ordering, and we ended up with a ludicrous number of containers.

"Are we feeding an army?" I asked.

"Just wait," she said.

Sure enough, when we got home and started unpacking the food, Mom and Phil wandered in within seconds, and before long, the whole family was chowing down. In a minor miracle, Phil had finally mastered the art of using chopsticks while on sabbatical.

"So you're definitely reopening the haunt tomorrow night?" Mom asked as we ate.

"It wasn't really a choice," Deborah said. "Beatrice made it plain that if I didn't, she'd find somebody who would. And if my people are going to be working with a murderer on the loose, I'm going to be there watching."

"Me, too," Sid said.

"Excuse me?" Deborah said.

He lowered his voice to a stage whisper. "I'm going in undercover."

"Dude, don't you mean uncovered?" I asked.

He ignored me. "I know you're adding monitors, but people won't talk in front of them. And your cameras won't pick up sound, will they?"

"No, I couldn't get cameras with decent sound at the last minute."

"Then what you need is a champion eavesdropper." He

poked his sternum with a thumb bone. "I'm just the skeleton for the job." He went on to outline his plan. It was kind of screwy, but even Deborah admitted that it might work. It would require some additional supplies, but Phil volunteered to take care of that.

Then Deborah turned to me and said, "What about you?"

"I think I'll go, too," I said, "but while Sid does his thing inside, I'll work outside and see if I can spot the people who wouldn't wait for the cops last week. The only problem is that I'm going to need a costume—I can't be Velma again." Mom offered to help me.

By the time we worked out all the details, all of us but Sid were ready to call it a night, and he even faked a couple of yawns to be sociable before going up to play on the computer.

19

As soon as I finished teaching my clump of classes on Friday, I headed home to help Mom put together my costume. Meanwhile, Phil had gone to get what Sid needed and the two of them were plotting in the attic. Fortunately, Madison was able to take care of her own preparations. After an early dinner of leftovers, we all got ready for the Howl. And I mean all of us—Mom and Phil were going to work the ticket booth so Deborah and her usual helpers could be stationed inside the haunt.

We must have made an interesting sight when we emerged from my minivan, even for the Howl. First up were Mom and Phil in orange McHades Hall T-shirts. Then came Madison in red-and-black vampire regalia, heavy on the eye makeup. As for Sid himself, he was in the duffel bag I was carrying. At least I think he was, but it was hard to tell because we were all carrying skeletons. Only Sid was real, but I wasn't going to start licking to verify which was him.

There was one other skeleton in evidence: me. Not just the

one I modestly keep covered with flesh and blood, but a skeleton costume. I'd intended to start with a bone-embellished hoodie Madison had given me for Christmas, add a mask and black pants, and be done. Mom was more ambitious. She'd gone through her closet to find a wide red-and-yellow skirt with a coordinating peasant blouse she'd bought on a trip to Mexico. Then she'd gone shopping to find long gloves and stockings with bones traced on them, spray-on black dye and a flower for my hair, and makeup to paint a skull and multi-colored swirls onto my face. The Day of the Dead might still be a couple of weeks away, but McQuaid had a campus calavera.

Deborah was waiting for us at the door of the haunt, and locked it behind us. "You're late," she said. "The rest of the cast will be here in half an hour."

"That's plenty of time," Sid said as he unzipped the duffel and extricated himself. "Let's get my Irregulars into place."

The plan he'd concocted was to plant fake skeletons—which he was calling his Baker Street Irregulars—in key spots along the upstairs and downstairs halls and in whichever rooms where we could fit one inconspicuously. The trick was that each skeleton would be up against one of the secret entrances hidden in the haunt. The real Sid would switch places with them throughout the night, hiding the fake ones behind curtains. So if he was suspicious of a customer, he would be able to follow him or her through the haunt. In order to keep in touch, he was going to have his cell phone.

"Just make sure nobody sees you texting on it," I'd told him when he revealed that part of the scheme.

"I'll use my feet," he said. "Nobody looks there."

"You can text with your metatarsals?"

"Of course. Can't everybody?"

We got the skeletons into place just as the rest of the crew started to arrive. Then Deborah headed to the control room for a last-minute check of the security cameras she'd installed, Madison joined her fellow crew members, Mom and Phil went to start setting up the ticket booth, Sid began his undercover stint in the cafeteria, and I left to patrol the grounds. All of us promised to be careful and to keep our eyes—or eye sockets—open. I could not imagine a more ridiculous set of sleuths, but I was still kind of proud of us.

There was half an hour to go before the Howl officially opened for the evening, but there were plenty of costumed characters already out and about in the crisp fall twilight. There were also a lot of campus security people and Pennycross police officers in view. I would like to have believed that the police had their own doubts about Linda's guilt, but thought they were probably there either to reassure anybody who might be concerned about safety or because the McQuaid Quintet had insisted.

If the inhabitants of Pennycross were haunted by the murder, you couldn't tell it by the number of people who continued to stream into the quad as it got dark. At McHades, the line for tickets was already twice as long as it had been the week before. I would have been disgusted by their morbid streak had I not myself been nosing into the murder, and dressed as a skeleton to boot.

So rather than stand on the moral high ground, I wandered through the crowd, accepting compliments on my costume and turning down a couple of invitations to join parties of revelers, including a trio of freshmen I recognized as regularly sleeping through my class. I hadn't had a chance to enjoy dressing up the previous week, what with worrying about Sid, and by all rights, should have been even more worried that night, but I got a kick out of being unrecognizable. When I saw Louis Raymond conferring with a couple of uniformed cops, I "accidentally" jostled him just to see if he would know it was me. If he did, he did an excellent job of hiding it as he accepted my apology and threw in a "Buenas noches."

I was starting to understand why Madison and the other scare actors liked their jobs. It was fun to be somebody else for a while, and trolling on people was a relatively harmless power trip. That led me to think about Kendall's murder. Had it started out as a prank that went very wrong? Then the killer panicked and ran? But then where had the bat come from? And would an accidental killer be willing to let Linda take the blame?

It was hard to reconcile my thoughts with the cheerful crowd of partiers—nobody was walking around with a T-shirt that said *I did it!* I sighed and kept wandering, though I didn't know exactly what I was looking for.

Over the next hour, I checked in with my family three times, ate a box of popcorn, and was propositioned once. None of that added in any way to the investigation. I was actually yawning when I spotted somebody, and was immediately torn between the urge to fist pump and cheer versus pure fear.

There, no more than ten yards away from me, was the ninja.

20

I pulled out my phone and texted all five Thackerys:

NINJA!

Deborah was the first to text back:

R U sure?

I snapped a photo to send. The long-sleeved top had white trim and gold cobras on the front, just like in the picture Louis had shown us.

See?

Sid joined the conversation:

Sid: Where is he?

Me: At hot dog stand.

Sid: Do not engage!

The ninja was talking to a Darth Vader whose costume was every bit as cheap-looking as his, and I tried to remember if anybody had mentioned Darth being around the night of the murder. Of course, Darth could have been dressed as something else that night.

They finished their hot dogs then headed toward the midway, and after a moment's hesitation, I followed, texting as I went:

Going to carnival.

Then I put away my phone, not bothering to check again when another message buzzed because I knew it would be someone in my family telling me to be careful, and that was already my plan.

The jostling crowd made it harder to keep track of Darth and the ninja, but it also meant that it would have been nearly impossible for them to realize I was in pursuit, had they been looking. As far as I could tell, they weren't.

Their next stop was a booth selling beer, and though I would like to have gotten close enough to see their licenses when they were asked for ID, I was pretty sure that wouldn't count as "being careful." They guzzled their beers, and got back in line for refills. Those didn't last much longer than the first two, and I was thinking they might go for thirds when Darth consulted a watch—which did not go with his costume—and slapped the ninja on the back before heading away.

The ninja paused, started walking purposely down the midway, then stopped and looked around in what I interpreted as an anxious manner, but could just as easily have been an urgent need for a bathroom after all that beer. Then he turned around and came right toward me.

I ducked behind the ticket booth, and realized that's what he was aiming for. Apparently he wanted to go on a ride, and for that he needed tickets. I watched as he purchased a long strip of cardboard tickets. Unfortunately he used cash, so I didn't have a chance to see a name on a credit card. Afterward, he started walking down the row of rides, stopping outside the Octopus and joining the line to go on.

I walked past until I spotted the ride exit, then settled in to watch for him. After a while he emerged, and looked around again. I was almost certain that he took note of me—my costume was pretty bright, after all. I ducked behind the nearest sign only to run smack into somebody in a purple Fenton's polo shirt.

"Hold on there, señorita," the guy said, then looked at me more closely. "Georgia? Is that you?"

So much for anonymity. It was Brownie, and much to my aggravation, he was blocking my view of the ninja.

"What's up?" he asked.

"I'm looking for someone," I said, craning my neck to see around him.

"Yeah?" He turned around, and naturally, the ninja saw the two of us staring at him. He jerked, then started away from us.

"Damn it!" If I didn't run, I'd lose him, but if I did, he'd know I was following him and would probably outrun me.

"Is there a problem?"

"I need to catch that ninja!"

Brownie started to laugh. "Seriously?"

"Yes, seriously!"

He stopped, looked curious, then nodded. "Okay." He pulled out a walkie-talkie that was considerably nicer than the ones Deborah had. "This is College Boy. We've got a towner in a ninja costume just leaving the Octopus. Anybody free to keep an eye on him?"

"Soda Pop here. I'm on him," a voice said in response. "What's the story?"

"Just stay with him. I'll explain later."

"Ten-four."

Brownie put the gadget down. "Now, tell me how I'm going to explain this."

"That guy might be the one who killed the girl in the haunted house."

"I thought the police arrested somebody."

"They got the wrong person. Besides, I'm sure that ninja was in the haunt the night of the murder. Well, fairly sure. I need to find out who he is."

"So you're following him? On your own?" I was afraid he'd spout some kind of macho nonsense, but instead he sounded admiring when he said, "You're fearless, aren't you?"

"Well, a friend of mine knows where I am." That was stretching it a bit, but Sid did know I'd gone onto the midway.

"Even so." His walkie-talkie squawked and he answered. "College Boy here."

"He's at the basketball joint."

"Stay with him." He looked around, then said, "Come on, I'll take you the back way." He led me between the Octopus and the Fun House, past *Employees Only* signs, and across a jungle of power lines littering the pavement, catching me handily when I tripped.

He pointed to a tent. "That's the back of the basketball joint." Then he got back on the walkie-talkie. "Is he still there?"

"Yup. Blowing through money. The guy's got no game at all."

"I'm behind the tent. Tell me if he moves."

"Ten-four."

Brownie said, "Do you always chase people you think are murderers?"

"Everybody has to have a hobby."

"Uh-huh," he said. "Nice costume, by the way."

"Thanks."

"A skeleton again."

"We're all skeletons under the skin."

"Are you going to tell me more about what's going on?"

"Not if I can avoid it," I said. "I could make something up but I'm terrible at cover stories."

He laughed. "Well, if I'm going to chase ninjas, I should let the boss know." He used the walkie-talkie again. "Boss Lady, this is College Boy. I'm taking a break."

His mother's voice replied, "On the lot or off? How long?"

"On, but not sure how long. Call it an hour."

"Good enough."

Then his father's voice said, "Is your break a towner or one of us?" He must have still been holding the button down, because I heard Mrs. Fenton say, "Leave him alone, you old fool!" before the walkie-talkie went dead.

It was my turn to laugh.

"College Boy, this is Soda Pop. The ninja is on the move, and I heard him ask about bathrooms."

"He had two beers really quickly," I said.

"Meet you at the donnikers," he said. Again he led me through a maze that only needed a minotaur to be complete, and we emerged at the carnival's selection of porta-potties.

A young woman wearing a fleece vest over her Fenton's polo shirt nodded at Brownie, gave me a curious look, then went back to texting on her cell phone. After a minute, the ninja came out of one of the porta-potties.

He spotted me instantly, then took off at a near-run. He'd have been gone, too, if Soda Pop hadn't "accidentally" gotten in his way and knocked him down. She helped him up, apologizing and brushing him off so thoroughly that he was trapped until Brownie and I got to him.

He looked at me and groaned. "Oh, come on, Bailey . . ." Then he looked at me more closely. "You aren't Bailey."

Brownie looked confused, and I imagine I did, too.

"No, I'm not Bailey," I said. "Why were you trying to run?"

"I thought you were Bailey. My ex. She's kind of stalking me because she wants us to get back together. She told a friend of mine that she was trying to find me tonight, and he said she was going to dress as a skeleton."

Brownie tensed as the guy fumbled in the pocket of his pants, but he came out with nothing more threatening than a dark blue case from which he pulled a pair of gold-rimmed glasses. He yanked the mask down to reveal an unremarkable set of features, and put the glasses on. A ninja in glasses isn't nearly so ominous as one without.

He said, "You're a lot older than Bailey. No offense."

"None taken," I lied. "Who are you?"

"His name is Hector Garza," Soda Pop announced. She was holding a wallet in one hand and a driver's license in the other.

"That's mine," Hector said.

"It must have fallen onto the ground when you toppled over," she said with an innocent look, and handed it to him.

"Okay, Hector," I said, "what were you doing at the haunted house?"

"What do you mean?" he said as he checked to make sure his belongings were intact. "I didn't go into the haunted house. I rode a ride and then played basketball. Man, that game is a rip-off. Anyway, what's it to you? Who are you people?"

"Somebody in a ninja costume like yours grabbed a couple of purses here last week, including this lady's," Brownie said. "We carnies don't like that kind of thing." He cracked his knuckles threateningly. "It gives us a bad name."

Hector held up both hands placatingly. "Hey, man, it wasn't

me. I was out of town last weekend for my mother's birthday, and I didn't find this costume until Monday."

"What do you mean, you found it?" I asked.

"It was in the lost-and-found at the student center. That's where I work. I waited all week to see if somebody claimed it, but when nobody did, I figured it wouldn't hurt to borrow it for tonight. It was just the mask and the top, and I needed something with a mask so Bailey wouldn't recognize me."

"What about the pants?" The photo Louis had shown us included pants.

"There weren't any," Hector said. "These are mine."

Now that I got a closer look, I could see he was wearing regular black jeans, while the top was a cheap grade of cotton.

Remembering Brownie's cover story, which was much better than the ones I came up with, I said, "I guess the purse snatcher ditched the costume so he couldn't be identified. And if you really were out of town last weekend—"

"I was, I swear. You can call my mom." He actually rattled off the phone number, which I dutifully entered into my phone. While I had the phone out, I quickly texted a message to my family.

Found ninja. Not our guy. Will explain later.

"One other thing," I said. "The cops have been looking for a ninja who was seen in McHades Hall last weekend when that girl was killed."

"Wow, I heard about that. But it wasn't me!"

"The cops still might be interested in hearing about how you ended up with that costume."

"But if you don't mind, keep the purse snatching on the down low. We like to take care of these things ourselves." Brownie cracked his knuckles again.

"Okay, I guess," Hector said, and I figured it was unlikely that he'd say anything to the cops. That was fine with me, actually—I'd only brought it up to soothe my conscience. Then he glanced behind me and said, "Oh man, there she is!"

Brownie and I turned and saw a young woman in a skeleton costume, but her outfit was nothing like mine.

The top was a strapless bodice with a ribcage painted on, and the tulle skirt was more of a tutu than anything else. She had stockings like mine, but hers stopped at the thigh, and she had a skull-themed domino mask. I think it was what Halloween catalogs call a Sexy Skeleton costume, and in my opinion, those are two words that should never be used together.

"Hector!" She started in our direction.

"Soda Pop," Brownie said, "why don't you take our boy out the back way as a little apology for knocking him down?"

"On it," she said, and grabbed Hector's arm to pull him into the shadows. It was the most ninja-like thing I'd seen all night.

"Don't worry—she'll get him out," Brownie said. "And in case you were wondering, not all carnies can pick pockets. Soda Pop is working up a magic act, and she's been practicing."

"That's good to know."

Bailey huffed up to us and said, "Where did Hector go?"

"Who?" Brownie asked.

"The guy in the ninja suit. He was right here."

"Oh, right, Hector," I said. "You know, I'm pretty sure he doesn't want to get back together with you."

"What? Who said anything about getting back together? That loser broke up with me in a text. A text!"

"Wow, that's cold. But if you don't want to get back together with him, why are you looking for him?"

"I wasn't looking for him. I have to go to the bathroom. I

just thought that if I saw him I could give him back the ring he left in my dorm room, but if he's telling people I'm chasing him, I'm going to drop the thing in the porta-potty."

"Tell you what," I said. "Why don't you give the ring to me, and I'll take it to the student center? He works there, doesn't he?"

"I guess I could do that. I mean his father gave the ring to him, so it's kind of important. No reason to lower myself to his level, right?"

"Right."

She dug around in a shoulder bag to produce a gold-colored signet ring with a *G* engraved on it, then hesitated. "How do I know you're not going to just sell it?"

"I'm a professor at McQuaid," I said, and went into my own bag to find my faculty ID. "I don't exactly look like the picture right now, but this is me. Or if you'd rather, you can take the ring to him yourself. Just don't throw it away, okay?"

She considered it, then handed the ring to me. "No, you do it. I don't want Hector thinking I'm making excuses to see him."

"I'll get it to him as soon as possible."

She nodded and picked out a porta-potty to go into.

"Nice," Brownie said. "You saved his ring."

"And gave myself an excuse to go see Hector."

"Georgia, you have unexpected depths."

"Did I come off as shallow before now?"

"Not at all. Just different. Do you have any other suspects we can chase? This was fun."

I wasn't sure if he was making fun of me or not, but he didn't seem to be. "Unfortunately no. My partner will let me know if anything else arises."

"Your partner? Tell me you're not talking about Charles."

"No, not Charles. Not that he wouldn't give it his best if asked."

"Would this be a romantic partner as well as an investigative one?"

"Definitely not."

"Good. Then would you care for a stroll around the carnival?"

"Yes, I would." I knew Sid would be annoyed that I'd abandoned my post, but I didn't have any more leads to follow anyway. He or somebody else would text me if anything came up, and in the meantime, why shouldn't I enjoy the carnival, especially in the company of a man with gorgeous blue eyes?

We started at the games, not to play, but so Brownie could show me how they were subtly gaffed.

"See the basketball hoop? From the front it looks round, but actually it's oval, which is why it's hard to get the ball in."

"Sneaky."

"And the balloons on the dart toss? They aren't inflated all the way, which is why they're hard to pop. If you aim for the tighter ones, and also arc up in your throw, you've got a better shot."

"What about the fact that your darts are crap?" I'd dated a serious darts player once, and we spent a lot of time at pubs.

"It's not a tournament target—it's a balloon."

"Fair enough. What about the duck pond? Is there some way you force ducks on people like magicians do with card tricks?"

"Nope, everybody is a winner. It's just that out of a hundred ducks, ninety win slum—"

"They win what?"

"Cheap prizes bought in bulk. Whistles, friendship bracelets, stuff like that. Anyway, of the other ten, eight are the next level up of prize and only two are flash prizes. Everybody wins, just not very much. Now in a rigged show, they'll let a plant win the flash, then pretend to throw the grand prize duck back into the water when what they've really done is throw in another dud. We don't do that here. Our games are fair, as long as you pay attention. Want to play one?"

"No way," I said. "I spent nearly fifty bucks winning my daughter a stuffed Powerpuff Girl doll a few years back, and my wallet has never been the same. Though I think I've still got the Scooby-Doo I got at this carnival when I was a little girl."

"You're a sentimentalist."

"Or a pack rat. I wouldn't be if I didn't have my parents' house to store stuff in. I've moved too often."

"I bet I've got you beat."

"Sure, but you take your house with you."

"Would you like to see it?"

I wasn't sure if that was an invitation just to view or to do something more active, but I wasn't ready for either. "Maybe another time."

We strolled farther, and he bought us an enormous piece of fried dough but warned me against patronizing the chili and churro booth, not that the juxtaposition of those two items appealed anyway. As we munched, conversation turned toward work, and the aggravations of the adjunct life. At least I was talking about aggravations—Brownie was mostly listening.

Eventually we reached the midway. "I like the way a midway sounds," I said.

"What? Loud pop music and screaming?"

"Okay, the music isn't always great, but the screams are mostly happy screams. Usually babies and toddlers are the only ones who scream for joy. Anybody older than that is too self-conscious."

"What about teenagers at a concert?"

"Equally loud, but carnivals have brighter lights, shorter lines for the bathrooms, and a better exit strategy. Once you're in a teen idol concert, you're stuck for hours."

"The voice of experience?"

I nodded. "Do you enjoy the midway? Or are you sick of the rides?"

"I only ride most of them to test them out, but I have one favorite. Want to see?"

"Sure."

Given his earlier invitation, I wondered if he'd suggest a dark ride or a scream fest like the Matterhorn. Instead he led me to the Ferris wheel. It was a big one, and since it was featured in the show's logo, I figured it was their centerpiece. I expected him to butt in line, but we politely waited our turn, though being the owner's son had some perks. When we got to the front of the line, the tattooed young man with a *World of Warcraft* ball cap didn't ask for tickets.

"Georgia, this is Gameboy."

We exchanged pleased-to-meet-yous, and then he handed us into a gondola.

As Gameboy checked that the gate was secured, Brownie said, "Don't rush the trip, okay?"

He gave us a knowing grin, and stepped back to start the ride moving.

"Do this often, do you?" I asked.

"If you mean coming onto the Ferris wheel, the answer is yes, at least once per stand. If you mean bringing a friend along, the answer is reserved."

"Fair enough."

I've never been a huge fan of Ferris wheels. Most of the ones I've ridden spend an endless time loading each gondola, meaning that you move a few feet, stop for loading, move a few feet, stop, and so on. But there weren't many people riding this Ferris wheel, probably because it was chilly to be up in the open air, and presumably Brownie's status as son-of-the-boss helped. We went around the whole way, only stopping at the very top.

I wondered if Brownie would make a move once he had me all alone, but what he did was lean over and look down. "Hello, Pennycross."

I mirrored him. "This is a great view."

"Every town is different from above. Down below, you see all the similarities—the duplicate malls and McDonald's and houses that could be anywhere in New England. Plus we set up the lot the same way every stand, or as close to it as we can given the space we've got. It's hard to tell where we are. When I come up here, I can see the shape of the town." He pointed toward downtown. "That's the oldest section—look at how the buildings are clustered around that dark spot. Town square?"

"Complete with a Civil War cannon. Not that there was fighting here. Somebody brought it home from the war as a souvenir."

"The cluster around the college is brighter, newer. How long has McQuaid been here?"

"Founded in 1950."

"McQuaid Hall looks older than that."

"That's because it predates the college. It was a defunct art school owned by the McQuaid family, and when somebody got the idea of creating a college, the McQuaids donated the building and grounds, along with some nasty strings." I explained the odder provisions of the bequest. "What is it about making big donations that inspires people to add strings?"

"If I ever have enough to give, I'll try to be less picky," Brownie said. "The more modern stuff is over there, by the highway. All those big box stores, and a mall."

"They aren't very pretty from up here, are they?"

"Not so much."

The wheel started downward.

"Want to go around again?" Brownie asked.

"Can we?"

He gave Gameboy a thumbs-up as we reached the bottom, and up we went, stopping a quarter of the way from the top this time.

"What else do you see?" I asked him.

He looked straight down at the midway. "Lots of people at the games, which is good for us. The bounce house is deflating, which means it's getting late enough that the younger kids have gone home. We have to close it or the partying college kids will go in, and since they've probably been drinking, at least one would barf in there. Nobody wants to clean that out."

"I can't blame you for that."

"No line at the haunted house, even this close to Halloween—they'd rather go to McHades. There's a long line at the popcorn stand, which means that JoJo is goofing off again. Look, my mother is going to read him the riot act."

Sure enough, I saw Dana Fenton striding in that direction, and even from above, her body language showed that she was not amused.

"From the macro to the micro," I said. The wheel started up again, but only went as far as the top before stopping. "And back to the macro."

This time Brownie leaned back and looked up at the sky. "This is the part of the view that gives me perspective."

I looked up, too. There were clouds around, and the lights of the town and the midway caused enough glare that I couldn't see many stars, but the moon was full and bright. "I could use a little perspective."

"I kind of thought so."

"Have I been whining?"

"Maybe a little. Can I ask you a question?"

"Sure."

"Do you like your job?"

"Of course."

He didn't say anything.

"Mostly," I said. "I like the work, but being an adjunct is tough."

"Why don't you do something else?"

"I don't know how to do anything else."

"Crap."

"Well, I could draw on my experiences to enter the exciting world of fast food."

"Don't you have a doctorate?"

"Sure, who around the adjunct office doesn't? It doesn't mean much."

"It means that you know how to learn, how to do research, and how to formulate an original thought. Apply that to another line of work."

"It's not that simple."

"Probably not," he agreed, "but it seems that way from up here."

"You can't see my bills from up here. Or my daughter, who I adore, but who keeps me from being footloose or fancy-free. I don't feel that I can take many chances with Madison depending on me."

"Is that why you're chasing ninjas? Giving yourself a chance to take chances?"

I stiffened, suddenly uncomfortable. I'd blithely eliminated Brownie from my list of possible murderers, but now I was feeling less sure. Being alone with him on top of a Ferris wheel didn't feel as comfortable as it had seconds before.

"Seriously," he said, "why are you sticking your neck out?"

"Why do you care?" I countered.

"I'm curious. Most of the time you've seemed focused on your work, your daughter, and yeah, sometimes your troubles. The only time I've seen you color outside the lines is this murder stuff."

"Okay, now I don't know if you think I'm really boring for doing my usual stuff, or a weirdo for my crayon techniques."

"Neither," he said with a laugh. "Your focus is admirable,

and if I had a kid as great as Madison must be, I'd give up a lot for her. As for the other, it's intriguing. Kind of hot, really."

"Yeah?" Nobody had called me hot in a long time, except for that one boy at Madison's high school, and that was just weird.

"Definitely hot. But if you don't want to talk about it, that's okay."

The wheel started turning again, and I enjoyed the view for a few moments before deciding I should color outside the lines a bit more. "It's complicated, but the short version is that my sister Deborah asked me to investigate and I don't believe the girl who the police arrested is guilty."

"Who do you think it was?"

"Maybe one of the other employees, or the real ninja, or some other customer. We've even been looking at the McQuaids."

"Why them?"

"That bequest I told you about. It turns out there's a missing heir."

"Really?"

I nodded. "So we've got all kinds of theories."

"I still don't understand why your sister wanted you to get involved."

"Would you believe that I've done this kind of thing before? And for some reason, I like it."

"I've seen you chasing a ninja while dressed as a calavera, so I'd believe just about anything about you."

That was said in such a nice way that I knew he meant it as a compliment, and it seemed like a great time for a kiss. Though Brownie's touch was gentle, he warmed me all the way down to my toes. The second kiss was nice, too, and I'd have been willing to bet that the third would have been even better, but there was a squawk from Brownie's walkie-talkie.

"Hey, College Boy, how's that 'break' going? You resting up there or wearing yourself out?"

Brownie sighed, and looked down at the ground. His father was standing below us, grinning. "I've got to go back to work."

"So I see."

Treasure Hunt was waiting to open the gondola when we got to the bottom. "College Boy, you've got some makeup on your cheek."

Brownie put his hand against his cheek dramatically. "I'll never wash it again." Then he took my hand and kissed it. "Farewell, señorita. I'll think of you every time I chase a ninja."

There was nothing I could say to that, so I pulled the flower from my hair, brushed it against my lips, and handed it to him. Then I glided away. At least I was trying for a glide, but I had to step over a spilled box of popcorn.

Treasure Hunt, for once, had nothing to say.

21

McHades Hall was still doing blockbuster business when I got back there, and since neither my ninja chase nor my Ferris-wheel-granted perspective had provided investigational inspiration, I asked my parents if there was anything I could do for them. They nearly dragged me into the ticket booth so I could spell one and then the other for bathroom breaks, and then enlisted me to bring back food. My idea of adding food delivery service to my resume was looking better and better.

The rest of the evening passed reasonably smoothly, if not quietly, considering the screams coming from both the midway and the haunt. Deborah kept a careful eye via security camera, and caught a pickpocket to turn over to the police, tossed out a guy who was trying to get too friendly with one of the scare actors, and stopped an argument between drunken customers before it came to blows.

When time came to cut off ticket sales, there was so much

protest that Deborah kept McHades open an hour longer than originally planned, and given the reaction when she did shut things down, she could have kept it going all night long.

We were in my minivan and gone ten minutes after the haunt closed. Though I'd been prepared to keep Deborah company while she oversaw cleanup and bookkeeping, I was just as glad when she shooed the rest of the family off so she could work in peace.

Since Phil confessed that he was so tired that for once he had zero interest in cooking, we went through the Aquarius Drive-In for burgers and throat-soothing milkshakes on the way back to the house. As soon as he and Mom finished their share, they were off to bed, but Madison, Sid, and I lingered at the kitchen table to compare notes.

"So your exciting chase led to naught?" Sid said.

"I did trace the ninja suit back to lost-and-found at McQuaid, and I've got an excuse to visit the student center to see if I can find out where the outfit was abandoned. That's a little more than naught."

"Not to mention getting a chance to hang with that guy Brownie," Madison said. "That's the first time you've had anything like a date in a looooong time."

"Hey! It hasn't been that long."

Funny how Madison and Sid, who I would not normally describe as resembling each other, made the exact same expression of disbelief.

Sid followed up with, "You know she's had the hots for him ever since he showed up at McQuaid."

"Sid! I never said one word—"

"Oh, please. As if I can't tell when you've got the hots for somebody. I remember that first crush you had on Steve Jones—your eyes sparkled every time you said his name."

"They did not. As for Brownie—"

"Sparkle sparkle sparkle," he said.

"Fine, be that way. I won't tell you about the sexy skeleton I saw."

"Big deal," he scoffed. "All skeletons are sexy."

Since there was no way I was going to win that argument, I said, "Did you two hear or see anything helpful?"

"I spotted the cowboy!" Madison said proudly.

"Why didn't anybody tell me?"

"Because it happened when you were off sparkling."

"I was not— Never mind. What happened?"

"Not much," she admitted. "I saw the guy, let Aunt Deborah know, and she had Sergeant Raymond meet him at the exit to question him. He didn't know anything—he hadn't realized he was running out on a lockdown last week because he thought it was all part of the McHades experience. Since he doesn't live in town, he didn't even hear about the murder until the middle of the week, and since he'd been drinking before he went into the haunt, remembered almost nothing about it."

"That would make a great cover story," I said.

"It would, but the guy had been drinking again tonight, so I don't think he was capable of making up stories."

"I don't know why Deborah tipped off the cops instead of letting us take care of him," Sid said.

"Be glad she did. He barfed all over Sergeant Raymond's shoes."

"Better his than mine," I said with malicious glee. I was still holding a grudge for Louis arresting Linda. "How about you, Sid? Anything good eavesdropping?"

"Nothing. I think I was able to spy on just about everybody, and nobody showed any signs of anything suspicious. Not that I expected anybody to start monologuing about how he or she had gotten away with murder, but I was hoping for some clue from body language."

"You're fluent in body language, too," I said, especially considering he didn't have a body.

"There is one thing. Maybe. I think I should stay overnight at the haunt tomorrow."

"Why?" I asked.

"To see if the rumors are true."

"What rumors?"

"Georgia, you know I'm a skeptic. I've always been a 'I'll believe it when I see it with my own eye sockets' kind of guy. But I heard several of the actors telling stories . . . What if the place really is haunted?"

"Sid, Deborah says every haunted house has rumors about being haunted. Okay, that didn't come out right. I mean, every haunt has rumors. They're usually old buildings, people are screaming, there's creepy makeup, it's dark. Add a real murder to that, and of course people are going to be a little uneasy. That's no reason to start believing in ghosts."

Madison started laughing. "Do you know how ridiculous it is to hear you two talking about skepticism and whether or not ghosts exist? I mean, just look at Sid!"

"I am not a ghost," he said haughtily. "Ghosts are intangible, tied to specific locales, and haunt people, whereas I'm tangible, go wherever Georgia takes me, and never haunt."

"But—" she started to say.

"Why don't we table the idea of whether or not ghosts exist?" I said. Sid didn't like to talk about why it was he was alive, and I was afraid that if he thought about it too hard, he might just stop living. Like Green Lantern, he was powered by force of will. "The question is whether or not this particular location is haunted. Madison, you've spent more time there than we have. What's your take?"

"I did hear that one of the McQuaids committed suicide in there when the original art school was running because she wasn't a good painter or her father was making her give up art or she had a broken heart or something."

"Vague much? Sid, you've climbed up and down the McQuaid family tree. Any family suicides?"

"Not a one," he said, "but remember what Paige McQuaid said at that meeting? According to her, a guy died from a knife fight at that building, and a girl fell down the stairs. And we know for a fact that Kendall died there."

"If those first two fatalities led to spirits haunting the building, it was a long time ago, and finding those ghosts wouldn't help us any. As for Kendall, didn't the ghost rumors predate her death?"

"Yeah," Madison said, "but things really have gone missing."

"You mean the bat and the rubber gloves that the murderer took?"

"Okay, that part wasn't a ghost. Still several cast members said they were hearing noises tonight, like something was moving behind the scrim when nobody was around."

Sid said, "I overheard a couple of people say that, too, but I didn't hear anything when I was back there."

I waited for them to connect the dots, but when it was clear that they weren't going to, I said, "Guys, did it ever occur to you that it was Sid who was making noises?"

Madison put a hand over her face. "Wow, I am an idiot."

Sid protested, "I was being quiet."

"I'm sure you were, but there's a limit to how quiet bare bones on the floor can be. We'll get you some socks or slippers to wear tomorrow, and see if we can exorcise the ghost. In the meantime, you guys have reminded me of an interesting question. If the killer wasn't a member of the cast or crew, then how did he or she get the bat and gloves?"

None of us had an answer to how somebody had gotten onto the third floor of a locked building, so after kicking it around uselessly, Sid went to play computer games overnight while Madison took Byron to her room and I took my memories of Brownie's kisses with me.

It was late when the breathing members of the family dragged themselves out of bed the next day, and none of us had the energy to do much more than get prepped for the next night's stint at the haunt. When we got to McHades, Deborah was in a state because a pair of her scare actors had canceled on her, so she had to shuffle the people she did have. Mom ended up helping out in the greenroom while Phil and I handled ticket sales, and since the crowd was even larger than it had been the night before, we were so busy we probably wouldn't have noticed if the killer had paraded by wearing a sash with sequined letters spelling out *It was me! Bwah ha ha!*

The worst part of the evening was when Louis came by and reported that they'd identified the other people he'd been trying to track down. He'd run into the witch himself, and found out that she'd zoomed out to get to a hot date, and the two guys without costumes had called the station to confess that they'd left because their parents had grounded them and they shouldn't have been at the haunt. As for the loser who'd tried to put the moves on Madison, Louis had cleared him days before. He'd left the haunt only to get back in line to go through again, thinking he'd be able to convince Madison to go out with him if he kept trying. Louis said he'd explained the difference between flirting and harassing.

I delicately brought up Scooby-Doo, and Louis said that he'd concluded he'd never be able to tie up that particular loose end, and had returned the costume to the rental place.

Though I was relieved the cops were no longer trying to find Scooby, and that my deposit would be credited to my charge card, the rest of the news was hardly cheering. We were running out of people to investigate, and the more time passed, the less likely it was that we'd ever get Linda out of jail.

Once again, we stayed open an extra hour, which meant that by the time Deborah chased off the last people insisting that she sell them a ticket, everybody was exhausted. Even Sid said he was tired, though he may have just been commiserating in his own way. None of us even had the energy for food, so we went home to collapse.

22

The situation looked a little better in the morning, partially because I remembered I still had Hector Garza's ring to return, but mostly because my father made French toast for breakfast. After that, a drive to McQuaid seemed like a fun thing to do. Sid, predictably, wanted to come along, so I indulged him by putting his skull back into my oversized handbag.

To make sure Hector was actually there, I'd had Madison call and ask for him, and when he responded, she hung up. I suspected real detectives didn't count prank calls among their usual techniques, but it did the job for us.

The McQuaid student center is a concrete-and-glass building, and it had been ultra-modern when it was built, but these days it was looking stuck in the seventies. The design clashed with the older parts of campus, which may be why it was located as far from the main gate as possible. I found Hector Garza at the center's information desk, looking worse for the wear. Either he'd been out later than I had or had woken up considerably earlier.

I plopped my bag on top of the counter to give Sid optimum eavesdropping range. "Hi, Hector."

He looked at me with absolutely no hint of recognition.

"We met Friday night at the carnival."

Nothing.

From in the bag came the whispered word, "Costume."

I thumped Sid. "I was in costume—the Day of the Dead outfit. And I helped rescue you from your ex-girlfriend." Of course, I'd also chased him down, but I preferred to lead with my strengths.

"Yeah, right."

"I stopped by to bring you this." I pulled his ring from my pocket. "You dropped it at Bailey's place. She was going to toss it, but I convinced her to let me give it back to you."

"Man, I'd totally forgotten I left it there. I've been going crazy looking for it, too. If Dad ever found out I lost it, he'd blow a gasket. Thanks! I owe you one."

"No problem," I said. "So did you talk to the police about finding that ninja suit in the lost-and-found?"

"Oh, hey, no. I meant to, but I haven't had a chance."

"It's probably not a big deal, anyway, what with them already having somebody in custody."

"Yeah, you're right." I had a hunch he didn't want to confess to "borrowing" from the lost-and-found.

"How did that costume end up here anyway?"

"What do you mean?"

"Don't you guys keep track of who turns stuff in or where it's found?"

"Why would we do that?"

"I don't know, I just thought you might. Were you on duty when the costume was turned in?"

"I don't think so. I didn't notice it until Tuesday, when somebody came by hunting for a missing textbook and I had to look in the box." He looked over my shoulder. "Hey, Oscar!"

"Hi, Hector, Georgia. What's going on?"

"We're not supposed to keep track of when stuff comes into the lost-and-found, are we?"

"Not that I know of. Why?"

"This lady here was asking about the ninja costume."

He blinked. "Beg pardon?"

"Somebody left a ninja costume in the lost-and-found, but I don't know where it came from. Do you know?"

"Can't say as I do." He looked at me quizzically.

"I was dropping off a ring Hector misplaced, and I was just curious." A thought occurred to me. "Oscar, do you have a minute?"

"Yeah, sure. Come on into my office."

The security forces at McQuaid had a small block of rooms right off the student center lobby, and Oscar opened the glass-fronted door to let us in.

"Are you running things all by yourself?" I asked.

"Not quite, but it's definitely a skeleton crew. I've had people working extra hours on the Howl, and they've got to get rest sometime. Have a seat." He waved me toward a chair and took his own behind a desk nearly as battered as the ones in the adjunct office. "What can I do for you?"

"I've been helping Deborah with the haunt, and a couple of the scare actors have complained about items going missing. Nothing valuable, but props and such. I know Deborah is careful about locking up, but I wondered how difficult it would be for somebody to get into the building."

"I'll be honest with you, Georgia," Oscar said, "McQuaid Hall isn't as secure as it should be. There's no alarm system, just smoke detectors, and the locks on the doors have been there since the place was built, so there's no telling how many keys are floating around. Of course my guys keep an eye out, but you know how it is. McQuaid is a busy campus, and a building that's left empty most of the time isn't our main concern. So when you ask if somebody could have snuck in there, I have to say that he could have, and it wouldn't have been hard."

"The cops know this, right?"

"Oh, they know. Sergeant Raymond didn't mince words when he told me what 'real cops' think of security around here. And what could I say? He's right, and there are going to be some changes. For one, we're requisitioning a new set of locks for McQuaid Hall. Of course that's locking the barn after the horses have run off, but in our defense, we'd never had a problem involving that building until now."

"You haven't gotten into any trouble about the murder, have you? I mean, it's not something anybody would have expected, and you guys responded right away."

"Thanks for saying that, and no, I'm not taking any heat from the administration. I just want to make sure nothing like this ever happens on my watch again."

"Deborah feels the same way."

"Yeah? She and I see things the same way a lot of the time. She's not, you know . . ."

"Seeing somebody? Not a soul."

"That surprises me. Sergeant Raymond said . . ."

My ears pricked up, and I felt Sid wriggling in my bag as if he, too, wanted to be sure he didn't miss the end of that sentence.

Unfortunately for both of us, Oscar's phone rang, and he said, "Sorry, I need to take this. Anything else I can do for you?"

"No, I'm good." I went past the information desk on my way out, but decided not to hector Hector any further. As much as I would have liked to know where that ninja costume was abandoned, I didn't think he'd be able to help me.

It was one of those glorious fall days that show up on travel shows, sunny with a bit of a breeze riffling the flamboyantly colored foliage, so rather than head straight for my car, I strolled toward the quad.

"Where are we going?" Sid whispered.

"Just getting some exercise. It's a nice day out."

"We're heading for the carnival, aren't we? You want to canoodle some more."

"Shush," I said. "Somebody might hear you." Nobody was close enough, but why take chances? And what if I was thinking of popping in to see Brownie? He'd come by McHades briefly the night before, but I'd been so busy there'd been no time to do anything but wave and accept the caramel apple he'd brought me.

I was nearly to the main gate when I glanced over at McQuaid Hall and spotted somebody familiar. Treasure Hunt was sitting on the stone bench in front of the building, looking up at it. I changed course to go toward him.

"Now where are we going?" Sid asked.

"Shush!" When I got close enough, I said, "Good morning, Treasure Hunt."

"Oh, hi, Doc," he said. "How's the skeleton?"

"Still dead. Are you considering coming to college? Or are you another stealth academic like Brownie?"

He snorted. "The boy can keep his books and papers. I was just curious about this place."

"Because of the murder? Yeah, that's where that girl was killed."

"That's not why I was looking at it."

"Oh?" I sat down next to him.

"I'm interested in the building itself. You see, it's mine."

"I beg your pardon?"

"That building belongs to me."

23

I finally put it together. "You're a McQuaid?"

"I used to be," he said. "Nelson Paul McQuaid the Third. Mannix is my mother's name, and nobody has called me anything but Treasure Hunt since before you were born."

"You're not— I mean, I would have expected—" I stopped. "You know, there's no way out of that sentence that won't end with me sounding like a jerk."

He grinned. "I don't exactly fit your image of a missing heir, do I?"

"Let's just say that you've got a very different style than the McQuaids I've met."

"I'll take your word for it. I haven't seen my sisters since my father's funeral, and never have met any of my nieces. I left all that family crap behind—at least I meant to. You see my mother died when I was young, and my old man and I never did get along. He had all kinds of plans for me, but I had other ideas. Plus I got into a little trouble. So I took off and joined a carnival. I never saw him again."

"Really? That's sad."

He shrugged. "Once or twice a year, I'd send him a letter to tell him that I was still alive, and then when I got married and had the kid. All I got back was a fat lot of nothing until he died, which is when his executor let me know that Dad had cut me from his will. That was what I'd expected, and I figured that was the last of my connections to the family until a couple of months ago.

"That's when some lawyer tracked me down and told me I was the heir of record for that building there." He nodded at McQuaid Hall. "Apparently Dad couldn't think of a way to disinherit me. Granddad wasn't what you would call a modern thinker, but he knew how to make a bulletproof will, and he wanted his aunt Persephone's legacy honored. So he specified that McQuaid Hall pass to the oldest male descendent. Meaning Dad, then me, and then Brownie. I might be the McQuaid black sheep, but I'm male. Of course, the building still belongs to the college as long as they play by the rules from Granddad's will.

"Except the lawyer claimed that the college had broken its side of the bargain by only using the place a few nights a year, meaning that it's mine after all. He called again after the murder, said he wants to handle the case. Dad must be rolling in his grave, and my relatives are probably burning up the phone lines to their lawyers, seeing if they can make it all go away."

"Something like that," I said, remembering how upset the Quintet had been.

"If things do go my way, we're talking serious money," he said with satisfaction, "but the best part is going to be messing with my relations. When I came for Dad's funeral—which I only did out of respect for my mother—they acted like I was dirt. My own sisters wouldn't talk to me! Brownie thinks I should let it go, but can you blame me for wanting to get a little payback?"

"Not really." Deborah and I didn't always get along, but I couldn't imagine her treating me that way.

He looked up at McQuaid. "It's a hell of a thing. For the past umpteen years, I've been going by a different name and never even living in a building for more than a month at a time. Now suddenly I own one with my old name carved into the bricks. At least I will until I sell it, assuming the college doesn't find a way to hang onto the place."

"I imagine they'll try to buy it back if all else fails."

"They can have it if they pay me enough to beat out any other buyers." He gave me a sideways glance. "I suppose you think I'm a louse for thinking of selling the building out from under the school."

It was difficult to know how to respond. Should I go on one knee and beg him to let the university keep the building despite the terms of the will, or berate him for trying to take it back? What I said was, "I do have some loyalty to McQuaid, since I work here, and even more because my parents are tenured here, but I can't say I wouldn't do the same thing if somebody offered me that kind of money." Even the idea roused my old dream of buying a house of my own someday. "Besides, there's nothing I could say to change your mind anyway."

He grinned again. "You're pretty bright for a college gal." He stood and stretched. "I think I'll be heading back toward the cook shack. You want to come along? Stewpot is making fried chicken today." He waggled his eyebrows. "College Boy will be there, putting on the feed bag."

"Thanks, but I've got plans." I didn't, but after Treasure Hunt's bombshell, I had things to think about and discuss with Sid. Besides which, Brownie had known of my interest in the McQuaid bequest, and hadn't said a word about his father being involved. He could eat fried chicken all by himself.

24

"I did not see that coming," Sid said, though at least he waited until we got into my minivan before speaking. "You realize that this gives Treasure Hunt a motive to commit murder. Ditto his wife and the mysterious lawyer. And um . . ."

"I know. It gives Brownie that same motive, especially since we know he was at the haunt on the night of the murder. But I'm not buying it."

"You could if you had that money."

"Look, the lawyer claimed there was a good chance of Treasure Hunt getting the building before the murder, so why get drastic? And it didn't even work—we reopened the haunt."

"Okay, that's a point."

"And say I've decided to sabotage the haunt. There are plenty of easier ways: arson, bomb threats, planting religious protesters saying that Halloween is the devil's day."

"That's two-thirds of a good point."

"How about planting rats or bugs and then calling health

inspectors? The risk would be a lot lower. Getting caught putting rats into a building is probably no more than a misdemeanor—"

"I could look that up when we get home."

"Don't bother. Whatever it counts as, it's less risky than murder."

"I guess," he said, not sounding convinced.

"Then what about opportunity? How would either Brownie or Treasure Hunt have gotten into McQuaid?"

"Didn't Oscar just say it would be pretty easy?"

"He said lots of keys are floating around, but how would they have one? Treasure Hunt said he'd been avoiding Pennycross for years."

"He did *say* that, but people have been known to lie. And doesn't the carnival have a pickpocket on staff? Maybe she picks locks, too."

"You're profiling. Even if Soda Pop can pick locks, the carnival only set up on the Thursday before the murder. They wouldn't have had time to do all this key finding, lock picking, and baseball bat arranging."

"Actually," Sid said, "you remember how I checked to see if there had been any other murders in towns where the carnival had been?"

"You actually wasted time on that?"

"I've got nothing but time! It turns out that Fenton's last stand was half an hour away, tops. That's an easy commute for dirty work."

I drummed my fingers on the steering wheel. "What about framing Linda? Why and how would they do that?"

"Now that is a worthy point, untainted by your wish to hook up with Brownie."

I stuck out my tongue at him, both because I thought it was justified and because he can't reciprocate. What he

THE SKELETON HAUNTS A HOUSE

could do was roll his skull over, which is the closest he could get to turning his back on me.

Our mutual silent treatment lasted until just before we got home, when I finally said, "Sid, do you really think Treasure Hunt or Brownie killed Kendall?"

"Bottom line? I think that just about anybody could kill given the right provocation—"

"Thanks a lot."

"What if somebody was about to shoot Madison?"

"Fair enough. We both know I'd kill in a heartbeat to protect her."

"So of course I think Treasure Hunt and Brownie could kill for the right reason, but I don't think the reasons we've found would be enough. Therefore you have my permission to suck face with Dr. Mannix."

"No, thank you."

"Don't tell me you think he's guilty!"

"I don't think he's a killer, but I know he wasn't honest and forthcoming with me. That's reason enough to forgo face sucking."

I meant it, too. Sure, Brownie was attractive and intelligent, and had a wonderfully quirky way of looking at the world, and was a good kisser—I made myself stop counting up good qualities, and concentrated on the failings instead.

The rest of the day was taken up with the trivia of normal life. I went grocery shopping, resisting all efforts by my mother to "help out" with some money. I did laundry, graded papers, and planned out lessons for the week. And I tried very hard to not think about murder or Brownie Mannix's kissing skills.

Once classes were over on Monday, I headed for the adjunct office, grabbed my mail, and went inside. As luck would have it, Brownie was at his desk chatting with Sara Weiss when I came in.

"Hi, Georgia," Brownie said.

"Dr. Mannix," I said and sat down.

Brownie was clearly taken aback and Sara's ears perked up like Byron's when he heard us open the bin where we kept his food. I ignored them both and set up my laptop to start grading papers.

A moment later, there was a ping from my phone and a text from Brownie appeared.

What did I do?

I deleted the message, and went back to work. A few minutes later, there was another ping.

This isn't fair. I give great apologies, but I can't apologize if I don't know what I did.

He had a point—I was angry, but he had a right to know why and I deserved the satisfaction of telling him to his face. So I turned toward his desk and said, "By the way, I ran into your father yesterday. He was outside McQuaid Hall, taking a good look at it."

"Oh," he said faintly. I went back to my laptop.

Five more minutes passed before another text arrived.

Would rather not discuss with Sara listening. Can we go somewhere?

Knowing he was watching, I started getting ready to go. Sara, who must have realized that Brownie and I were communicating in some way that did not enable her to listen, said, "Leaving so soon, Georgia?"

"I just remembered a lunch date," I said. I walked out slowly, and a couple of minutes later, Brownie caught up with me, though we didn't speak as we walked. We continued not talking until we were seated at Hamburger Haven and supplied with drinks and burgers that I suspect neither of us had an appetite for.

"So, Dad told you."

"That he's the lost McQuaid heir I was telling you about the other night? Yes, he did."

"Do I get any credit for not pretending that I didn't know?"

I held up my thumb and index finger so there was just a sliver of light showing between them. "You get this much credit."

"Look, I knew about this lawyer tracking down Dad with a song-and-dance about getting a lot of money, but we all figured it was gaffed. That will has been in place for a lot of years, but no money had made its way into Dad's grouch bag, so we didn't expect anything was going to happen now. He didn't even want to take the stand in Pennycross—you heard him say so yourself."

"He did say something about that," I allowed.

"Still, I can't say I wasn't curious about McQuaid and Dad's relatives."

"You're a McQuaid, too, so they're also your relatives."

"I'm a Mannix—that's the name Dad was using when Mom and he got married, and that's the name he gave me. I've never had anything to do with the McQuaids. But once we got this gig and I heard through the grapevine that the school had an opening in my field, I figured what the hell? Getting paid to teach here would be the first money the McQuaids had ever given us."

"They don't own the university."

"I know, but it still feels like poetic justice. I don't care about meeting any of them, but I did want to see the building."

"I can see why you'd be curious."

"That's all it was, too. After the murder, the lawyer called my father again with a lot of talk, but neither Mom nor I really think anything is going to happen. The only people who make money off a deal like this are the lawyers. Who needs the aggravation? Dad just wants to stir things up."

"You still haven't explained why you didn't mention this the other night."

"Other than it not being any of your business?"

"Oh." I took a bite of my rapid-cooling cheeseburger. "You know I'm trying to find out who killed Kendall?"

He nodded.

"And even more important, I'm trying to get an innocent girl out of jail."

He nodded again.

"That means I'm finding out all kinds of stuff that isn't any of my business."

"Are you saying this stuff with my father has something to do with that girl's murder?"

"It might."

"Do you think my father killed her? Or that I did?"

"If I did, I wouldn't be eating lunch with you."

"That's good, anyway."

Neither of us spoke for a while, but finally I took a deep breath and said, "I think an apology is called for."

"You're right. Georgia, I'm—"

"Brownie, I'm sorry."

"Okay, that wasn't what I was expecting."

"The fact is, I've been being a pain in the coccyx. I have no right to be offended. We've been having fun together, and I hope you consider me a friend, but we haven't known each other long enough for me to expect you to trust me, especially when your family is involved. So I apologize."

"Oh. Okay."

I was expecting him to look gratified rather than non-plussed. "Was I not abject enough? I really am sorry."

"No, I accept your apology unreservedly. I just feel bad because I didn't trust you."

"Wait, you can't apologize to me—I'm the one apologizing."

"I can apologize if I want to."

"No, you can't."

"Yes, I can."

"Can not."

"Can too."

"Can not."

"Can too."

We started laughing at the same time, which ended the argument nicely, and when he did make an attempt to apologize again, I stopped him the best way I knew how.

He really was a good kisser.

After lunch ended much more pleasantly than it had begun, Brownie had to run to make it to his next class, and I knew I probably had students waiting at Mom's office. Sure enough, when I got there, one was leaning against the wall looking terribly aggrieved. I'd have felt more guilty if he hadn't missed the past three classes with no good explanation.

When the line petered out later that afternoon, I remembered that I'd been so busy shunning Brownie that I'd forgotten to look at the assortment of envelopes I'd picked up outside the adjunct office.

It was mostly made up of the usual notes from students asking for more time to complete papers and/or extra credit assignments, and questions that would have easily been answered by their reading the syllabus I'd handed out on the first day of classes. Of course, if they'd read the syllabus, they'd know I preferred that such communications come by e-mail.

The last piece was a plain business-sized envelope, with my name written on the front in printed, capital letters. No postmark or university interoffice stamp, so somebody had put it into the mailbox personally. I opened it up and pulled out a single piece of white paper with three lines of text:

STOP LOOKING FOR ME OR YOU'LL BE SORRY.
THIS IS YOUR ONLY WARNING.
THE NINJA

25

I stared at the letter for a solid minute before the snickers started. A full-out laugh wasn't far behind. I knew anybody passing by would think I was insane, but I just couldn't stop myself. Okay, sure, Sid and I had dressed up as Scooby and Velma, but getting a note from "the Ninja" was over the top. The only thing that stopped my giggles was seeing a student outside my open door, so I tried to pull myself together to help him with his paper. Was it my fault if his essay comparing Hong Kong action films to American superhero movies mentioned the prevalence of ninja in both genres?

I headed home as soon as my student left, and went straight to Sid's room to show him the not-so-threatening letter.

"You weren't scared?" he asked.

"Of this? Sacrum, Sid, the only way this guy could have made it cornier is to have cut letters out of a newspaper to spell it out, ransom-note style."

"Yeah, but it means that somebody knows you're asking questions about the disappearing ninja."

"*The Disappearing Ninja* would make a great Hong Kong movie title."

"Georgia, you're not taking this seriously," he said, waggling a finger bone.

"Sid, do you really think a cold-blooded murderer would be silly enough to leave a note like this? This is like something the Creeper or the Ghost Clown would leave on the windshield of the Mystery Machine. My guess is that somebody thought it would be funny."

"Who? Who knew you were looking for a ninja?"

"Okay, that's a good question." The more I thought about it, the odder it seemed.

My family all knew, but I felt pretty safe in ruling them out. Hector might have thought I had an unhealthy interest, but since I'd done him a favor by getting him his ring back, he would have no reason to scare me.

Brownie knew, but I couldn't seeing him playing that kind of prank, especially when he was still feeling apologetic. Soda Pop? She wouldn't have known where my mailbox was. Brownie could have told his parents, and I could see Treasure Hunt playing the joke, but he'd have wanted to see my face when I found the note.

Who did that leave? For about five paranoid minutes, I worried that somebody might be following me and planting listening devices on my phone, spyware on my computer, and a tracer on my car. Common sense prevailed when I tried to imagine somebody who had the wherewithal to keep me under high-tech surveillance but would still send such a ludicrous note.

So who?

Sid and I speculated for a while, but came up with nothing. The evening passed, and I still didn't have a clue. When I went to bed, I lay awake for an hour, mentally going down the list of everybody I'd discussed the ninja with. Finally, just as I was about to doze off, the answer came. Of course, I'd want to discuss it with Sid to see if my reasoning held, but I was confident enough to be able to go to sleep.

When my alarm went off, the first thing I saw was Sid sitting in a chair next to the bed. "What are you doing in here?"

"I've figured out who the ninja is!"

"Me, too."

"Who?"

"You go first."

"How do I know you won't just agree with whatever I say, and pretend you figured it out, too?"

"Sid! We're not in junior high school."

"Then you go first."

"Tell you what. I'll count to three, and on three, we both go."

"Okay."

I held up one finger. "One." I added a second. "Two." I put up the third, and we spoke. Then we grinned at each other. We really had come up with the same name.

Of course, knowing who the ninja was didn't mean we could prove it. It didn't even necessarily mean that the ninja was the killer, though I both hoped he was and hoped he wasn't. While I wanted to solve the case and get Linda out of jail, I liked the guy. But for safety, we were going to act as if he were a killer when we approached him. That took planning and involved both Deborah and my parents. And of course, Sid wasn't going to let anything happen without at least part of him in attendance.

At four thirty, after my afternoon class was over, we had all our pieces in place for me and Deborah to confront the ninja together. Sid's skull was in my bag so he could listen in, and he had a hand and his phone in there, too, so he could text for help if needed. For backup, Mom and Phil were sitting at a table in the student center where they could watch the only available doors.

We'd discussed bringing in the cops, of course, but didn't feel as if we had enough information to go to them, and were afraid our explanation would be more suspicious than our suspicions. Besides, Mom was still angry at Louis for taking Linda out of her office, and wasn't inclined to throw him any crumbs.

"Ready?" I said to Deborah once we were all set. I'd been worried when I realized that the ninja was someone Deborah might be fond of, but whatever inner turmoil I'd caused her was deeply hidden.

"Just knock on the door already!"

I did so, and a minute later, heard Oscar say, "It's open."

We walked in, and I imagine we didn't looked overly friendly, but he said, "Hey, Deborah, Georgia. What can I do for you?"

"I've got something I need to show you," I already had the ninja note out, or rather a photocopy of it, so I handed it to him.

He looked at it, and without even taking the time to read it, asked, "Where did this come from?"

"I'm guessing it came from your printer."

"Excuse me?"

"Come off it, Oscar," Deborah said. "We know you're the ninja. What we don't know is why you killed Kendall Fitzroy."

"What? No, I didn't kill anybody!" He ran his hands through his hair, leaving it a mess. "Please, sit down and let me explain."

With our safeguards in place, we felt safe enough to do so, but both of us watched closely as he shut the door and went back behind his desk.

He took a deep breath. "Listen, I did not kill that girl. I only found out that she'd been killed after I left McHades."

"But you were there that night?" I said. "In the ninja costume?"

"Yeah, I was. How did you find out?"

"That note. When I found it in my mailbox, I tried to figure out how 'the Ninja' could have found out I was looking for him. The trail led back to you, from when I was talking to Hector about the ninja costume being in the lost-and-found."

"I panicked," he admitted, "and I wanted to scare you off."

Deborah snorted. "You don't know my sister very well." I was genuinely touched until she added, "She never knows when to give up. So tell us what happened that night."

"Okay, here's the thing, after working with Deborah, I wanted to go to McHades, but I was worried about how it would look because of my job. I mean, if I went and got scared, I'd never live it down. So I picked a costume that would hide my face and nobody would know it was me. And I had a great time. You did a super job, Deborah."

She gave him a look, clearly in no mood for compliments.

Oscar went on. "Anyway, I'd just come out into the court-yard when your security crew asked everybody to stay put. I didn't want to be found out, so I made a break for it."

"Wait," I said. "You knew it was a security issue, and you're a security officer, but you ran away anyway?"

"I didn't know why there was a lockdown," he said. "It could have been nothing more than a missing pocketbook or a fight or—"

"Any of which I would expect you'd want to deal with."

"Look, it was embarrassing for me to be there in costume, okay. And I had a previous engagement I had to get to. And—"

"Just stop. You're a horrible liar." His pretexts were worse than mine, and that was saying something. "Just tell us why you ran away."

He hung his head in defeat, and mumbled something, but I didn't understand him.

"Spit it out, Oscar," Deborah said.

He pulled himself together and sat up straight. "I got so scared I wet myself. Okay? I was doing all right at first—maybe I jumped a time or two and got a little bothered by the rats—but I was fine until I got to the room with the heads. Then that guy with the chainsaw came at me. So yeah, I wet myself like a little kid. I didn't want anybody to know, because how can anybody on campus take me seriously when I get scared at a fake haunted house?"

"Seems to me that there's nothing to worry about as long as none of the students come after you with a chainsaw," Deborah said.

"Deborah, that's not funny," I said.

"Of course it's not funny. Nothing about this is funny. So what if Oscar had an accident? The chainsaw gag gets every-body. I peed myself the first time I saw it."

"What?"

"Yeah, I said it. I peed myself, and I was lucky that was all I did, if you know what I mean."

"Then you— I mean you don't think—" Oscar said, clearly surprised that we weren't mocking him.

"I think you got scared at a haunted house, just like I did. That's what haunted houses are for. We go, we get scared, we come home safe again. And if we have an involuntary physi-cal reaction, it doesn't make us cowards. Or do you think I'm a coward?"

"God, no, Deborah. I think you're—" He stopped himself just in time. "No, I don't think that."

"Good. Right back at you. But I've got to ask this. Did you see anything at the haunt that night that would tell us who killed Kendall Fitzroy?"

"Absolutely not. When I found out what had happened, I tried to remember every detail, and there was nothing I saw that would help the cops with their case. I never even saw Kendall or her friends. I did see Linda Zaharee, but that was earlier, so I can't tie her to the crime or clear her. I swear, if there were anything whatsoever I could add, I'd have come forward, wet pants or no wet pants."

Deborah looked at me, and I nodded. I believed him, and could tell she did, too.

"So how did the ninja costume end up in lost-and-found?" I asked.

"The only thing on my mind when I left McHades was to get back here before anybody spotted me. I had a spare set of clothes in my desk, and had just finished getting cleaned up and changed when I got the call that the body had been found.

"That's when I realized the cops would be looking for the ninja, thinking he might be involved."

"And they'd be the last ones you'd want to tell about your accident," I said.

"You got that right. So I had to hide the costume pronto. The pants were plain black cloth, nothing to distinguish them, so I figured I was safe shoving them in a trashcan, but the flashy top and hood would be too noticeable. I couldn't leave them here because the other guys in the department use this office, and I didn't want to take the time to go all the way to my car because it was an emergency. I figured lost-and-found was my best shot. There's stuff in there that's been there for years—it never occurred to me that anybody would pick now to rummage around." He sighed heavily. "I guess you're going to have to tell Sergeant Raymond about this."

I said, "I don't see why we should. They're happy with their arrest, and if you're sure you don't have any information for them—"

"I'm sure."

"Then what would be the point? Of course, they might find you on their own, but I doubt it. So we can keep this between us." Well, and my parents and Sid, plus we'd have to tell Madison, but Oscar didn't need to know everything.

"I can't tell you how much I appreciate that." The words were meant for us both, but he was looking at Deborah when he said them. Unless I missed my guess, as afraid as he'd been about the campus community and the police finding out about his accident, I think he'd been more worried about Deborah finding out.

I made some noises about it being time to go, and Deborah and I left before he could thank us any more. My parents weren't in sight when we left the office, but from the vibrations in my bag during the conversation with Oscar, I knew Sid had been keeping her and Phil apprised via text.

"Poor guy," Sid said as I drove us back home. He was still in the bag, but we'd unzipped it so he could join in on the debrief. "He must have been so embarrassed!"

"Speaking of embarrassment, Deborah," I said, "after all the teasing for me not going to your haunt, you never told me you peed yourself at a haunted house!"

"That's because it never happened."

"You said—"

"I just said that to make Oscar feel better. He's a good guy, and hasn't got a thing to be ashamed of. It's not like he pushed his wife into the path of the chainsaw or abandoned his kids, which I've seen bigger men do."

"That wouldn't keep you from dating him? Because you know he's interested in you."

"I don't care about the chainsaw phobia, but if he wants to go out on a date, he's going to have to man up enough to ask me out."

"Why don't you ask him?"

She just shrugged.

"Seems to me that Oscar isn't the only one who needs to man up," Sid said.

Deborah's only response was to lean over and zip up the bag.

26

My parents were in a celebratory mood when we got home—they'd stopped on the way to pick up a bottle of wine and my father was getting steaks ready to grill. Once she heard how we'd uncovered the ninja, Madison joined in on the conviviality, though not the wine. Over dinner, Mom and Phil read Sid's tweets aloud to general hilarity, and toasts were drunk to our success. It was a lovely evening.

But Sid caught my eye more than once, and I knew what was on his mind. After Deborah went home and my parents and daughter went to handle dishes, homework, and television, I joined him in his attic.

"Are you going to tell them, or am I?" he said.

"No need. They'll figure it out."

He nodded sadly.

What he and I had already realized was that with both the secret McQuaid heir and the ninja out of the picture, we were back at square one.

"Who do we have left to look at?" I asked.

"The people who were at the haunt during the pertinent time window. Plus the haunt crew. Which adds up to—"

"To more people than we'll ever be able to investigate."

"We could get to them all eventually."

"By which time Linda will be tried and convicted, Roxanne will have missed her shot at a doctorate, and I'll have retired and will have plenty of time to investigate."

"Hey, I'm not getting any older."

I sat and thought, trying to figure out what we'd missed. "We decided early on that Kendall Fitzroy wasn't the real target because we couldn't come up with a single reason why somebody would have killed her. Right?"

"Right."

"But we're pretty sure she wasn't killed to get the haunt closed, because there are so many easier ways to do that. So that lets out the missing McQuaid heir. Right?"

"Right again."

"It's not the ninja, and Louis eliminated our other random suspects."

"Still right."

"And we played with the idea of either Linda or Roxanne being the real target, but didn't find anything."

"Georgia, if you're trying to cheer me up, you're going about it the wrong way."

I ignored him. "So unless this was a random killing, which I don't believe, then somebody really did want Kendall Fitzroy dead. Does that make sense?"

"It makes sense to the police—that's how they got Linda."

"They got Linda because somebody led them to her. Without the planted gloves, they'd never have thought twice about her. The fact is, they still haven't found the real reason Kendall was killed. Neither have we."

"They would have looked at her family and boyfriend,

but I guess we could look at them ourselves. I can see what I can find online." Sid didn't sound enthused.

"I doubt there's anything there. Maybe Louis hasn't handled a lot of murder investigations, but he's working with the state police and they've got plenty of experience. They'd have caught a whiff of any motive."

"You talked to those adjuncts at Brandeis. Maybe you could network with more of Kendall's instructors."

"I could, but I've got a better idea. Louis thinks that Linda held a grudge against Kendall dating back to high school. Do you suppose he's done anything to verify that?"

"Maybe not," Sid said. "He's got the gloves, the e-mails, and the phone call. The details of the motive aren't as big a deal for him."

"We, on the other hand, have nothing, so motive is high on our list. Let's find out if something really did happen in high school."

He grinned. "Ms. Rad?"

"Ms. Rad."

Ms. Marie Raduazzo, who went by Ms. Rad out of pity for her students and their parents, had been at Pennycross High School for over a decade, and had taught most of the students who'd graduated from there. I'd met her when she was Madison's freshman English teacher, and she'd been a coworker during my short stint as high school substitute. Not only was she a terrific teacher, but I had great faith in her powers of observation.

As soon as my classes were over the next day, I dropped by PHS, and was lucky enough to catch Ms. Rad in her classroom.

"Dr. Thackery!" she said when she saw me. A perpetually cheerful woman, despite a specialty in Holocaust literature, she was a couple of inches shorter than I was and had tightly curled black hair.

"I thought we'd graduated to Georgia."

"That was when you were a fellow teacher. I have to be more formal with parents." She grinned, which showed how seriously she took the rule, even if she was following it. "Since I don't have Madison in my class anymore, and she's doing great with Coach Q, what can I do for you?"

"I'd like to pick your brain about some former students."

"That sounds intriguing." She sat down behind her desk, and waved me to one of the student desks.

"I suppose you heard about what happened to Kendall Fitzroy."

"Oh yes, I heard. Poor girl."

"You may not know that my sister Deborah is in charge of McHades this year. She wants to write a note of condolence to the family, but has been having a difficult time since she never actually met Kendall. So she asked me to find out what she was like so the note would sound better."

"I see." Ms. Rad reached over and patted the stuffed lion on her desk. Lance the Lion was her personal mascot, and a fixture in her classroom. Madison said the teacher spoke to him during class, and I'd seen her pat him before when she was stalling. "Georgia, how long have you been teaching?"

"Um, full-time since Madison was a baby, but I taught while in grad school, too."

"How long did it take for you to develop a sixth sense for knowing when a student is lying to you?"

I winced. Sid had told me my cover story was weak, but neither he nor I had been able to come up with anything better. "That was lame, wasn't it? Can I just say that I'm trying to find out more about Kendall and why she was murdered?"

"Now, that's honest. And given some of the events during your tenure here, I think I can safely assume you have reasons for working outside the official route." Obviously Ms. Rad had figured out that I'd had ulterior motives for spending so much time at PHS before. "What do you want to know about Kendall?"

"Then you're okay with my snooping?"

"If you hadn't snooped before, a murderer would have gone free. So ask your questions. If you ask something I'm not willing to answer, I'll let you know."

"I don't have anything specific. I just want to know what Kendall was like."

She pulled Lance into her lap, and patted him some more. "Kendall was a good student. She was always polite to me and as far as I know, to the other teachers. Not an original thinker, perhaps, and focused more on grades than on learning, but she was hardworking and meticulous. She also stayed active in extracurriculars—softball and choir and I think the Spanish club."

"What about friends?"

"She was fairly popular. I don't recall her dating anybody seriously, but she had a couple of boyfriends. She did have three close friends she ran with."

"Alexis Primo, Nadine Seger, and Vanessa Yount?"

Ms. Rad nodded. "They were very close, and in fact, the only instance when any of them had to be disciplined was for talking to one another in class. They spent so much time together that I had mixed feelings when they ended up at four different colleges. On one hand, they'd have a chance to learn and grow as individuals, but on the other, I was worried they'd be lonely. I read in the paper that they were all there the night Kendall was killed, so obviously they kept up the relationship, but that must have made it so much more devastating for the three survivors."

I remembered the girls' faces when the police had brought them to Stuart Hall after the murder. "Devastated" was the right word.

Ms. Rad said, "That's really all I can tell you about Kendall.

A good student, popular in school, and I never had any problems with her."

"What about Linda Zaharee? Did you teach her, too?"

"I did, and I would never have expected her to do something like this. Not that I expect any of my students to be murderers, but all teachers get those who go bad, and sometimes you're surprised and sometimes you're not. This time I was shocked."

"My family knows Linda, and we're just not convinced that she's guilty. The police think she was jealous of Kendall and that led to the murder."

"That's their idea of a motive? Has there ever been a high school student who wasn't jealous of somebody?"

"Verena Rose was the one I envied," I admitted. "She was prettier, made better grades, and dated the boy I had a crush on, but she's still alive as far as I know."

"Exactly. Now it's true that Linda was a troubled girl. Her grades were good, and she really did seem to enjoy literature, but she never seemed happy. She didn't have many friends, and I suspected she was a cutter."

"Oh, dear."

"I may have been wrong, but she showed the signs: too many Band-Aids, wearing long sleeves in warm weather, and so on. I spoke to the guidance office, they spoke to her parents, and they got her into treatment. I never heard anything else officially, but after a while, I stopped seeing Band-Aids."

"But she was never violent toward other students?"

"No, never. I'm no expert, but self-injury sufferers usually turn their pain inward, not outward. As for Linda and Kendall having some sort of rivalry, they were in my English class together and I never saw any signs of problems between them. In fact, I don't remember them interacting at all. Linda was very self-contained."

"What about any other students? Did anybody else show signs of disliking Kendall? Did she ever get into fights or feuds?"

"Not that I ever saw." Then she started patting Lance, which meant she was either stalling again or thinking.

So I prompted, "But?"

"But Lance didn't like Kendall."

I looked at the stuffed lion, almost expecting him to join in on the conversation.

"I know it sounds silly," Ms. Rad said, "but there are some students that I have no particular reason to dislike or distrust, yet on a subconscious level, I find myself getting anxious when they touch Lance. Kendall was one of those students." She shrugged. "I can't tell you anything more definite than that. Lance didn't like her."

"What about Linda?"

"Oh, he liked Linda. In fact, on those days when I could tell Linda was particularly sad, I'd leave him with her during class. That's why this all seems so inexplicable. Does any of this help you?"

"I think it does." Ms. Rad did have a way of figuring people out. If she'd thought something had been off about Kendall, then something probably was. "Thank you."

"Any time. Stop by again when you get a chance, and let me know how it all turns out."

"You bet. Just one other thing—"

"Lance likes you just fine, Georgia. And Madison as well."

"Glad to hear it," I said, reaching over to rub his fuzzy head.

As soon as I got home, I ran up to the attic to tell Sid.

"So the toy lion didn't like Kendall," he said. "And you take this seriously?"

"How many friends have I dumped on the advice of an ambulatory skeleton?"

"Are you comparing me to a stuffed lion?"

"Nope. You're far better educated and intelligent and talented—"

"And I know when I'm being buttered up."

"Perceptive, too."

"What do you want?"

"If there's something nasty to be found about Kendall, there must be a sign of it, and since you said she was active on social media, there might be something there."

"You want me to dig?"

"Like you've never dug before."

"Then hold my calls and bring me a shovel."

27

Sid wasn't kidding about holding his calls. He didn't come down for dinner or to watch TV, and when I yelled good night on my way to bed, he was still typing as he yelled back. I'd intended to check on him in the morning, but I found a text on my phone that said, I may have something. Do NOT interrupt.

I followed his instructions, and didn't text once all day. But when I got home after work and he was still at it, I had to resort to folding laundry to keep myself distracted. By the time dinner was over, I was thinking I'd need a sleeping pill or a strawberry margarita to keep from bugging him. Then, as I was grading papers, I heard loud music and bony pounding from the attic.

"What is that?" Mom said.

"I believe that's 'Shut Up and Dance'! Sid's having a dance party!"

"That's nice," she said doubtfully.

"It's more than nice. It means he found something!"

Leaving my papers where they were, I zoomed up the stairs and into the attic, where I joined in on general principles. As impatient as I was to find out what he'd learned, I kept on dancing through the end of that song, "Bang Your Drum," and "What the Hell?" before reaching over to turn off the music blaring from his computer.

"Please tell me this means you found something."

"Georgia, I will never doubt Lance again. Kendall Fitzroy was not what she appeared to be." He paused dramatically, waiting for a breathless prompt from me.

Considering how long and hard he'd been working, I was willing to oblige. "Really?"

"Big time, but it wasn't easy to find."

I took this to mean that he was going to go through the whole investigative process before spilling the goods, so I sat down and got comfortable.

He said, "I started with Twitter, thinking that people can be looser in their tweets, but that didn't help. Kendall was more a re-tweeter than a tweeter."

"Ms. Rad said she wasn't much for original thinking."

"So then to Facebook, where I went through hundreds of posts. Maybe thousands." He held up his fingers. "Are my finger bones shorter? They feel shorter."

"They look fine."

He looked at them as if doubting my veracity, then continued. "Mostly it was the stuff everybody puts on Facebook. What she ate, the movies she saw, the clothes she wore, the work she had to do, how bored she was. Which was nothing to how bored I was."

"I can only imagine."

"But I persevered, and a couple of patterns began to emerge." Again he paused to look at me significantly.

"You're only allowed one dramatic pause per conversation."

"Fair enough. The first pattern was while she was still at PHS, when she and a lot of her friends made references to online bullying. A couple of kids mentioned trolls spamming them with things—making fun of their weight, their clothes, their grades. All the usual attacks. There was a lot of it going on, apparently."

"Who was doing it?"

"Nobody seemed to know, and there was considerable discussion of who it could be. Lots of names were bandied about, including Linda's."

"Linda was a cyberbully?"

"Bear with me a while longer."

"Do I have a choice?"

"No. So the bullying was the first pattern. I know trolling is common, so I wasn't sure it meant anything until I saw the second pattern."

"Which was?"

"Several times, Kendall was discussing something and would then make reference to taking it offline or having private time."

"So there was nothing online?"

"That was what I thought at first, but then I had an idea. Maybe Kendall was part of a secret Facebook group."

"You can do that?"

"Groups can be public, private, or secret," he said loftily. "But while Kendall's settings allow me to see her public and private groups, I couldn't see her secret groups. I had to hack her account."

"Since when do you know how to hack Facebook accounts?"

"Since about three in the morning," he said with a totally fake yawn. "It turns out that there are quite a few ways to hack an account, but the easiest is to guess the user's password."

"How?"

"Kendall created that account when she was a young

teenager, and most young teenagers aren't overly sophisticated when they choose their passwords. A lot go with '12345' or 'password' or 'qwerty,' because they think those are clever. Which they were the first time somebody came up with them, back in the dawn of time. If not one of those, they pick an obvious piece of personal information, like a pet's name or their middle name or their favorite band. Since I'd gone through years of Facebook posts, I knew all that stuff about Kendall. I was prepared to keep trying as long as I had to, but as it turned out, it was her cat's name. Which was Fluffy."

"Of course it was."

"Once I was in her account, it was easy to find the secret group. It was called the Devil's Divas, and had exactly four members."

"Four? Would the other three be Kendall's BFFs?"

He tapped his nasal cavity. "On the nose. Alexis, Nadine, and Vanessa."

"So what was the group for?"

"Nothing good. While I hate to speak ill of the dead—" He stopped. "Hey, you speak ill of me all the time! Why don't I get a pass?"

"You can either stay in a grave and get a pass, or hang with me and take your chances."

"Okay, I can live with that. Well, not technically live—"

"Focus, Sid."

"Focusing. Now I know why Lance didn't like Kendall."

"Why?"

"Because she was a bully. An internet troll. The Devil's Divas existed solely to torment people. And they weren't content to just mock people behind their backs. No, they'd plan and carry out elaborate harassment campaigns. Once they picked a target, they were merciless. They made fun of other girls' weight and clothes and looks. They told a gay guy he ought to kill himself because he was an abomination.

They spread rumors that a girl's boyfriend had screwed around on her, and that somebody else was sleeping with a teacher to get good grades. They posted screenshots and links. They doxxed people. Alexis seemed to be the real strategist, but they all participated eagerly and often."

"Are you serious?"

"Dead serious, if you'll pardon the expression. And they didn't limit themselves to PHS students. Neighbors, kids they met at softball tournaments, fellow parishioners from their churches. Even random people. If they could find you on Facebook, you were a potential target."

"How did they get away with that?"

"By hiding their identities. Vanessa is good with computers, and guided them through creating multiple Facebook and Twitter accounts purely for the sake of bullying."

"Those ossifying pieces of sacrum!"

"And they didn't even believe in half of their own insults. Telling that gay guy he was an abomination? Nadine is bi, and the others don't care. Anti-Semitic screeds? Vanessa is Jewish. They just like torturing people. If it was somebody they saw every day, like another PHS student, they'd watch to see if they were getting a good reaction. No reaction, and they'd move on to somebody else, but if a victim started to look sad or cried in class for no reason, they'd double down. One of their victims ended up in the hospital, either from the stress or just a coincidence, and they all posted 'LOL LOL LOL.' Laughing out loud! It's a game to them, Georgia. Literally. They keep score! Who hurts the most people, who hurts them the worst." He shuddered noisily.

I didn't blame him. I felt sick to my stomach. "This is vile. At least when you bully somebody in person, people recognize you as a bully. But when you make up an online identity and bully without even telling people who you are, it's that much worse. I bet doing it in secret added to their kicks."

"You know that happens all the time online," Sid pointed out.

"That doesn't make it any better."

"So what do you think? Did I find a juicy murder motive or what?"

"I hate to say this, but maybe not."

"Georgia, she was a part of a commando team of Internet bullies! The only mystery is why nobody went after her before."

"Did any of their victims realize who was behind the fake e-mail addresses? Were any of them at McHades Hall the night of the murder?"

"Well . . ."

"Sid?"

"Okay, I started the dance party too soon. I read enough of the posts to see what the Divas were up to, and got excited. I haven't started finding the victims yet. Back to work!"

"Why don't you take a break, Sid? You've been amazing to find all this stuff out. Come down and watch some TV or read."

"No, thanks," he said. "The premature dancing was enough of a break for me."

"Are you sure?"

"Hey, I'm a researching machine. You go back to doing what you were doing."

"Okay, but yell if you need me."

I didn't really expect to see Sid for the rest of the evening, but about an hour later, I got a text:

Can you come to the attic? I need to talk to you.

This time I cleared up my papers before heading up. "Is it time for another dance?" I sat down on the couch, expecting him to launch into his latest discovery. Instead he sat down next to me and fiddled, popping his fingers off and reattaching them. "What's wrong?"

"I've gone through about six months of posts from the Divas—and if we get a chance tomorrow, I want a skull bath. Reading that stuff makes me feel dirty."

Sid didn't bathe regularly, for obvious reasons, but he did like a good wipe with hydrogen peroxide every once in a while to keep himself white and clean. I got the job of swabbing out the inside of his skull.

"We can do that. So what did you pull out of the muck?"

"I found a bullying victim who was at McHades that night."

"Great! Who was it?"

"It's Madison, Georgia. The Divas went after Madison."

28

"Sid, tell me you don't think Madison killed Kendall Fitzroy!"

"Of course not! I'm just worried that other people might think she did. And by other people, I mean the cops."

"Who's going to tell the cops?"

"You might have to if the bullying turns out to have something to do with the murder."

"We'll cross that bridge when we come to it," I said. "What did those pieces of sacrum say about her anyway?"

"I'm not entirely sure. It was Kendall who was going after her, and she mostly talked about her attempts failing. Some of the others offered to join in, but Kendall said it wasn't worth it. She really didn't post much these past few months. As far as I can tell, Madison was one of her last victims."

"That's odd. I wonder why." Before we could discuss it further, we heard Madison and Byron coming upstairs, heading for bed. "I'm kind of concerned Madison didn't tell me about this. I think we need a mother-daughter talk."

"I'm sorry, Georgia," Sid said, his bones loosening. "It never occurred to me that Madison would be brought into this."

"I asked you to dig into Kendall, and Madison was already involved because she was at McHades during the murder. This is just another complication, that's all. I'll go talk to her and let you know what I find out."

"Give her a hug from me."

M adison was already wearing the oversized T-shirt she slept in when I tapped at her door.

"I was going to come kiss you good night," she said.

"I wanted to talk to you about something first, if you're not too tired."

"Sure." She climbed onto her bed, pushed Byron to one side, and patted the other side for me to sit next to her.

"Madison, you know I've stopped monitoring your online stuff—e-mail and Facebook and all. I trust you to tell me if anything bad is going on."

"Geez, has there been another incident of a girl running off to meet a hot guy from online, only to find out it's some gross perv instead? Mom, I know better than that."

"No, not perverts. I mean, of course I'm glad you're wary of things like that, but I was talking about bullying."

"What about it?"

"I know there's a lot of online bullying going on, and it can be really upsetting."

"Well, yeah. Some of my friends have gone through it."

"Not you?"

"Why are you asking?"

"Okay, first let me say that I have not been snooping, but Sid—"

"Sid's been snooping?"

"No. Well, yes, but not snooping into your stuff. At least not on purpose." I took a deep breath. "Have you had problems with online bullying?"

"Me? No."

"No? You're sure?"

"No—wait, there was one time. Back around December or January, I got some Facebook messages that said the only reason I'd gotten that solo in the Christmas concert was because I'd given Coach Q a . . . Because I'd orally pleasured him."

"Madison! Why didn't you tell me?"

"It wasn't that big a deal, Mom. I blocked the account, and reported the abuse to Facebook, and that was it. I did ask Samantha if she'd heard any rumors like that around school, but she hadn't, so I forgot all about it. How did Sid find out?"

"He's been seeing what he can find out about Kendall, and it looks like she was your Internet bully. In fact, she and those three girls from the haunt had special accounts that they used to harass people anonymously."

"Seriously? What a—! Can I swear?"

"You have special dispensation." Not that I believed Madison never used profanity, but we had an agreement that she wouldn't do so in front of me, Deborah, or my parents. Her fluency with the vernacular both impressed me and confirmed that she did a fair amount of cursing when I wasn't within earshot. "Feel better?"

"Much better, thank you."

"Good. Now I don't want to sound as if I'm blaming the victim, but do you have any idea why Kendall targeted you?"

"Not a clue. I only met her the one time after the choral ensemble's holiday show. She said she thought I did a terrific job on the solo, I thanked her, and that was it."

"What about her sister?"

"Bianca and I have never had any problems. Except . . ."

"Except what?"

"Bianca tried out for that solo, too, and Samantha heard her telling somebody that she was sure she was going to get it."

"Do you think Bianca blamed you?"

"Why would she? Coach Q made the call. And she never said anything to me about being mad about it."

"Kendall could have been mad, even if her sister wasn't. Like that time you invited Julie Hu to your birthday party, but when she had a much bigger party two weeks later, she didn't invite you. You didn't care, but I was outraged."

"Mom, tell me you're not still mad about that. I was six. Let it go."

"I'm over it now. Mostly. But the point is that sometimes people get angry on a loved one's behalf, whether or not the loved one does."

"But you didn't do anything to Julie. Did you?"

"No, of course not. But Kendall was already an experienced Internet bully, so maybe she was glad to have a fresh target. Good for you for not letting her get to you."

"I just wish I'd known it was her so I could have told people about her. At least I can spread the word about those other three losers. Samantha said the year before last, she got a lot of online garbage making fun of her being in a wheelchair and saying her mother should have aborted her instead of giving birth to a cripple. A cripple! Who even uses that word anymore? Anyway, I'm going to tell everybody I know."

"You can't, Madison, not yet anyway."

"Why not? I know it's not cool to dump on dead people, but those other three need to be taken down."

"I know, but Kendall being a bully may have something to do with her murder."

"You think one of the people she harassed retaliated?"

"It's a theory, anyway. But while it looks as if she trolled on a lot of people, the only one we've found who was in

McHades Hall the night of her murder is you." I held up a hand. "Not that we suspected you for a millisecond, of course."

"If I'd known for sure that she was the one to go after Samantha, I might have. Whoever did kill her was probably justified."

I didn't say anything, and after a second, Madison looked chastened.

"Wow, what am I saying? Of course she didn't deserve to be murdered. Smacked around, maybe, but not murdered. Can you forget I said that?"

"Said what?"

She grinned. "Seriously, I can't believe I even thought that, let alone said it out loud."

"That's what happens when bullies attack people. They turn everybody mean." I stopped. "That sounded amazingly pompous."

"You're a mother. You're allowed to be pompous now and then."

"Thanks so much. I will now pompously remind you to get some sleep."

"Don't overdo it."

I started for the door, but Madison said, "Hey, I had a thought. I could talk to some of the other people at McHades Hall, see if any of them had problems with Internet bullies."

"No way. The killer isn't likely to admit it, is he or she? And if he hears you asking questions about Internet bullying . . . No, you are not going to do that."

"I'll be careful."

"That's right. And nothing could be more careful than not bringing up the subject. At all. Ever."

"Then how are you going to find the killer?"

"We'll think of something. Sid's on the job, and I am too pompous to fail!"

29

After such a heavy conversation, I was exhausted emotionally if not physically, but I knew Sid would be waiting to hear what had happened. So back up I went, only to find him typing away with no apparent signs of concern.

"You were eavesdropping, weren't you?"

"Just to the first part," he said. "Once I heard that Madison hadn't been upset by the Divas, I made myself scarce."

"There are times when I want my conversations with my daughter to just be between the two of us."

"Understood. If you tell me that, I will abide by your wishes. Cross my chest cavity and hope to crumble."

That was the best I was going to get. "I assume you're delving into the Divas' deviltry. Any other leads?"

"I've got a few names, but nothing that looks familiar, and I'm not seeing any signs that anybody had figured out who the Divas were. It must go back a while, anyway, because like I said before, Kendall hadn't been posting much in the group."

"I guess even bullies take time off. Though it seems strange that somebody discovered Kendall's deep dark secret while she was inactive." Then I thought of something I'd been told. "Sid, when did Kendall stop posting in that list?"

He started scrolling through entries. "About six months ago. The last one was kind of incoherent, too. She said she'd been out drinking. Why?"

"Remember how I spoke to Kendall's English instructor, Caroline? She said Kendall was a real party animal the first part of spring semester, but seemed to turn herself around about six months ago. Go back to her public Facebook page. I want to check some of her status updates from around then."

He got to the right spot, then moved aside so I could share the chair with him.

"Look at this one, back around the first of February. 'I got sick and tired of being sick and tired.' And this one the next day: 'I only have to change one thing—EVERYTHING.'" I scrolled on. "'First Things First.' 'One Day at a Time.' 'Gratitude Is an Attitude.' 'Pain Is the Resistance.'"

"She could have had a great career creating bumper stickers."

"She didn't come up with any of these, Sid. They're all Alcoholics Anonymous sayings."

"Are you sure?" He opened up another window on the laptop, and searched out a few. "You're right. How did you know that? Is there something you're not telling me?"

"A woman I knew in grad school was in recovery, and she had a lot of these slogans posted in her apartment. If Kendall was a twelve-stepper, it would explain why her grades were starting to improve."

"I would think Bullies Anonymous would have been more appropriate, if there is such a thing?"

"Not that I know of, but I do know that twelve-step

programs have a step about apologizing to people you've hurt."

Sid's phalanges flew across the keyboard. "Got it! Step Eight is to make a list of people harmed, and become willing to make amends to them. Step Nine is to make amends to the people you've wronged. That's how the killer found out that Kendall was a bully! Kendall confessed so she could apologize."

"And that was why she wanted to meet with Linda. I bet she's one of the people the Divas bullied. Ms. Rad said she was lonely and depressed in high school, which would have been the Diva equivalent of waving a red cape at a bull."

"Wait, do you think Linda killed Kendall after all?"

"Not necessarily. The Divas bullied a lot of people. There's no telling how many people would want to kill them if they found out who they were."

"Okay, then I'll go back into the muck to find more names." He cracked his knuckles in preparation. "At least I can skip the most recent victims, since only the other three Divas messed with them."

"I'm surprised they didn't stop or at least slow down when she went on hiatus."

"Not these vicious beasts. They enjoy their games too much. You may as well go on to bed."

"Are you sure?"

"Absolutely. Unlike me, you need your beauty sleep."

"Was that a crack about my beauty?"

He grinned. "Sleep well."

"Thanks, Sid. I couldn't do this without you." I started down the stairs, then stopped.

"You okay?"

"What did I just say?"

"That you couldn't do this without me."

"Which is true. Everybody who knows us—at least

everybody who knows both of us—knows that we're a team. Now what did you call the surviving Divas?"

"Vicious beasts."

"Vicious beasts who like their little hobby, and part of their fun is that nobody knows who they are."

"Right."

"But everybody who knows them, knows that the four of them were BFFs. Madison immediately figured out that if Kendall was a bully, then so were the others. Therefore if Kendall confessed to being an Internet bully, it would come out that the other three were, too."

"That makes sense."

"Do you think that possibility would make Vanessa, Nadine, and Alexis happy?"

He snorted. "I bet they were enraged. Wait, you don't think—?"

"Do I think that a vicious beast would kill in order to keep from having her fun spoiled? And then frame one of her previous victims? It sounds like just the kind of thing a Diva would do."

"Maybe they teamed up and killed her together."

"Was any mention made of it on the Divas' list?"

"No, but surely they're not stupid enough to put something like that on the Web."

"They were stupid enough to put all their bullying plans on the Web. Even if they were more circumspect, I think they'd have said something about things being clear or how now they can keep going. No, I bet the murder was a solo act. But which one was the killer?" I gave Sid a meaningful look. "If only we knew more about the three of them."

He cracked his fingers again, with more enthusiasm. "Go to bed, Georgia. I've got work to do."

After all that, I didn't expect to be able to get to sleep,

but it had been a long day and I was out in minutes. It was a good thing, because Sid woke me up an hour before my alarm was set to go off, and waking to a skull hovering over you is never a good sign.

"What's wrong?" I asked.

"Nothing. I just couldn't wait any longer. Sleeping really eats into your time, doesn't it?"

"You were the one who said I needed beauty sleep. What have you got?"

He held up three neatly printed dossiers. "You tell me."

"Is this another competition?"

"Maybe."

"Hand them over." They made for interesting reading, even at that hour of the morning.

"Well?" Sid said when I finished the third one. "Who's your pick?"

"Vanessa goes to college in Connecticut, and according to what you found on her Facebook page, went back to school immediately after Kendall's funeral. That means she couldn't have framed Linda, so she's out of the running."

"I concluded the same thing."

"Nadine's school is in upper New York state, but she was so upset over her friend's death that she stayed in Pennycross a few extra days. Therefore she could have set up the frame. But according to her Facebook posts, she didn't get to town until late Friday afternoon, just before the Divas went to the Howl. So she's out, too."

"I concur."

"That leaves Alexis. She attends McQuaid, so she was in town in time to case the haunt and plant her weapons, and she had the best chance to frame Linda."

"Alexis lives in the same dorm as Linda, as a matter of fact."

"Can't get more convenient than that. Of course, we don't know how she snuck into McHades, but—"

"I bet her mother has a key."

"Her mother?"

"Somebody wasn't reading carefully," he said in a sing-song voice.

"If you'd have waited another hour to wake me up, I might have." I flipped back to the first page of Alexis's dossier. "How did I miss that?" Alexis's full name was Alexis McQuaid Primo. "Is one of the Quintet her mother? No, don't tell me. It has to be Vivienne—Beatrice said Vivienne knew Kendall's parents, and of course she would if their kids were close friends."

"Bingo! As part of the Scholar's committee, Vivienne would have had access to a key to McQuaid Hall and Alexis could have 'borrowed' it. Plus Alexis being a McQuaid gives us her motive for deciding to frame somebody. She probably didn't know about the weird bequest until after she'd killed Kendall."

"So she framed Linda to make her mother happy?"

"Maybe, though I'm not willing to put even that much of a positive spin on it. I'd guess that she's got that whole family pride thing going, or maybe her mother's fussing was getting on her nerves. Either way, she probably got a kick out of framing Linda. She was handy, and Alexis could claim she had a motive for killing Kendall, which she actually did, even if she didn't know about it."

"So that's it? Alexis killed Kendall?"

I looked at Sid—he looked at me—and though we didn't turn on any music out of consideration for my sleeping daughter next door, we did indulge in a brief but enthused dance party.

Finally we collapsed onto my bed, out of breath. At least I was out of breath. Sid had as much breath as usual, which upon reflection, meant that he too was out of breath.

Reflection also put a damper on my spirits. "So what do we do now? We don't have any proof. I suppose we could point the cops at the Divas' Facebook group, but that would just confirm that Linda had a reason to hate Kendall. As for Alexis being a McQuaid, that would make the police suspect her less, not more. We can't prove her mother has a key or that Alexis used it to sneak into the haunt before the murder, or that she snuck into Linda's dorm room to plant the bloody gloves. What can we do?"

"No worries," Sid said. "While you were a-snooze in your bed, Sherlock Bones was on the case. I have devised the perfect solution, a way to fool Alexis into incriminating herself." He sat up, the better to make grandiose hand gestures. "Picture this . . . Tonight, at dusk, Alexis gets a private Facebook message. From her murder victim!"

"You can do that?"

"Of course. The message says, 'Why, Alexis? Why did you betray me?' An hour later, another message. 'I don't like being dead, Alexis. It's dark, so dark.' Another hour. 'It hurts. You hurt me, Alexis.' Next up, 'I'm coming for you, Alexis. I don't want to be alone.' Every hour, another message, until just before midnight, I send the final one: 'I'm waiting for you, Alexis. Look outside.'"

I started to say something, but Sid put his bony hand over my mouth to stop me and went on.

"Alexis fearfully looks out the window, and sees a shadowy figure wearing a Brandeis hoodie, just like the one Kendall was wearing when she died. She gasps in terror! A hand beckons to her.

"Of course she doesn't come down right away. She's too scared. She hides from the window until the next text: 'Come down, Alexis. Or I'll come up for you.' Swallowing her fear, she forces herself down the stairs of the dorm, belting her robe around her long, flowing nightgown. Or maybe a short, revealing one. I'm not sure what she sleeps in.

"Anyway, as she approaches 'Kendall,' the apparition

turns and walks away. Alexis follows her across the darkened college grounds until she realizes they're in front of McQuaid Hall, with the McHades sign dangling over the wide-open door.

"Kendall gestures for Alexis to follow, and then disappears into the gaping darkness. The murderous coed swallows visibly, then steels herself. Maybe she'll belt that robe again.

"As she goes inside, she finds a line of candles tracing a path into the building. We'll use electric candles, by the way—they're safer. She follows, follows, follows, and finds herself in the zombie party room. The lights are on—not house lights, but the disco ball and strobes. A blood-stained baseball bat is on the floor in front of her next to a pair of rubber gloves just like the ones she used to frame Linda, and just a few feet away is Kendall, her back turned.

"'Kendall?' she whispers. There's no reaction. 'Kendall!' she calls again. And slowly the figure turns. But where Kendall's face should be, there's only a bare skull. A handsome skull, mind you, but still not what she was expecting. A skeletal hand points at her, and the specter speaks. 'Alexisssss. . . . Why did you kill me, Alexissssss?'

"Fear makes the killer both brave and angry, and she says, 'It's your own fault, Kendall! You were going to spoil my devilish fun tormenting innocents. I couldn't let that happen. You had to die!' She reaches for the baseball bat and says, 'I killed you once, you ossifying piece of sacrum, and I'll do it again. Die! Die! Die!'

"She swings the bat at me in the role of Dead Kendall, and I fall apart, my bones hitting the floor with a clatter. And around the room, lights flash from behind the scrim, showing the outline of witnesses who were watching the whole thing. 'Noooooo!' Alexis cries, and falls to her knees. 'I've ruined myself.' Then we call the cops, and your parents, Deborah, Madison, and you tell the cops what you heard, and play the tape recording you cleverly made. Of course, I'll have to make myself scarce so you can replace me with one of my skeleton Irregulars, but Alexis will be too busy weeping and beating her breast to notice. Maybe she'll faint, which would make it that much easier." He paused, probably for applause. "So? What do you think?"

"Wow."

"I know, right? See what a person can accomplish if he doesn't waste time sleeping? Now, I know it's not perfect, so if you've got any tweaks, I'm willing to take notes."

"I've only got one major comment."

"Yeah? What?"

"That is the most ridiculous plan I've ever heard."

30

"What's wrong with it?"

"Seriously? First off, Alexis would never fall for something like that. If she were to get messages from a dead friend, she'd think one of her living friends was trolling on her."

"From a dead person's account?"

"You got into it—somebody else could, too. Kendall might have written the password down somewhere, or given it to her sister, or forgotten to log out of her Facebook account on a public computer. All kinds of ways."

"I guess."

"And if Alexis saw somebody waving at her from outside her window at midnight, she'd call campus security. Do you want to have to run away from Oscar?"

"I could beat him, but it would be risky."

"You said yourself that Alexis is a strategist. So she'd know a living person was behind this, but would have no reason to reveal her hand when the 'ghost' hadn't shown a single card. If we don't have proof to threaten her with, we've got nothing."

"You don't think her guilt would propel her to confess?"

"I don't know that she feels any guilt."

Sid sat back·down on my bed, and drummed his fingers across his jawbone. "Maybe I've been watching too many horror movies. My plan would totally have worked in *The Ring* or *It Follows*. Maybe you should be Sherlock after all."

"Hey, who found the Devil's Divas? Who did the background check to show us that Alexis is the killer? The deerstalker is still yours."

"I don't know. If the real Sherlock— And yes, I know there's no real Sherlock. But if there were a real one, and he'd been at the haunt, he'd have found a clue instead of messing around and asking the other customers for Scooby Snacks."

"And the real Watson wouldn't have stayed outside. He'd have been there with you and spotted a fact you could use to make a brilliant deduction."

"I just wish one of us had seen something," Sid said.

"Me, too." I paused. "What if you had seen something? What *could* you have seen that would point to Alexis?"

"But I didn't see anything."

"I know. Just imagine for a minute. Come on, you've got the best imagination of anybody I know." He'd imagined himself back to life, after all. "Imagine what would help us the most."

He put his hands over his eye sockets so he could concentrate. "Not the murder itself—I would have said something right away. So maybe something leading to the murder . . . Alexis ducking behind the curtain to get the bat? No, she would have seen me, too, and wouldn't have done anything in front of a witness."

"Probably not, and if she had, it would still beg the question of why you didn't come forward sooner."

"What about Alexis popping back out from behind the curtain after the killing?"

"We don't know that she did that. She could have taken the back way to the next room."

"Right." He thought some more. "I've got it! The gloves! We know Alexis took the gloves with her because she used them to frame Linda. So she must have had them in her hand at some point. What if I'd seen her with the gloves?"

"And you didn't come forward until now because it was only a couple of days ago that the story about the gloves being found in Linda's dorm room made the news. So it took you until now to realize it was important."

"Perfect! I mean, it would be if I'd actually seen her with the gloves."

"You know you didn't, and I know you didn't, but Alexis doesn't."

"And this helps us how?"

"Because now I've got a plan, or part of one. It's going to be a lot easier to carry out than yours, but we still get to haunt Alexis."

31

Though I'd assured Sid that my new plan was simpler, it still took most of the day to gather the necessary equipment and recruit the help we needed. And of course, I had to teach my Thursday classes and deal with accompanying tasks. We got it all put together by the skin of our teeth, and at six o'clock, after Sid had checked Alexis's most recent Facebook postings to confirm that she was on campus, he sent her a message:

> I saw you with the gloves.
>   Come meet me at Hamburger Haven by 7 tonight or
> I'm calling the cops at 7:15.

The name of the sender was Scooby-Doo@McQuaid, thanks to the account Sid had created that afternoon.

If Alexis had followed the story of Kendall's murder—and of course she would have—she'd know about the "stolen" Scooby-Doo suit. If that wouldn't lure her out, nothing would.

We'd purposely given her as little time as possible to respond so she couldn't come up with any kind of counter-measures. Mom and Phil were stationed near her dorm, and texted us to let us know when she left, and Deborah and Madison were hidden along the way to track her progress. With all the advance warning, we were in place long before Alexis came in.

I'd expected her to look scared, or maybe mean and deter-mined, but she looked normal. She was the shortest of the Divas according to the pictures I'd seen, with bouncy blond hair, blue eyes, and dimples. Being cute somehow made her scarier.

She glanced around the room, which was about half filled with people eating burgers, but when she saw the stuffed Scooby-Doo perched on the end of the middle booth on the left wall, she went right over. "You sent me a message?" she said, and slid onto the empty side of the booth.

"That's right," said a scruffy-looking individual in a NAS-CAR T-shirt and a ball cap that had seen better days.

"So who the hell are you?"

Brownie smirked. "Just call me Scooby."

I'd wanted to play the part of Scooby myself, but had been overruled by Sid and my own common sense. I'd been teaching at McQuaid for over a year, and Alexis could have seen me around campus and might know about my associa-tions with Deborah and Madison. Brownie, on the other hand, was a recent hire, and his current clothes and demeanor were nothing like the attractive adjunct I'd come to know and be fond of.

At least I'd be able to listen in on their conversation. I was in the corner of the restaurant, on the other side, and I had on reading glasses and a black beret—neither of which I usually wore. Madison had wanted to apply old-age makeup, too, but I decided I looked quite old enough with the glasses. I had a book in front of me and earbuds that looked as if they were attached to my iPod, when in reality they were picking up the transmission from the gadget Deborah had taped under Brownie's shirt.

Sid was in the duffel bag under my table, also listening in. I'd expressed concern about his ability to use earbuds, since he has no ears, but Deborah had found earphones that worked via bone conduction. Which was good. I think he'd have walked to campus if I hadn't brought him along.

"What do you want?" Alexis said.

"Money. It seems to me that my seeing you with those bloody gloves might be worth a few bucks. You're a McQuaid, right? If your family can buy a university, you can afford to spare some cash."

"My family doesn't own this lousy school. It's just named after us, okay? And what makes you think I know anything about those gloves?"

"Oh, sweetheart, that ship sailed as soon as you came rushing down here."

There was a pause. "Tell me what you saw."

Now Brownie could launch into the story we'd concocted. "I was working the duck pond at the carny the night your pal got snuffed, and when I was taking a break, I saw some old geezer toss his costume into his car and forget to lock up. So I thought I'd 'borrow' it and have some fun. He'd left a ticket for the haunted house next to the costume, so I grabbed that, too. Then I saw you and your friends in line, and you better believe I noticed you. Four sweet blondes? Oh yeah." The script said he was to leer next, and when I heard a slight sound of disgust from Alexis, I deduced that Brownie had done his duty.

He went on. "I wanted to be in your group, but they stuck me in the one after. I was thinking I'd see if I could join up with you ladies, maybe save you from a monster or two and see how grateful you were." Either his next leer wasn't as convincing, or she ignored it. "Problem was, a pair of rug rats attached themselves to me because of the costume. First chance I got, I dumped them and the costume and hotfooted it after you, so I was right behind you when you left the building. Too late to rescue you, but just in time to see."

"See what?"

"Do I have to spell it out? The gloves."

"What about them? I didn't have them that night."

"Come again?"

She made a sound of pure exasperation. "I don't know who you are, but you don't know squat. If this is some sort of trick little Linda dreamed up to try to get off the hook for murdering Kendall, tell her she can forget it. And if you bother me again, I'll have you arrested and get my father to sue your whole freak show carnival."

I didn't need to see Brownie to know he was as confused as I was. Alexis had come running in response to our message about the gloves, but was now saying "Scooby" couldn't have seen anything on the night of the murder. What did she mean about not getting the gloves until later? Had we picked the wrong Diva?

I had nothing else to use on her, and I knew she was going to leave in another second if I didn't do something. So I left my book and Sid behind, grabbed a chair to drag over to the booth where Brownie and Alexis were, and sat down at the end of their table.

"Mind if I join you?"

Alexis said, "You can sit with this loser if you want—I'm leaving."

She started to slide out, but I blocked her. "Don't go yet. I want to talk to you about Kendall Fitzroy's murder."

Her eyes narrowed. "I know you. You've got something to do with the haunted house."

"What did you mean when you said you didn't get those gloves that night?"

"Who are you people? Is that guy wearing a wire?"

"Yes, and we're recording everything you say, including your admission that you had the gloves in your possession."

"Fine," she spat out. "I had the gloves, but not until Tuesday."

"And you planted them in Linda's room the next day?"

"So what? It's not like they got an innocent person in trouble. Linda Zaharee is as guilty as sin."

"Why are you so sure of that?"

"Hello? She was there! As soon as I realized she was working at McHades that night, I knew she had to have done it."

"Why didn't you tell the police?"

She shrugged. "I couldn't prove anything."

"It was so you wouldn't have tell people about her motive, wasn't it? You didn't want anybody to find out about the Devil's Divas."

"I knew it!" she snarled. "I knew Kendall told Linda about us. She swore she was going to say she worked alone, but I never believed her. Just because she decided to go all twelve-steppy and confess everything she'd ever done. We were in high school when we messed with Linda. What difference does it make now?"

"Because you're still bullying people every chance you get."

"So what? We have a little thing called freedom of speech in this country!"

"Harassment is not free speech, but never mind that. The fact is, you didn't want anybody to find out what you and your pals have been up to, and when Kendall told you she was going to confess, you decided to get rid of her. And after all those years of playing softball, you knew just how to swing a bat."

"Are you mental? I didn't kill Kendall. Linda did. She's the one who worked in that haunted house and could set it all up, not me."

"You've gone through McHades every Halloween for years, so you knew all about the setup, and you had plenty of time to explore because you could get the key from your mother. You snuck in the Thursday before the murder, found the gloves and bat, and hid them where you could reach them. Afterward you broke into Linda's dorm room and planted the gloves to frame her."

"Nobody saw me plant those gloves!"

"But you did plant them."

"Prove it," she said with a nasty smile.

"You mean like producing a witness who saw you in Linda's dorm? We could do that." Well, we could if we actually knew of somebody who'd seen her, but I was hoping Alexis was mad enough not to see that I was bluffing. For once, it worked.

"Fine, I planted the gloves. That doesn't mean I killed Kendall."

"Then how did you get them?"

"In the mail! That a-hole sent them to me, and I've still got the box and the note she wrote."

"Excuse me?"

"A couple of days after Linda murdered Kendall, she mailed me the gloves with a note that said, 'You're next.' I wasn't going to wait around and let that freak come after me. Not to mention the fact that Mom was going mental because my great-great-grandfather's will gave McQuaid Hall to somebody because the haunted house was closed. So I figured

I'd kill two birds with one stone. Linda would go to jail and the haunted house could open back up. I mean, it's not like Linda didn't do it."

"Linda did not kill Kendall! She had no reason to because she didn't know Kendall bullied her in high school." Part of the day's preparation had included Mom getting in touch with Linda's lawyer to pass along the question to Linda, and then get the response back. It was all third-hand, of course, but the lawyer was firmly convinced that Linda was telling the truth. She'd been flabbergasted to find out that Kendall was a bully. "Kendall may have intended to tell her when they met the next day, but she never got a chance."

"Oh, sure, Linda says that now. Why would you believe her?"

"Why would I believe an Internet troll who just admitted to framing somebody for murder?"

She glared at me. "I am so going to get you fired."

"You can try."

"Just you watch me. And nobody is going to believe this insane story of yours, anyway. As for your little recording, I'm pre-law, which means I know your tape is inadmissible."

"You are absolutely right—the recording is useless." I waited just long enough for her to start to get nervous, then said something I'd been dying to say ever since Charles taught me the phrase. "Hey, rube."

Soda Pop hopped out from the booth behind Brownie, Treasure Hunt and Dana stood up behind Alexis, and Charles and an out-of-uniform Oscar rose from the table behind me.

"Since I figured you'd deny everything you said, I thought it would be better to have witnesses along."

"Some witnesses," she sneered. "A lousy adjunct, a rent-a-cop, and I don't know who those other creeps are." Then she caught a glimpse of the shirts Treasure Hunt, Dana, and

Soda Pop were wearing. "Are you serious? Carnies? As if anybody would believe carnies over a McQuaid."

Treasure Hunt smiled wider than I'd ever seen him smile. "You think people will take a McQuaid's word over anybody else's?"

"That's how it works in this town, old man."

"Glad to hear it. Now let me introduce myself. My name is Nelson Paul McQuaid the Third, but you can call me Great-Uncle Treasure Hunt."

32

I was never sure which lever Deborah had used to get Oscar to help: the opportunity to repay our discretion in regards to him being the ninja, a chance to show up the "real cops," or the hint that she might not be unwilling to go out with him. Whatever the reason, him being there meant the police showed up with admirable speed, and they listened to our explanations with a lot less skepticism than they might have had otherwise. With so many witnesses, they had to arrest Alexis.

The charge was going to be police obstruction or lying to the police or whatever applied when somebody framed another person for murder, but everybody seemed pretty sure that that was just a preliminary for the murder charge to come. Which caused considerable cheer. I joined in as best I could and ate my share of Stewpot's special party cupcakes, but my heart wasn't in it. That was part of the reason I begged off from spending a little quiet time with Brownie for a special celebration for two. The other part was knowing that Sid was waiting in the duffel bag.

So I smiled, gave Brownie a pretty decent kiss, and drove my parents and Madison home. Sid bounced out of the bag for more congratulations, and my parents even joined in on the resulting dance party. We kept it short because it was a school night for Madison and a work night for me.

I'd thought I was faking my happiness pretty well, but Sid can see through me almost as well as I can see through him, and he pulled me up to the attic for a chat.

"So, high five for another successful case?"

I obliged.

"You call that a high five? More like a low one and a half. What's wrong?"

"I don't know, Sid. It just doesn't feel finished. What if Alexis didn't kill Kendall after all?"

"Do you think that story about the gloves being mailed to her could be true?"

"I admit it sounds phony, but she sounded sincere. Rude and awful, but sincere. You're better than I am with voices. Did you think she was telling the truth?"

He hesitated, but finally nodded. "I hate to say this, but either she was telling the truth or she is the best liar in the world. Besides, the way she reacted when Brownie tried to pretend he'd seen her the night of the murder makes no sense if she was the killer."

"I think she was expecting 'Scooby' to blackmail her for planting evidence, not for killing Kendall."

"If Alexis didn't kill Kendall, then who did?"

"I have no idea. I'm too tired to even think straight."

"Buck up, Georgia. If nothing else, we've cleared Linda. Louis said she'll be out of jail by morning. And that'll make Roxanne happy, or at least less of a pain. That's good, right?"

"Absolutely," I said, and managed to muster up enough of a smile to reassure him. It just didn't last long enough to reassure me.

33

The next morning I kept up the pretense of satisfied delight for the benefit of my parents and Madison, but stayed away from the adjunct office because I knew news about the night's adventures would have spread and I didn't want to deal with Sara Weiss and her gossip mania. I wasn't really up for talking to Brownie or Charles, either, so I decided to go home after my third class. Nobody was likely to show up for office hours on a lovely Friday afternoon anyway, especially not when it was the final weekend of the Halloween Howl.

My cell phone rang as I was driving home.

"Hello?"

"Georgia, this is Oscar. I thought you'd want to know that Linda Zaharee has been released, and Alexis Primo has been charged with tampering with evidence and whatever else they can pin on her."

"What about the murder?"

"Yeah, about that. You know how she said she got the bloody gloves in the mail? She actually produced the box they were mailed in. Stains on the box prove the gloves were placed in the box while the blood was wet, and the box was postmarked the Saturday of the murder."

"She could have mailed them to herself."

"We thought of that, but we did some checking on the package."

"We?"

"The real cops let me sit in."

"Good for you."

"Anyway, the package was mailed from the self-service machine at the Elm Street post office, and the time stamp is seven o'clock."

"Before the body was found?"

"That's right. Nadine Seger and Vanessa Yount swear Alexis was with them at that time, and before you say they could be lying, we've got outside verification from some people they were talking to at that time. Alexis did not mail that package."

"I don't suppose postage was paid for with a credit card."

"No such luck."

"Any security cameras at the post office?"

"The sender was in costume, including a mask. Would you believe it was Batman?"

"Was there a Batman in the haunt?"

"According to your sister and several scare actors, a number of Batmen went through McHades. Apparently it's a hot costume this year."

"What if Batman was Alexis's confederate? She could have passed the gloves on to him as soon as she left the haunt and then—" I sighed. "Sorry, I'll stop. Alexis didn't kill Kendall, did she?"

"I'm afraid not."

"Coccyx!"

"Beg pardon?"

"Sorry, I'm just frustrated. Thanks for letting me know, Oscar."

Mom and Phil's car was missing from the driveway when I got home, which was a relief. I didn't want to give them the bad news right away. There was no escaping telling Sid, though, so after a quick dog-patting break, I trudged up to his room.

As soon as he saw me, he said, "Don't say it. I can tell from the way you're walking. Alexis didn't kill Kendall."

"No."

"And we have no idea who did."

"No."

"And you need a hug."

"Yes."

Sid really is a good hugger, despite his lack of padding, and this time I think he needed the hug as much as I did.

"On the good side," he said, "we have one less suspect."

"I'm not entirely comforted by that."

"Take what you can get."

"All right, then, we can eliminate two other suspects while we're at it: Nadine and Vanessa. They all alibi one another."

"Good. Are we still assuming the cops would have found any viable motives among Kendall's family and boyfriend?"

"I think we have to."

"And are we still thinking there's a connection with the Devil's Divas?"

"There has to be, Sid. Kendall never did anything else to make somebody want to kill her."

"The problem is that the cops have the Diva data now, so they'll be all over that."

"Maybe not. They probably have to jump through legal hoops to get access to the information."

"You're right! We've still got the edge—I've got a list of the Divas' victims for the past year. If I correlate those with the people who were at the haunt . . . First things first. I'm going to need a new spreadsheet."

He started tapping energetically.

First things first . . . "Sid, if you were trying to make amends to people you'd harmed, who would you go to first? The oldest or the most recent?"

"Why?"

"Kendall went after Madison after she stopped harassing Linda. But she never apologized to Madison, which means she wasn't starting with her most recent victims."

"So you think she started at the beginning of her reign of terror, not the end? That would mean there are people out there to whom she has already confessed, and so I should be looking for earlier victims. That makes sense."

"Can I help?"

"I wouldn't mind your company."

"Sure. It's the least I can do." I looked over his shoulder as he scrolled through posts and put names into his spreadsheet.

One post was nothing but the names of the Divas and numbers. "What's this?"

He looked disgusted. "You remember how I said the Divas were keeping score? This is their running tally for how much pain they caused their victims. Getting somebody upset enough to reply counted as a point, with another point if the person tried to troll back, blocked them, or reported them to Facebook. For people they saw in person, they scored for causing major change in behavior like screwing up grades; getting kicked off a sports team; or fighting with a friend, teacher, or significant other. And get this! They got twenty points if a victim came to one of the Divas and confided that she was being bullied."

"That's just evil."

"They spent an inordinate amount of time arguing over

points. Did crying in class count more than crying during lunch? Did failing an exam count for more than just failing a normal test or a quiz?"

"Why is Kendall's score so much higher?" It was almost a hundred points higher than Alexis's, who was in second place.

"I wondered about that, too. I can't see that she bullied any worse or more often than the others, but I saw a couple of references to her 'big score,' so she must have really gotten to one of her victims. Maybe somebody flunked out completely or left town."

He kept working, and I thought about all the essays my students had written about the effects of bullying. I'd read examples of everything the Divas had scored for, and worse. "Sid, what about suicide? An awful lot of teen suicides are caused by bullying, and I bet the Divas would give Kendall a lot of points for that."

"Sacrum, Georgia! Even if Kendall was trying to reform, she couldn't ever make amends for that. What could she do? Apologize to a tombstone?"

"She could apologize to somebody's family. Maybe that was who she spoke to first—not the oldest victim or the most recent, but the one she hurt the most. What if that person's family wasn't willing to accept her apology?"

"I'll keep looking."

While he scrolled, I continued to make connections. "Remember how the crew was talking about the haunt really being haunted?"

"I didn't mean to scare everybody."

"It's not your fault—they was nervous that night. Besides, I'd heard them talking about the place being haunted before. Somebody claimed there had been a suicide in the building."

"None of the McQuaids committed suicide. I checked."

"Did you check to see if anybody else killed himself there?"

"I never thought of that. Let me see what I can find. Search terms 'suicide' and 'McQuaid.'"

He started typing so quickly that he forgot to muffle the sound of bone against key, going from screen to screen faster than I could read. "Found it! A suicide six years ago. No, false alarm. A Pennycross student hanged herself, but she wasn't at McQuaid when it happened. She was at home."

"Why did that show up in your search?"

"Hang on." He winced. "Strike that. Okay, now I see. The victim's body was discovered by a McQuaid student."

"So is the victim connected to any of our zillion suspects?"

"Her name was . . ." His eyes widened impossibly. "Oh, my spine and femur. The victim was Doreen Beale."

"Beale?"

"And her body was discovered by her sister: Roxanne Beale."

34

"Our Roxanne Beale? Why did I never hear about this?"

"Where were you living six years ago?"

"Umm . . . Okay, I don't remember offhand, but wherever it was, it wasn't Pennycross. And if I had heard, it probably wouldn't have meant anything because I didn't know Roxanne then."

"Right. I didn't find a lot of hits for the story, so I guess it wasn't considered that big a deal. I know I never heard anything about it."

"Unless the victim is a celebrity or it takes place in public, a suicide doesn't get that much attention. What happened?"

"Hold on, I'm reading. Okay, high school student Doreen Beale, parents thought she'd been a little glum but chalked it up to teenage angst—"

"It says that?"

"Not in so many words, just that they didn't think her moodiness was that serious. Doreen was supposed to meet her sister Roxanne at the movies, but Roxanne was late. When

Roxanne finally arrived, she assumed Doreen was somewhere in the theater and took a seat in the back to watch the rest of the movie. She couldn't find Doreen afterward, and she didn't answer her cell phone, so Roxanne went home to see if she was there. That's when she found Doreen hanging in her closet. There was a note, which referred to nobody liking her. As a contributing factor, when the police looked at the e-mails on her computer, it turned out that she'd been bullied online. There were messages calling her a nerd, a geek, ugly, fat, and stupid. They said she ought to kill herself and make the world a better place. The cyberbully was never found, but I think we both know who it must have been."

"No wonder Kendall was the reigning champion. She convinced somebody to commit suicide. Then years later, she tried to apologize."

"I can't even picture that. 'Sorry I caused your sister's death.' Or maybe she went to their parents instead, which is even worse." He shuddered noisily. "Remind me why we care about Kendall's murder?"

"It's getting hard for me, too, Sid, but she did seem to be trying to change. And let's not forget that Roxanne was willing to let Linda suffer, so I'm not giving her a pass."

"Right. So how did Roxanne know Kendall was going to McHades?"

"She could have called to find out when Kendall was going to be in town so they could talk in person. It would be natural to ask what she'd be doing while she was here, and McHades would be the perfect place. Roxanne has been on campus for over a decade, and probably went through McHades multiple times over the years and could easily have had an opportunity to get a key to the building."

Sid took over. "So she went in beforehand to scope the place out, and got the bat and gloves ready. Then, on the night of the murder, she dressed as Batman to conceal her face and even make it fuzzy whether it was a man or a woman. She waited until she saw Kendall and the other Divas getting in line, then got right behind them so she'd be in the same group or the next one. How did she know Kendall was afraid of zombies?"

"That may have just been luck. Maybe her original idea was to club Kendall out in the open, thinking nobody would pay attention in the middle of all the zombies running around. Or maybe she planned to get her in that hallway between the detention hall and the zombie party and then escape through the passages. But when Kendall was so scared she backed up against the curtain, that was the perfect opportunity. Afterward, Roxanne left the bat but took the gloves to mail to Alexis."

"Do you think Kendall told her about the other Divas?"

"Either she did or Roxanne figured it out herself. We don't have to work out every detail this time, Sid. We're telling the police everything we know and letting them take over. Agreed?"

"Agreed. We're not taking any chances with her."

"I just want to tell Mom first. I don't know when she's coming back—"

"She and your father are back. I heard them come in while I was typing."

"Then let's get this over with. Mom's going to be so upset that she's been working with a murderer. I'm creeped out just knowing she's been in our house."

"Yeah, that's too much Halloween for me."

"Give me a couple of minutes' head start and I'll make sure the drapes are all drawn."

It turned out to be a good thing that I went down first. Roxanne Beale was sitting at my dining room table, right next to my mother.

35

Not only were Roxanne and her inevitable scatter of papers and books in the room, but Linda was there, too. I managed not to scream or faint, and even held back the curse words that sprang to mind. I just said, "Oh, hey. What's up?"

"Roxanne pried Linda away from her family somehow so we could try to make up for lost time," Mom said.

"I figured it was the least I could do for you Thackerys," Linda said. "My lawyer said it was your efforts that got me out of jail." The undergrad looked paler than she had the last time I'd seen her, but she was smiling.

"We were glad to help," I said. "Um, Mom, can I borrow you for a little bit? I need to talk to you about something."

"Now?" Roxanne said with a frown. "We've got a lot of work to do."

"It shouldn't take more than a minute," I lied.

"There have been too many minutes wasted already."

Mom looked bemused at her student's rudeness, and said,

"I was going to go get us something to drink anyway. Georgia can talk to me while I'm pouring." She stood up, but Roxanne shoved her back down into her chair.

"That's it! Neither you, nor Linda, nor I are going anywhere until my dissertation is done. Do you understand? No more murders. No more arrests. No. More. Distractions."

"Roxanne, really!" Mom said.

I started toward them, then froze when I saw Roxanne pull a gun out of her backpack and aim it at Mom.

"You stay here, Dr. Thackery," Roxanne said. "Georgia can get the drinks. I'd like a Diet Coke." Then she actually added, "Please."

"Roxanne, what are you doing?" Mom said. Linda just stared.

"I'm trying to get my dissertation done. Is that so hard to understand? Doesn't anybody realize how important my work is?" Her voice kept rising, and before I could warn him, Phil came in with Byron to see what the ruckus was about. As soon as he saw the gun, he stepped in front of me, and when Byron started growling, he grabbed his collar.

"You're going to help us, too," Roxanne said to him. "Sit next to Linda. Georgia is getting drinks. Maybe some chips, too, if you've got them. But don't try to leave or call the cops. In fact, you better bring me all the phones, including everybody's cell phones."

"Roxanne," Linda said, "I don't understand."

"Roxanne killed Kendall," I said.

Roxanne nodded. "It was a mistake—I see that now. I should have waited until after I finished my dissertation. It's just that I already had my plans in place before Dr. Eberhardt denied my extension, and I wanted to get it over with before Dr. Thackery got back so I wouldn't be distracted. I'd already decided to take care of Kendall's friends later, after my oral defense. Then Linda got arrested and I had no way to do the statistics. I thought her getting out of jail would be a good thing, but that means the police are still looking for Kendall's killer, and I realized it was just a matter of time before the police came after me."

"But why?" Linda asked, "Did Kendall send awful e-mails to you, too?"

"Not to me—to my sister. Doreen killed herself because of it, and my parents blamed me. So what if I was a little late getting to the movie that night? It was only half an hour, maybe forty-five minutes. I was working. I was wonderfully focused then. But afterward, I was so distracted my first thesis advisor said I should take time off. Which I did, but when I came back, she was gone, and it was harder to get the work done. Then my second advisor left, and I got Dr. Thackery. And then Dr. Thackery went off on sabbatical. So many distractions! When Kendall came and tried to apologize about Doreen, I was so mad. She'd done more than kill Doreen—she'd derailed my life's work! But still, I should have waited. It's like you said, Dr. Thackery—I need to focus on the work. Killing Kendall was just a distraction."

Roxanne was saying such awful things that her voice should have sounded anguished or angry. Instead she just sounded annoyed.

"Anyway," she went on, "none of us are leaving this house until I get my dissertation done. Linda, if you try to do anything on your computer other than statistics, I'll shoot you in the leg. It'll hurt a lot, but you'll still be able to do the work. Dr. Thackery and Dr. Thackery, the same goes for you two. And no offense, Georgia, but I need your mother and Linda, and your father can help, but you're only an adjunct. I don't need you. So I'll shoot you in the head. Now give me the phones."

I gathered up the handsets from our landline and put them into Roxanne's backpack, and we all gave her our cell phones. My hands weren't the only ones shaking.

Roxanne said, "Now everybody tell Georgia what you want to drink."

"I don't think I care for anything right now," Phil said politely.

"No, you should drink something. We need to keep our strength up. So what'll it be?"

"I know what my parents like," I said. "Is Coke all right for you, Linda?"

She could only nod.

I got drinks, dumped potato chips into a bowl, and found napkins, all the while knowing that I should be doing something, anything, but every scenario I devised ended with somebody getting shot. Somebody other than Roxanne, that is. I wasn't particularly worried about her welfare.

As I came back into the dining room, Phil was saying, "No, we're the only ones in the house. Madison has gone to McHades with her aunt. They won't be back until late."

The idea of Madison coming home to an armed madwoman made me want to throw the chips at said madwoman's head, but not when she was that close to Mom. So I said, "If it's easier, I can call Madison and suggest she spend the night with Deborah. That will give you one less person to worry about."

Roxanne thought it over for what seemed like an eternity. "Okay, but we should do it by text." I hadn't intended to blurt anything out on the phone, but I couldn't fault Roxanne for her attention to detail.

She wouldn't even let me do the texting. Instead I had to guide her through it, giving her my phone's password, telling her which number to select, and dictating the message. She did it one-handed, so as not to have to put the gun down.

"Have I got this right?" she asked me when she'd typed it all in. "'Madison, Mom and Dad are helping Roxanne with her dissertation, and it's going to be an all-nighter. Why don't you spend the night with Deborah so you won't have to worry about being quiet?'"

"That's it."

She sent it, and a few minutes later there was an answering text from Madison:

Message received. I love you!

"There, that's settled," Roxanne said.

"Could you text back that I love her, too?"

"Is it really necessary?"

"We always do that. I don't want her to think anything is wrong." I was hoping she wouldn't take the time to scroll through previous texts and figure out that Madison and I were more likely to end our text exchanges with bad jokes.

Apparently Roxanne decided to get the distraction over with as soon as possible, because she texted and said, "Now can we get going? Dr. Thackery, what do you think of this passage?" She handed my mother a piece of paper, and proceeded to act as if it were perfectly normal to work on an academic paper with a gun in her lap.

Mom and Phil played along as best they could, but it was harder for Linda. I could tell she was having to correct a lot of mistakes as she tried to calculate the statistics Roxanne wanted. As for me, I stayed busy filling Roxanne's requests for refills on drinks, more snacks, and so on. At one point, she told me to go lock all the doors, to make sure nobody could sneak out quickly, and had me raise all the blinds and draw all the curtains so she could see if anybody approached the house. Then I had to shut Byron up in my parent's office so he would stop growling at her. I had to admit that once she put her mind to something, she really thought it through.

In between my errands, I tried to figure out what Roxanne had in mind for her endgame. Did she expect to be able to keep us captive until she finished the paper? And if she did, what then? Did she think the police wouldn't arrest her afterward? Or had finishing the dissertation become her only goal? Would she shoot herself afterward? As awful as that would be, I hoped that was the plan, and that she didn't intend to take the rest of us with her.

I determinedly stopped that line of thought. We had an ace in the hole. Or rather, a skeleton in the attic. I'd left Sid waiting for an all-clear signal, but knowing him, he wouldn't have waited very long. So chances were that he'd crept down to check for himself, seen and heard enough to know what was going on, then retreated quietly to the attic. So what had he done next? Why hadn't he called the police?

As time went on, I started to think that he'd been afraid to spook Roxanne. I hadn't heard sirens, no SWAT team had burst through the door, and no hostage negotiator had called to speak in soothing tones. I didn't know if Pennycross even had a SWAT team or hostage negotiator.

After what felt like a year, but which was probably more like an hour and a half, I felt a tiny nudge from under the table and was just able to stop myself from jerking. I looked down at my feet and saw a bony finger. Since it immediately started to move, I considered myself safe in assuming it was Sid's. Moving like nothing so much as a skeletal inchworm, it wriggled away toward Roxanne's chair.

Over the next half an hour or so, more of Sid's bones propelled themselves silently across the floor, passing me on their way to pile up close to Roxanne. I tried to decide if there was something Sid wanted me to do, but since I didn't know what he was planning and I didn't want to get in his way, I did nothing. Doing nothing is a lot harder than it sounds.

In my efforts not to look at Sid, I hadn't been looking at anything, so I hadn't noticed that the neighborhood was getting unusually quiet. But Roxanne had.

"It's not always this empty around here, is it? I haven't seen a car go by in ages," she said, swiveling her head to look out the windows. I don't know what she saw, but whatever it was, it was enough to convince her that the jig was up. "Damn," she said mildly. "I told you people not to call the cops. Now how am I going to finish this?" She sighed, sounding more exasperated than frightened. Then she picked the gun up from her lap and aimed it at me. "Maybe this will keep them away."

At the time, the next few seconds were a blur, but later I was able to figure out what happened. My parents must have had one of their silent conversations in the midst of everything else, because they reacted instantly. Mom threw herself over Linda while Phil threw himself over me. At least he tried to, because I was doing my best to throw myself over him. But as fast as we moved, Sid was faster. He rose up behind Roxanne's chair, grabbed both her arms, and jerked them upward. The shot, when it came, went into the ceiling instead of any of us.

Roxanne was so shocked that she let Sid wrestle the gun away from her, and Phil and I untangled ourselves so we could grab her.

"This is the police! We're coming in!" said a voice via megaphone. "Hands up, and put down your weapons!"

"Armoire!" I said to Sid, and put my hand over Roxanne's eyes in a bizarre game of peek-a-boo so she wouldn't see him slide the gun across the floor, scurry away, and shut himself up in his hidey-hole. Mom still had Linda, who'd burst into tears, and she was patting her and making comforting noises as she blocked Sid from view. Phil and I kept a tight hold on Roxanne as what seemed like two dozen police officers with bulletproof vests and large weapons burst in, with Louis in front. In seconds, they had the gun and Roxanne was flung to the floor and handcuffed.

36

It got confusing after that, as if I were watching a slide show of random events instead of living through the next half an hour. A pair of EMTs came in to make sure nobody had been shot, and seemed vaguely disappointed when they didn't get to bandage anybody. Then Linda started hyperventilating and came perilously close to fainting, so they got to carry her out on a stretcher to where her family was waiting. Speaking of family, Deborah and Madison pushed their way into the house a few minutes later.

"You should have stayed at the Howl," I said to Madison.

"I figured if I wasn't here, Aunt Deborah would want to charge in with the cops, and she'd just get into trouble."

"You may be right," I admitted. I could tell my sister had been worried—when I'd hugged her, she'd actually hugged back instead of just enduring it.

"Your daughter picked up on your clue right away," Louis said.

"The text? I was hoping she'd catch it. She knows I hadn't called Phil *Dad* in decades."

"Though how she and Deborah realized you were being held captive just from that is beyond me."

"My daughters and granddaughter are just that clever," Phil said complacently, and Mom nodded while Madison, Deborah, and I tried to look both clever and modest. Not one of us so much as glanced in the direction of the armoire.

The officers who'd been dealing with Roxanne started to lead her out, and Mom said, "Excuse me, Louis," before marching toward Roxanne. "Under the circumstances, Ms. Beale, I will not be continuing as your thesis advisor and will, in fact, recommend that your enrollment at McQuaid be terminated immediately. And on a personal note, I want to advise you that my daughter, Dr. Georgia O'Keeffe Thackery, is ten times the scholar that you are, and the quality of her doctoral dissertation makes your unfinished jumble of concepts look like an elementary school composition." Then she turned away from her with an air of finality. "Now, Louis, if you could get this person and her pathetic papers out of my house, I would be most grateful."

Roxanne opened and shut her mouth a few times, like a fish who was wondering where its water had disappeared to, but before she could find anything to say, a couple of officers hustled her out.

I wish the rest of the police had gone with her, but of course they couldn't do that, not when they had questions to ask, and ask again in a different way to see if they'd get a different answer, and then go back to the first version to ask one more time. At last they decided we were telling them the truth, which we mostly were. The only parts we were leaving out were the Sid-related ones. As soon as the door shut behind them and Madison ran around to close all the curtains, the door to the armoire started to open.

"Man, it's about time—"

The doorbell rang.

I shoved Sid back inside the armoire and shut it while Deborah opened the door. Oscar was on the porch, with Louis standing right behind him, looking exceedingly aggravated.

"Deborah, are you okay?" Oscar said.

"Why wouldn't I be? I was outside during the shooting."

"I told you that," Louis snapped.

"I just wanted to be sure," Oscar snapped back. "Her family was in danger—she might be upset."

"I'm fine, Oscar," Deborah said, "but thanks for asking."

"Is there anything I can do for you?" Louis asked, apparently not wanting to be outclassed in the thoughtfulness competition.

"Not a thing, Louis. Thank you for asking."

The two men stood there, and I would have given even odds for one of them either embracing Deborah or slugging the other. Or maybe they were planning to stand there all night.

Deborah finally said, "Do you two have phones?"

"Of course," Oscar said, and Louis nearly broke a finger trying to get his out of a pocket.

"Good. Now if either one of you—or both of you—care to do something other than make cow eyes at me, you can call me like a regular person and ask me out on a date. But not tonight. I have plans with my family." She shut the door on the two astonished faces.

Sid shoved the armoire door open and started hooting. "Way to go, Deborah. You've got those two—"

The doorbell rang.

"Sacrum!" Sid said, but he went back into the armoire while Deborah answered it again.

"Now what?" she said.

Only it was neither of her smitten swains. It was Brownie.

Deborah lifted one eyebrow and stepped aside for him to come inside.

"Is everybody okay?" he asked, looking at me.

"We're fine," I said. "I take it you heard what happened."

"Most of it. Maybe someday you can tell me the whole story."

"Bring me some of Stewpot's chicken and dumplings, and I think something can be arranged."

"It's a deal." Unlike Oscar or Louis, he had no problem figuring out what to do next. He leaned over to give me a kiss on the cheek, and when I pulled him closer for something more thorough, he was happy to comply. He probably thought the cheer came from Madison or Phil, but I knew it was Sid. After that, he said he had to get back to the carnival, but shook hands and offered hugs all around.

Then, at last, Sid could come out of the armoire, and there was even more hugging. Though everybody was praised for presence of mind and/or bravery, Sid got the prize for jumping Roxanne, and I'd never seen him look prouder.

The next day was Halloween, and Deborah and Madison insisted they were up to working at McHades Hall. They even talked Mom and Phil into helping out again. Sid and I stayed home to deal with trick-or-treaters. I was in charge of handing out treats, and Sid took care of the tricks. He kept it mild, though. The only ones he really scared were the two boys who started to run off with the jack-o'-lantern Madison had carved that afternoon. I was almost certain they had to change their pants after they escaped my favorite screaming skeleton.

Sunday was considerably quieter, and passed in a relaxed glow of movies, Phil's finest cooking, and leftover Halloween candy. The following week was more or less normal, punctuated by more questions from the police, phone calls from reporters, and much curiosity at work. On the good side, I got those chicken and dumplings—on the bad side,

Sara Weiss cornered me for an interrogation that made the police's questions seem like idle chitchat.

The happy finale was when Brownie asked me out on an honest-to-God, makeup-wearing, no-Mom-jeans dinner date on Friday night. I think Mom and Madison were more anxious about my outfit than I was, finally settling on a pair of black slacks, simple but elegant flats, and a sapphire blue sweater they said had just enough depth in the neckline to entice without looking cheap. They actually had it laid out for me when I got home Friday evening, which turned out to be a good thing because I was running behind schedule. I did insist on doing my own hair and makeup, though I had to lock my bedroom door to keep them out.

With all that, I was slow getting downstairs, which gave Madison time to complete her usual what-are-your-intentions-toward-my-mother interview. Brownie acquitted himself admirably, but seemed just as glad to get going.

"Sorry to rush," he said, "but we've got reservations."

"No need to apologize. It's my fault for being late."

"I hope you're in the mood for Italian."

"Always."

After we were seated with our orders put in, I said, "I expected Fenton's to be packed up and gone by now. Not that I mind you still being around."

"This is our last stand of the year, so we can take our time. Besides, my parents have spent most of the past few days meeting with the powers that be at McQuaid."

"Are your father and his lawyer going to pursue his claim on McQuaid Hall and the environs?"

"Nope. For one thing, the lawyer backed out of the deal. Apparently his daughter's involvement caused a conflict of interest."

"His daughter? Who's the lawyer?"

"A guy named Salvatore Primo."

I finally put it together. "He must be Alexis's father, which makes him Vivienne's ex-husband. I bet the rest of the Quintet was furious about his involvement."

"Is it any wonder why I didn't want to meet my so-called relatives?"

"Treasure Hunt could get another lawyer."

"He could, but Mom and I talked him out of it. She told him how much he'd have to pay a lawyer, plus how much time he'd waste. Then I gave him a better idea for getting back at his family."

"Does it involve smoke bombs?"

"That would have been good, too, but no. He's going to sign over his property to the university for good."

"So McQuaid Hall is safe?"

"Not exactly. What he's giving them is the Dana Fenton Building."

"Excuse me?"

"He thought Mom deserved to have a building named after her more than any of the McQuaids."

"That's brilliant! A present for your mother and a slap in the face to the McQuaids, all in one fell swoop."

"That's only half the deal. The other half is a present for you."

"For me?"

"For you, for me, for Charles, for all the adjuncts. The university has agreed to convert the Dana Fenton Building for use by adjuncts. That means each of us gets our own cubicle with walls at least five feet tall for privacy. Plus there will be conference rooms where we can meet with students; a break room with a refrigerator and microwave; a copier and a printer; and new furniture."

"The university agreed to spend that kind of money?"

"Mom added up how much they'd save by agreeing instead of fighting it out in court. Plus it seems that some of the tenured faculty have been pushing for treating adjuncts better, and they were threatening to make a public stink."

"That would be my parents' work," I said, remembering all the time they'd been spending with colleagues. "But what about McHades Hall?"

"Not our problem. The McQuaid Quintet has a year to come up with a new location. Dad suggested that they use the family mansion, but I don't think that's happening."

"Probably not. That's really good news, Brownie."

"Yeah? You don't sound that excited."

"No, I think it's terrific. I just wish I were going to be here to enjoy it."

"What do you mean?"

"The reason I was late tonight was because I had a meeting with Dr. Eberhardt this afternoon. The department won't be renewing my contract next semester. Eberhardt says that with my parents back from sabbatical, they won't need as many adjuncts. So they picked a duck out of the pond, and I lost."

"That is such bull."

"Of course it is, and I called him on it. He eventually admitted that the McQuaid Quintet had insisted. Because of me, Alexis was exposed as an Internet bully who framed an innocent girl for murder. Appropriately enough, the story has gone viral, so their fair name has been besmirched."

"Fair name! Alexis isn't the only bully in that family."

"Yeah, I'd say the acorn didn't fall far from the tree. Anyway, Eberhardt is embarrassed by the situation, but due to the black eye the department has been given because of our murderous grad student, he doesn't feel he can fight it. So he's promised to use his connections to find me another position close enough to Pennycross that I won't have to move out of town."

"You know what?" he said. "As soon as we're finished eating, we're going to go talk to my parents and get them to modify their agreement with the university to say that they have to keep you."

I considered it, but only for a moment. "That's really sweet, but no. I don't want to queer the deal for the building, and if the department kept me, they'd have to fire another adjunct and I don't want that on my conscience. Plus I'd just be on borrowed time until they could find an excuse to get rid of me, and when that happened, Eberhardt wouldn't lift a finger to help me find another job. In fact, he'd probably go out of his way to spread dirt about me to every college within range."

"You've really thought this through."

"Sometimes I don't need a Ferris wheel to give me perspective. I've been fired before—I've always survived."

"Of course, if you're going to be close to Pennycross, then you'll be within the range of the show's stands."

"I'm glad to hear that. I'd really miss Stewpot's cooking."

"Is that's all you'd miss?"

"There might be something else." I leaned over and showed him. Several times. Unfortunately our food arrived, and we had to break it off long enough to eat. Dinnertime conversation was considerably less intense, but very pleasant, and afterward Brownie took me back to the carnival. It was shut down, and most of the rides were in the process of being disassembled, but the Ferris wheel was still lit up and operational, and Gameboy was on hand to give us a long, private ride. It was a crisp, clear night, and we spent a good while up there trying to pick out my next school. Eventually the wind started to blow, overwhelming Brownie's efforts to keep me warm, so he suggested hot chocolate in his trailer.

I don't know where Charles spent that night, but it wasn't in Brownie's trailer.

In deference to my parent's sensibilities and Madison's presumed innocence, Brownie got me home before daylight.

I was trying not to disturb anybody, but Sid was waiting for me in the living room.

"So?" he said. "How was your date?"

"Very nice."

"Was there canoodling?"

"What is canoodling, anyway?"

"You were the one who was out all night. You tell me."

"Why don't I tell you about what Treasure Hunt, aka Nelson McQuaid, is planning?"

"I'm all ear holes!"

Sid was much impressed by the solution Treasure Hunt had come up with. "I just wish I could have been eavesdropping when they broke the news to the Quintet! They must have been livid."

"Unfortunately, the Quintet still has power in town," I said, and explained what Eberhardt had told me.

"That ossifying piece of sacrum! And the Quintet! Mail me to them, Georgia, let me show them what a real haunted house is like."

I patted his femur. "It's okay, Sid. I'm not thrilled about having to job hunt, but it could be a lot worse." I was a good teacher. I had a guy worth canoodling. I had a daughter strong enough to blow off a bully, parents who considered me a worthy academic, and a sister who didn't think I was completely useless. And my house was haunted by my best friend.